Cole Morton was born in East London in 1967. He lived there most of his life before realizing a childhood dream by moving to the seaside. He now lives in East Sussex. His debut, *Hungry for Home: A Journey from the Edge of Ireland*, was shortlisted for the John Llewelyn Rhys Prize.

My Father Was a Hero

The true story of a man, a boy and the silence between them

COLE MORETON

PENGUIN

PENGUIN BOOKS

Published by the Penguin Group
Penguin Books Ltd, 80 Strand, London WC2R 0RL, England
Penguin Group (USA) Inc., 375 Hudson Street, New York, New York 10014, USA
Penguin Group (Canada), 10 Alcorn Avenue, Toronto, Ontario, Canada M4V 3B2
(a division of Pearson Penguin Canada Inc.)
Penguin Ireland, 25 St Stephen's Green, Dublin 2, Ireland
(a division of Penguin Books Ltd)
Penguin Group (Australia), 250 Camberwell Road,
Camberwell, Victoria 3124, Australia (a division of Pearson Australia Group Pty Ltd)
Penguin Books India Pvt Ltd, 11 Community Centre,
Panchsheel Park, New Delhi – 110 017, India
Penguin Group (NZ), cnr Airborne and Rosedale Roads, Albany,
Auckland 1310, New Zealand (a division of Pearson New Zealand Ltd)
Penguin Books (South Africa) (Pty) Ltd, 24 Sturdee Avenue,
Rosebank 2196, South Africa

Penguin Books Ltd, Registered Offices: 80 Strand, London WC2R 0RL, England

www.penguin.com

First published by Viking 2004
Published in Penguin Books 2005
1

Set by Palimpsest Book Production Limited, Polmont, Stirlingshire
Printed in England by Clays Ltd, St Ives plc

What we call the beginning is often the end
And to make an end is to make a beginning.

T. S. Eliot, *Little Gidding*

I

I am pinned down, unable to move. The Jerries control the balcony and their fire is merciless. My brothers-in-arms are nowhere to be seen as I crouch low among the dustbins, gulping down fetid air, trying to work out an escape from this damned mess. The lid of a bin shakes as it takes a hit and grit flies, stinging my eyes. The shots are getting closer. There is nowhere to run; nothing to do but go down in glory, taking a few of them too: so I check the ammo, pull up the hood of my army parka and rise, screaming, scrambling into no-man's-land, dashing for the staircase that will lead to the enemy above.

And that's when I get half a brick in my face.

It feels cold and numb at first. They're all just standing there, up on the first floor, staring down through the railings, not even bothering to hide. The skinhead looks horrified. There's blood all over my chin. The pain begins to burn. My broken lips are swelling fast, my front teeth are jagged to the tongue. My shirt is wet and red. Now I know I'm dead. Mum is going to kill me.

The games we played were all about Us versus the Hun. We fought out on the wasteland, crawling between bushes, or knelt in piss-pools at the bottom of stairwells, waiting to ambush each other. Huge gangs of boys, and a few girls, fighting all over the estate for hours. Usually it was pretend, just pointing twigs or plastic rifles for the lucky few, and shouting bang:

'You're dead, I got you. Go down!'

'No you bloody didn't.'

'Did!'

'Sod off!'

Sometimes it got rough, then sticks and stones were thrown, and bricks.

'I'm telling on you!'

If you wanted to catch the eye of the girl from the flat downstairs you would fake a heroic limp, or get your mum to put your arm in a sling and say it was a war wound. At least I did. It never worked.

My point is that we were not cowboys and indians. We were not Flash and Ming. This was the year before *Star Wars*, before light sabres and heavy breathing, long before mutant turtles and power rangers and all the other fantastical substitutes for war. Before the primal urge to form a tribe and beat the crap out of the rest was sublimated into football, or driven indoors to individual game consoles. We were Tommies and Jerries, yelling phrases from the speech bubbles of *Commando* magazine or the *Victor Book for Boys*:

'Achtung, Fritz!'

'For you, Englischer pigdog, ze war is over.'

'Eat lead, sausage guzzler!'

We were the last generation to be brought up on the folklore of the war, the last to collect shiny tin medals from the covers of comics, the last to know the names of battles from three decades before. Our fathers encouraged it. Mine did, anyway, pausing from his scale models of Stukas and Spitfires to paint my little plastic Airfix soldiers in their authentic colours. The conflicts played out on the carpet always looked right. He bought my Action Man a tank – a big lump of moulded green vinyl with black caterpillar tracks – and he painted that too, in the right camouflage with the right serial numbers, and rolled-up netting on the back that Sergeant Scarface could use to keep out of sight of spotter planes when he made camp under the coffee table. Dad was so pleased with this transformation that he couldn't help but share it.

'Come here, mate, I've got something to show you.'

It was an evening in late November and my mother was out. I was impressed when he lifted the tank from a cardboard box in the bottom of his wardrobe, if a little confused about who it was for.

'Is it mine, Dad?'

He was turning the turret, lifting the gun and making quiet firing noises.

'Can I have a go?'

'Yeah. Yeah,' he said, not looking up. 'Just let me show you this bit . . .'

And that's how I learned to act surprised on Christmas morning, a life skill that still comes in handy.

Slowly, though, I began to realize that this was not just a game; that the soldiers on the television who clutched their chests and fell writhing to the ground were actors, yes, but they were acting out a version of something real. Somebody had really died, sometime in the past. The survivors were still alive, and you could see them out in force once a year; old men in berets and raincoats marching to a Remembrance Day service in loose formation behind the Boys' Brigade band, then standing to attention with tears in their eyes as the Last Post was played. Each was alone again the following day, bareheaded, shuffling with a stoop, carrying dinner for one home from the Wavy Line.

Neither of my grandfathers would talk about what he had done in the war, but that just added to the glamour. It must have been top secret, or so traumatic they couldn't bear to relive the memories. Frank, my mother's father, had driven a truck with the Eighth Army, the Desert Rats. He drove at El Alamein and Monte Cassino, Frank came home to Gladys, who was waiting in the East End of London, and never drove any kind of vehicle ever again. He never said why.

Bert was also silent, about the war anyway. My father's father was fitter than Frank, latterly at least, and therefore easier to believe in as a soldier. He didn't lay on the sofa on Sunday afternoons snoring, with fag ash spilling down his string vest. He was usually at the swimming pool, or exercising in the garden, soaking up so much sun that we used to say he looked like an Indian. He even wore a uniform, the blue-black tunic of the Salvation Army with the words 'blood and fire' on his cap and a silver cornet under his arm. When I played I would often pretend to be him, wading ashore in the rainbullet splatter of the Normandy landings with the bodies of my comrades twitching all around me as they fell. The war had happened and he had been in it and so there was only one obvious conclusion: my grandfather was a hero.

2

There is a silence peculiar to families that keep secrets. It is like the silence you hear when you enter a room just after a raging argument, when the angry words have died away but the air is still agitated in their wake. For those of us born long after the secret, the peculiar quality of the silence may be the only clue that anything ever happened. It offers a sign that something in the past changed the lives of the people we love, and made them who they are. Perhaps even crippled them. Perhaps determined the shapes of our own lives. The silence is passed down, from father and mother to son and daughter, and on. So it was for the men and women who came home at the end of the Second World War but could never talk about what they had been through, nor explain why it was so hard to settle down again. Their families could only imagine what had happened, by watching the person who had come back to live with them. In these acts of imagination, both heroism and guilt were exaggerated. Any fragments of memory that did spill out into words were forgotten or misremembered; but the consequences of both the war and the return continue to echo through the beliefs and fears, thoughts and actions of children and grandchildren. The air is still agitated long after the disturbance, like the draught that lingers when a door has been slammed shut.

As for my father, he must have been a hero to me, too; but when I try to remember those times, a big playground bully of a memory pushes all others out of the way and takes me to a room with a high ceiling and the sea visible through a long window. I am holding a new Action Man, a present for my eighth birthday, and I'm sitting at a large, hexagonal Formica table made low enough for children. There are many of us in the big room, and all the others are talking like friends. The oldest is next to me: Robert Amos. I remember the name as clearly as the raven hair and ratty face. He is twelve. We are both patients at a sanatorium for the asthmatic children of postal workers and telephone engineers, in a small town on the south coast.

'How long you here for?'

The question puzzles me. I try to remember what the doctor in the black suit and waistcoat said in his rooms, but all I can recall is a cold metal stethoscope and the rattle of the lift cage on the way back down to the street. I think of the matron of this place, York Lodge, snow-haired in a white dress, drinking tea with my parents as I fingered the scar on my Action Man's rubber cheek. The meeting took place in a room I was later forbidden to enter. There is a pain in my chest as I am telling you this, a faint but insistent sense of panic.

Back in 1975 I give my answer: 'Two weeks. That's what they told me: a fortnight, see how it goes. Two weeks. If I don't like it I can go home.'

He laughs. In my memory he laughs like a demon, like Captain Hook or the Sheriff of Nottingham. He was a child, I must remember that. But you don't laugh the way Robert Amos laughs unless you are happily aware of causing havoc and pain.

'Nobody comes for two weeks.' His crow eyes shine. 'Six months, at least. A year sometimes.'

He is right and I know it even as he points to a shaven-headed boy in the corner whose face is red with eczema.

'One year, so far. I'm going home soon.'

And he was. Robert Amos left us. The rat king fled the pack, by which time I knew its rules all too well. One parental visit a month, on a Saturday afternoon, 'because some of you have mummies and daddies who live too far away to come more often than that so we've got to be fair'. One Saturday a month, to eat jam sandwiches on the beach at Birling Gap, run from wasps, skim stones, swim with Dad, laugh at my little sister and cry all the way back to bed. And between times, a telephone call every night. Sitting under the stairs, whispering.

'You put the phone down.'

'No, you.'

I never could. Neither could my mum.

'We've got something to show you,' she said one Saturday visit. 'It's a house.'

I could see that. A house with a blue door and a rectangular window.

'Yes,' I said. 'Whose is it?'

'Yours,' they said, together.

And so, when I finally took my things out of the dormitory cupboard, and gave away the remains of a big plastic jar of sweet peanuts that had lasted a month (two every morning break) and wrapped myself up warm with the football scarf I had begged for Christmas (a red, white and black one like Robert Amos had, although I could not have said where Manchester was and would never support United) and got into the back of the car, and was driven away with a wave but no sadness, and got back to London, we did not go to Selwyn Avenue. We did not go back to the old place. I never said goodbye to Mrs Walker and the class that had written to me in what they called hospital. There was no last battle, no goodbye to the girl downstairs. Instead, we pulled up outside a terraced house on an estate on the other side of our town.

It was a dump. Literally, in the case of the neighbouring front garden whose tenants collected car spares like other people keep gnomes. Instead of the long green grass of the old recreation ground we had a concrete square to play in, with broken railings and weeds growing through. There is nothing to be romantic about, in retrospect: this was not a nice place to live. I didn't realize it then – I was too busy setting up an assault course in the garden, was flying over the coal bunker, jumping from milk crate to crate, reaching for the sky on a rusty swing and burrowing through the scrappy bushes that served as a fence – but I realize it now. I've been back, driven around, and it hasn't changed much. I know why they moved there, too: the doctors said my asthma was aggravated by the central heating, so we became one of the few families on the borough housing list prepared to do without radiators. Consequently the house was very cold, particularly that first winter.

I think about it now and realize the sacrifices my parents were prepared to make, but little boys don't see such things. Particularly little boys who weep every night because they want to go home, although they don't know where home is. The old flat had faded from my memory. At York Lodge I used to love to look out of the classroom window at the ferries leaving Newhaven, crossing the grey Channel, and the longing to be by the sea would never leave me; but I had bad dreams about being ordered back to that dormitory. I also had nightmares in the new place, where shapes on the wall-paper throbbed in the dark and frost glittered on the ceiling.

There were good days. Sometimes Dad would finish his work as a telephone engineer early on a Friday afternoon and he'd come for us. We would be halfway down the A127 on the way to Southend before the rush hour started. The empty beaches were wide expanses of mud at low tide, but my father, sister and me played on them anyway, wearing cold-weather coats with fur collars. We built muddy castles then undermined them with tunnels until the wet sand cracked and they fell. Only the turrets and battlements remained, isolated and vulnerable as the tide came back in. Then we heard Mum's call and ran to chips or candyfloss in the finger-thawing warmth of the van. All the way home I would lay on my back among oily tools and rolls of wire, watching lights sweep across the roof.

But all my fantasies were of escape. The sea was my way out: an irresistible higher power that would carry me away from these people whose rules I had no choice but to accept. I loved and hated them at the same time, but it was easier to express hate at high volume than admit the other. Most of all I felt detached, as though I didn't belong with them any more. When there were arguments I would roll up on my bed and pound my forehead with my fists in rage, silently screaming that I wanted to go home. Wherever that was.

3

'Where's Dad going? Where's he going?'

Mum doesn't answer. She's looking at the wall, at the cupboards, anywhere but at me. My sister has wrapped both arms around my mother's waist and is crying. Dad is upstairs, slamming wardrobe doors.

'Where's he going?'

He's coming down the stairs, not shouting any more, standing in the doorway. Saying nothing. There's a black bag in his hand.

'What are you doing?'

He's turning his back, opening the front door. Closing it very carefully, as if coming in late after a curry with his friends. Only he is on the outside. I can see his body through the glass, filling the porch. Quite still.

'Mum?'

He's gone. I pull open the door and run out on to the pavement, still high with fury and fear from our argument, tongue still burning from the names I called him.

'Dad, wait . . .'

The Purple People Eater starts up. That's what we call our Escort estate, after an old rock and roll song. I drew a picture of it on the cover of my English composition book. The door is locked and the window closed. He won't look at me.

I run behind as he drives off, my bare feet coming down on tarmac, stones, and coloured glass from somebody's broken rear light. Running to try to catch him. Stop him. Holding on to the side mirror.

'Dad!'

The car brakes. As I fall forward, unable to stop, his right hand is rolling down the window. The left is on the steering wheel. The engine dies, stalled.

'I'm going,' he says, calmly. 'I need to think.'

I have no words, no breath. I want to say sorry. I want to ask why. There is no need. As the ignition key turns and the car jumps forward our wet eyes meet and my father speaks:

'You are breaking up my marriage.'

They didn't split up. He came back after three or four days and they stayed together. He never repeated what he had said to me out in the road and I never mentioned it. We both used to say things we didn't mean. Everybody does, don't they? I didn't want to be held accountable for some of the statements I had made. And I certainly didn't want to believe he had been right.

'You ought to show a bit of respect,' my mother would say.

'I will,' was the answer. 'When he does something I can respect him for.'

If I met my thirteen-year-old self today I would give him a thump on the nose. But although Dad took off his belt and raised it one night, as I threw some apocalyptic teenage fit, I do not recall a blow ever landing. I cannot remember ever being hit, despite my eagerness to provoke.

I came home in tears one day, having been threatened in the playground. He tried to teach me the best way to throw a punch, using your body weight and the momentum of your opponent; and it was not very long before I was using this useful technique, not to thwart a school bully but to land Dad a blow in the stomach. He was a big bloke with a gut, an obvious point of weakness that I exploited with all the cruelty of ignorance. The punch was the climax of a row that had raged all over the house for reasons I couldn't even remember by the middle of it, but what came next was pathetic: I watched him fold up and reach out for support and I ran for the bathroom, sliding the door behind me with a crash and pulling across the bolt to lock it.

'Come out of there now!' he shouted when he had got his wind back. 'Let me in!'

Not on your life, I thought. 'I'm not stupid.' That was debatable. 'I'm not coming out until you promise not to hit me back.'

He was never going to hit me, but nor would he promise. The siege could have gone on for hours, but Mum knew how to end it: she put the chip pan on.

Our arguments were about the usual teenage things: loud music, untidy bedrooms, the washing-up, nuclear disarmament, religion, the state of the Labour Party. 'Never be frightened of asking questions,' he would say as he stood in front of the mirror putting on a tie for that night's council meeting, exchanging the overalls and instruments of an engineer for the suit of a civic grandee.

'Question everything people tell you.'

I thought it rich that a man who taught his son a mantra like that should get so offended when the boy began to question the things he believed in. Dad was the son of a Salvationist but he had chosen not to follow his father's faith, expressing his inherited sense of social justice through politics instead. So he became an Alderman, a representative of the London Borough of Waltham Forest, and for one year its deputy mayor. This meant I got to see the look on the faces of my friends as I rode at the head of the borough carnival in the back of a mayoral Daimler driven by a chauffeur in a peaked cap. It also meant Dad's address and number were in the council yearbook. The telephone rang every night and at weekends, and voices poured out their problems, demanding to know how they were supposed to pay the rent or live with the fungus on their walls. We knew all about that: green mould growing in the bedroom of our damp flat had given me bronchitis as a baby and first triggered my asthma.

'Is Councillor Moreton in?'

They came to the door, sometimes when I was watching the telly with Mum. The two of us played along with *A Question of Sport* on Wednesdays while Dad was out at the council.

'Can I leave him a message?'

My mother must have been annoyed and slightly fearful at having to go through the drawers in the sideboard for a pen while some strange man she didn't know stood in the shadows outside. He was still talking as she closed the door:

'It's just we've got a problem with the drains.'

The hate was far louder than the love by the time I was sixteen. That is how sons are with their fathers. Each of us grows up believing ours is the greatest man in the world, a colossus who can fend off any enemy on our behalf. We long to be like him. Then we begin to see his faults: the vanity, the weak will, the ageing body and ready temper, his impatience. Never mind that these are flaws we already share, and that will grow bigger in us; we are gloriously unaware of that just yet. Our task is to challenge the old man, to bring him to account. To take his place at the head of the household. And then to leave it.

When I was fifteen years old Dad arranged work

experience for me at the local newspaper. He was friends with the editor, through politics. A year later I was invited to join the staff as a trainee reporter, which seemed to make a lot more sense at the time than doing A levels. I was only a child, but tried so hard to fit in, staying out and spending my new money with my new grown-up friends from the paper who appeared to enjoy indulging the amusing puppy panting at their heels. At eighteen I got on my knees and prayed, embracing the very religious tradition my father had rejected, Evangelical Christianity. At nineteen I went to work in refugee camps on the other side of the world, taking this new faith to extremes that alarmed my parents. I discovered that the starving poor could be as devious and manipulative as the undeserving rich, perhaps more so since they had nothing to lose; and that many of my fellow missionaries would only give bread in return for the promise of a soul. My naively simplistic belief system was broken on the rocks of other people's suffering and cynicism, but I was in too deep to admit that for a while, so I tried to drown out the doubts by becoming louder about my faith. That must have really wound up my father. Our relationship improved after I got married, at twenty-three, but we were still not exactly close. We could debate each other to a standstill, and often did so while our wives looked on and shook their heads, but we never really talked about the things we felt were important. Not as equals. We couldn't be in the same room for too long before a real argument started. Many of my friends have lost their fathers and say this is how it ends: at first you don't really want help or answers from Dad because you're too busy trying to find new ones for yourself. Then he dies. And after the big bright burning shock of emptiness and panic comes the slow untreatable burn of loss, the gradual revelation of things you never knew about the person you had no choice but to live with. This is the love that comes too late.

I was lucky. My dad had a heart attack.

4

The party at the top of the Post Office Tower was a rare honour, but then he was retiring from the organization after thirty years. Arthur had started as a labourer, trained as a telephone engineer, become a salesman and won promotion after promotion, finishing as something relatively big in public relations. He was diligent but a charmer too, and the drinks party in the rotating room with views overlooking London was going to be packed with old friends. Most of them knew he had been pushing for early retirement for quite a while, hoping to get out before his rapid rise and the aggressive new ways of working took their toll. They had persuaded my mother, Marion, to lend them photographs from the old suitcase under the bed, and were ready with a slide show. The one of Arthur outside a holiday chalet some time in the sixties was bound to make people laugh: winklepicker shoes, pork-pie hat, goatee beard, a white T-shirt and blue jeans like a West Coast beatnik stranded on the Kent mudflats; and the old trim waistline he had before all those working lunches and late-night post-council pints. Somebody had even arranged a red folder, with gold lettering on the front that said 'This Is Your Life'. And it very nearly was.

The telephone rang far too early in the morning to be anything but an emergency. The green LED by the bedside said five something. It was the day of the party. I groped my way into the front room, guided by the yellow light of the street lamp outside, and grunted into the receiver.

'Dad's not well,' said my sister, just about keeping control. 'You'd better come.'

Whipps Cross hospital was a familiar place. Somewhere on the first floor my wife's grandmother was managing to smile and think of kind things to say to the poor suffering people in the beds around hers. She would slip out of the world soon, watched by her family, leaving her daughter holding the hand of the body she left behind.

Dad was in a cubicle in casualty, hidden behind a floral curtain. The heat from a heavy iron radiator pushed all the air in the room up into the corners of the ceiling where the cobwebs were. Rain stuck to a tiny window high in the wall. Bright light from a neon strip explored every blemish of my father's body, which was naked to the waist. Starched green hospital sheets creased at his groin. A butterfly needle had been taped into his left hand, and as a nurse bent across him I noticed two liver spots by a knuckle.

When she moved he saw me for the first time, through dazed eyes that seemed to plead. Underneath the clear plastic breathing mask he made an embarrassed attempt at a smile, as if he had been caught out doing something really bad or stupid. There were so many wires and drips I had to step round behind him to kiss his forehead, resting my cheek for a moment on his thin black hair.

'All right?'

Of course not. The ambulance had come just in time. I thought of a man I once saw laid out on the floor in the lobby of a concert hall, arms wide as if to embrace someone, while the woman he would have embraced hid her face in the shoulder of a female paramedic whose team had arrived too late. They put a red blanket over the man's head and cancelled the show.

*

'What the hell do you think you're doing? Do you think you're the only one that matters here? Why didn't you listen to the doctor when he told you to lose weight, go for a walk occasionally, drink a bit less? Why didn't you just tell those bastards where to shove their job and walk away? How could you let this happen? How dare you?'

Those are the questions I never asked.

My hands formed into fists on the way to the hospital the next day, and all the days after, and I wanted to punch the bus driver and shout, 'No, he can't go, I need him. There's stuff I don't know, arguments we haven't had. It's too soon. I need somebody above me.'

Those are the things I never said.

Everything goes warm in a hospital ward. Water – poured twice a day into plastic jugs which become so scratched and worn from being used to irrigate a thousand other parched throats that they always look dirty. Lucozade – which doesn't come with that crinkly orange wrapping any more. Fizzy water flavoured with fruit – which tastes foul when it is tepid. Everything is warm except the tea, brought in green cups with saucers, which is cold. And the food. They tell a man to eat properly or he'll die, then he nearly does die and they feed him stale sausage roll, baked beans in a sugary sauce and mashed potato he has to chew.

'Any chance of a kebab?'

He was smiling when he said that, giving the orderly the works: eye contact, full-beam grin and a wink. She giggled and moved on to the tracheotomy in bed three.

'I want to show you something,' he said when she had gone. He was sitting up in bed in his own pyjamas, bought new because he went naked at home. It was about the third or fourth day I had come, putting off work to sit at his bedside. Here in this awkward, enforced situation we were finding a new way of conversing: quietly, but urgently, leaning close at the shoulder but looking away from each other, surprised at this intimacy. We talked about my work, his work, football, politics, the family, anything, for the sake of talking. As though we were building up to something.

'Give us up that bag, will you?'

From the holdall he took out an exercise book with a shiny red cardboard cover and flicked through the pages.

'I've been writing things down.'

'What things?'

'The stuff I think about in the night. Bits and bobs about my childhood, the things I wanted to do. Dreams, really.'

I looked at the pages and saw dense, hieroglyphic writing rising free of the ruled lines, curved arrows, exclamation marks, diagrams and ink sketches that could have been stick people standing by a house.

'I'm trying to get it out of my head, on to the page. It helps. I want to tell you about it, now we've got a bit more time.'

But he didn't. We promised each other these conversations would go on after he left hospital but they did not. We were both busy. We were both, perhaps, unsettled by the glimpse of something uncomfortably true. We said we wanted to keep on talking like that but maybe we didn't really. Maybe it was too much of a reminder to him of the nights in that ward when the pipes rattled and the dying men moaned and the walls closed in. Maybe I was afraid of what he might say and unwilling to listen. For whatever reason we let it slip, let ourselves ease back into a way of being that was less tense than before, more understanding, more grateful, but still conveniently distant. The moment had passed.

*

Wait. Another memory presses in. Dad is at home, on the brown and gold velveteen sofa under the serving hatch, lying on his side with his knees brought up to his chest and his arms wrapped into each other. He has not shaved or washed today. He is wearing a clean sweatshirt and jogging bottoms because my mother brought them to him this morning and made him put them on. They are soaked with sweat although he has not really moved from the sofa all day. He doesn't talk much, she says, he just cries and cries. There are long silences, when his eyes drift away and nobody can catch his attention. Then he cries again. I kneel on the floor beside the sofa and try to put my arms around his great big shoulders, try to reach around his neck, try to embrace him. He moves his head slightly to register my presence but remains on his side, trembling. I am trembling too, almost lying on top of him, my face in the nape of his neck, squeezing hard as if trying to force something up from the core of him. There is nothing to say but 'I love you'.

That is how he was on the worst of days. They gave him drugs and the dead man breathing on the sofa came back to life, slowly, over weeks and months. The nervous breakdown actually happened before the heart attack, as is often the case, but one intense memory bleeds into another. The doctors blamed stress: the long working days and the nights when I heard him crying with frustration downstairs because the next exam was one push too far; the committees and full council meetings, the canvassing and decision making. But nobody ever said why he was like that, what had driven him so hard. Then again nobody else wanted to know as much as I did. We were so alike, that was why we found it so hard to get on. When I looked at him on the sofa and on the casualty trolley I saw my future self. That was frightening. There was another kind of future waiting, however, in which our similarity would be a strength. It was the next stage in the cycle of father and son, the one we nearly didn't get to. I became a father myself, after a long time trying. We both moved one step up the ladder of life. He became a grandfather. I had lost my childish faith in him as a hero but now at last, as a man who had a son of his own, I would begin to recognize the struggles he had been through. I was going through them, too.

My father did eventually have his party at the top of the tower, and he completed the traditional East End journey from council flat to council house to private house, then a bigger one in the suburbs and finally a bungalow in the Essex countryside. It is in a quiet cul-de-sac where all the houses have loft extensions that mean they're not really bungalows at all; a sort of seaside retirement village without the sea. There is a phrase he likes to use, when they come home from the shops with brass dimmer switches or ornaments like the porcelain fairy castle on their mantelpiece that lights up inside:

'That's it. We've joined the middle classes now.'

Some days, though, he is like a tightrope walker who just looked down. Some nights he wakes up sweating and the bedroom is like a cauldron to him although the radiator is off and the windows wide open. Then he starts scribbling page after page of notes that will be unreadable in the morning, just like he did in hospital. He has unfinished business.

So have the older men and women who come to the museum he helps to run, which is dedicated to the airfield on the edge of his village. They come with their grandsons and daughters, who sit in the corner while Gramps or more rarely Granny talks into a tape recorder, telling tales of another life that might otherwise have been forgotten. There is something safe about grandchildren: they are interested enough to listen but don't know enough to ask the really awkward questions. The experiences of the three generations since the war mirrors those of many immigrant families across the world. The adults of 1945 behaved like the first generation of settlers, who typically do everything they can to engage with their new homes, preferring not to tell stories about how they got there. They teach their children to look only to the future, so that those sons and daughters become detached from the old ways. Some reject their heritage entirely, while others are sustained by falsely romantic versions of it.

Then grandchildren come along. They challenge their own parents and feel the need to look further back, to understand their roots. By now their grandparents are old, preoccupied with memories and only too willing to talk. Something similar has been happening in museums and oral history groups all over the country in the last decade or so. People who would always say nothing of the war have been volunteering their stories in remarkable numbers, often through their grandchildren.

I saw this for myself at a squadron reunion held at the museum one day in the summer. Old Spitfire pilots in hound's-tooth sports jackets cut the air with their palms to relive the briefest of dogfights, while on the other side of the room stood men with rougher accents who were once their ground crews, charged with pumping fuel and loading guns even as the bombs dropped around them. 'He jumped out of the plane and said, "Where the bloody hell's my sergeant?" Nobody knew. He was furious. We found the fella sitting in a latrine with a piece of shrapnel through his head.'

The grandchildren left them to it after a while and retreated to the pub, but they had all gone by the time we closed the museum and went for a drink. Dad nurtured his pint glass, balancing it on the ledge of his stomach, as the two of us sat alone outside. Foam slid down the side and stained his rugby shirt. After each mouthful he stroked his beard, which was growing out, becoming a little wild. The silver flashes had almost driven out the black. He wanted something, but seemed unable to ask for it. I think he was searching for a way to start the conversation we had been putting off for so long. He needed to fashion a useful, healing story from the mess in his head.

'It's almost like a cleansing that's going on. It is a relief.'

He was talking about the oral history volunteers. At least I thought he was.

'They know their time is nearly up,' he said.

Neither of us mentioned what we had recently learned: a consultant had discovered a tumour in his eye. It was malignant. He would go blind. He might not have long to live.

'After telling nobody these things for so long they are now saying, "I need to get this off my chest and away from me before I go."'

He paused, and looked into his beer.

'While I still have time.'

5

My father was offering the chance to talk properly at last, to confront fears he himself had put in my mind; to answer a challenge he had made a couple of years earlier, dropping it into a casual chat like a hand grenade through a letterbox. Back then we had been discussing where he was born and went to school, his first job; the mundane details. Matters of record that were necessary for an application I was making on his behalf. He leaned back in a pine chair that bent under his weight, and shielded his eyes from the sun streaming in through the window. I sat opposite, with a notebook and a red felt pen, writing things down and not looking him in the eye. It felt peculiar to be interviewing my own father about his life, even on such a superficial level. I knew he didn't like to talk about his childhood. Instead he would usually make a joke or promise to tell the whole truth when he thought I could take it.

'One day. Not now.'

That was the answer I expected when I asked, half-heartedly, about his mother. Instead he gave a response that changed both our lives, although we did not know it at that moment, nor even for a long while afterwards. He said something about her struggles. I asked if he meant depression. I knew what it felt like to experience sudden moments of utter desolation for no apparent reason. He seemed about to agree but shook his head instead, as if to say this was a thing far greater than I would understand:

'She had the family curse. I have got it. So have you.'

We drank more coffee and talked about something else and got up from our yielding chairs and said no more about such things. The red felt pen notes were typed up but as the weeks and months passed by that same moment, the exchange that had slipped by, kept coming back to me. I had been cursed by my father. Should I laugh it off? Should I be afraid?

'Tell me more about this curse,' I said more than once, but he would not do so. Not for a long time. Not until the night he decided he was ready.

The photograph had been in his loft room for years. Dad would sit up there by it on warm evenings with a telescope pointing out of the skylight, listening to voices breaking through the hiss of a short-wave radio as pilots flew their vintage warbirds low overhead. They were coming down to land at the airfield, hobbyists copying the flight paths of the fighters who had descended there half a century before. Small pewter or plastic models of their aircraft were arranged along low shelves at the point where the sloping roof met the floor. There were books and videos everywhere too, mostly concerned with the aeroplanes of the Second World War. The photograph was not out of place but it was sinister. The docks and yards of East London were laid out with the clarity of a map, as the Thames slipped tight like a noose around the Isle of Dogs, but the cityscape was scarred by the black shape of a bomber with white crosses burning on its wings. He lifted the photograph from its hook, carried the frame carefully with his fingertips, set it down on the floor and began to describe its significance to me for the first time. The image had been captured from a second aircraft flying directly above the bomber at 5.48 p.m. on Saturday 7 September. Only a few clouds of smoke could be seen rising from the docks because this was still the first hour of an onslaught that would last fifty-seven days and nights. This moment in his room was another kind of beginning. Perhaps for want of a clue about how to start talking, for want of the words to say things he dared not tell himself, he was showing me the picture that reminded him of everything he would rather forget.

'See that dark line?' He traced it with his finger. 'That is the Grand Surrey Canal. My mum and dad were down there, walking along it, when this was taken. The first day of the Blitz.'

6

This is how I think of them. On a towpath beside a canal, on a hot and cloudless day, a man and a woman are walking, talking. The sky is deep hot blue above their heads, over the timber stacks and factories, the church spire and the dockside cranes that claw the horizon. Boathouse Walk is wide and the young man keeps to the edge of it, watching light splash in the water. Enjoying the free luxury of sunshine. Midges spiral over his head, attracted by the sweat glistening on his high forehead, but he is cool enough. Down to a clean white undershirt and glad of it, khaki draped over one shoulder. He reaches out behind him, without looking away from the light on the water, but she is not there.

A few steps back in the shadow of a barge sail, Violet is keeping out of the sun. Still unsure of him, she is conscious of the way the cornflower blue dress rides on her hips. They were married nearly a year ago, but have been together as man and wife only a few times since then. He kissed her on the steps of the register office on a Saturday morning and left in the afternoon, catching a bus as though he were going to work, not to fight.

'I'm frightened,' she says.

'Eh?' Splintered crate wood floats at his feet, disturbing the rainbow surface. A skinny boy of nine or ten, with a scar on his back, pulls himself up out of the water on the far side. His friends are laughing.

'I know,' says the soldier gently, when he has registered her words. 'I know, mate.'

There is something else he doesn't want to say: so am I.

She looks at the back of his head, at the shoulders that have grown stronger since he went away.

'I don't know what to do.'

They are both believers, as sure of heaven as of the blue sky, but neither is sure that prayer will save them from being promoted to glory too soon. Asleep at night he sees ruined French houses. A ruined house. Chicken feathers in the yard, water seeping from a broken well, a dead dog and roof tiles in the bushes. A girl bent double in the dust. They were lovely houses, some of them. She has nightmares too, of parachutes blossoming overhead and tanks juddering down Rye Lane, but it is not the prospect of invasion that wakes her before dawn. That's not what she is afraid of.

'Bert? Play a game.'

'I don't get you.'

'Listen. What do you hear?'

Bottles clinking and the clop of a horse stepping forward, pulling a lemonade cart along the path. The beating of wings echoing under a bridge. The lap of water on stone. 'Nothing,' he says.

'Say what you hear.' Her smile is strange.

'What? Everything?'

'Anything.'

A saw whining in the timber yard at Eagle Wharf. An ambulance bell. An uncommon throbbing sound behind it all like the slow beat of a giant heart.

'Pigeons,' he says. 'Under there.'

They both look back into the shadows.

'What else? Quickly.' She is afraid it will stop.

Somebody whistling. 'A baby crying,' he says.

A baby. He might have noticed the way her eyelids closed and her face turned from him when he said that, but he doesn't, because the words of a fisherboy have more urgency: 'Bloody hell, look at that lot. They'll give the bastards a treat.'

They look up, with all the other Saturday afternoon walkers, across the canal and over the factory rooftops to the east. High in the sky, a flock of silver birds suspended in the blue. Hundreds of them. The massed aircraft of the Royal Air Force going off to give the Germans hell.

'Puffing out a lot of smoke, aren't they?'

That's when he notices the growing, throbbing, uneven sound and feels a lurch in his stomach. Those gentle black smoke rings are not coming from the engines, they are shells exploding in mid-air. Fired by the mates who stayed behind on the guns while he took a day's leave.

'They're not ours, Vi.'

The muscles around his chest contract and his sweat goes cold.

'Come on.'

'Where? Where do we go?'

'I don't know. Under here. Run, girl.'

The soldier and his shy lover, a boy with war eyes and a girl carrying a child, catch their breath under the bridge. The sound is familiar, but not in that volume. How can there be so many?

Up there a shutter opens to receive the dazzle and glitter of a city in summer, seen from high above. The camera operator cannot believe it has been so easy for three hundred bombers to get this far, crossing the coast of Kent and swinging to follow the line of the Thames on their way to Zielraum G, the docklands of London. They form a line twenty miles wide, in wings of three, with twice as many fighter escorts dancing above and below them; but few of the bomber crews have seen any opposition, apart from the belated bubbling of anti-aircraft shells far below. All leave has been cancelled and every available plane recruited for the attack, ordered as revenge for the outrageous bombing of Berlin. As they crossed the Channel their newly self-appointed commander was apparently on the clifftop at Cap Griz Nez with his officers to see it for himself. There was a radio transmitter with him so that Goering could broadcast to their parents, children and lovers back home. 'Today I have heard above me the roaring of the victorious German squadrons which now, for the first time, are driving towards the heart of the enemy in full daylight.' The claws beneath the Heinkel open. The first of many bombs begins to fall, confusing earth and sky on the way down to the terrible impact it was made for. The words scratched into its metal casing will never be read again: 'Heil, London.'

Down falls the bomb, and down, towards the canal. Bert and Vi lean close against the damp wall of the tunnel, muttering breathless prayers out loud. Thy kingdom come. They look out through streaming eyes as firefly incendiaries flutter, clang and clatter against pipe and tile. The ground under their feet moans, groaning with the pain of it all as the night comes early. Thy will be done in the burning dark. Deliver us from the evil of the cloud descending, thick, black choking smoke rolling down, dropping all around. The docks are burning, a mile of Canada pine stacked high as houses now crackling, sending flames up and the cloud westward on the wind, full of embers, sparks and glowing splinters carried in the air. Somewhere on the road above them a baby cries or a woman cries like a baby or a man does and the smoke slouches over the side of the bridge to rest on the water, sucking up breath. The horse on the empty towpath, abandoned, stands dead still as it is enveloped. The power and the glory screams from above, forever and ever, jealous of life, shaking the earth, disturbing the waters like angels playing. With a hideous din a plague of rats pours from a fence, all face and teeth and whining, chirping, complaining; black body upon body tumbling towards the waters foaming with the thrashing mass. A thousand rodent eyes reflect the pink flash of a mine exploding in the churchyard of Saint Chrysostom the golden-mouthed. The air cracks, breaking through the roar, bursting eardrums. Oh my love. Throats burn, lungs are shrivelled by the fumes from flaming oil and tar and rubber and paint and varnish in the blazing yards. The bombs fall again and again.

When at last the steady blast of the all-clear comes they begin to walk, dazed, through night streets blind with blood and oil and shattered glass, past smoking bricks and upturned prams, flooded craters and raging timbers. The dying of the sun turns the sky from blue to red as low, slow-turning clouds reflect the flames reaching into the air at Surrey Docks a few miles away, where burns the fiercest fire ever recorded in London. Crews hurry there from far away, to cover their mouths with cloths and join the men who watch their water turn to steam in heat that blisters the paint on their engines. The burning barge, the smouldering pub, the fizzing rosettes left by incendiaries among the rubble will have to go untended. Bert and Vi walk past them, stepping carefully in the half-light, feeling waves of heat then the rushing cold. In an empty street they hear the sound of their own footsteps against the thunderous rumble of unseen walls falling. Blackout curtains are closed, shelters are full. Then they turn a corner and see the side of a house sliced off, the fountain of a burst main pipe, a broken-backed bed on what used to be the pavement. A coat spread out on the rubble and under it the shape of somebody's old man. The wife is hysterical, thrashing in the arms of an ARP girl who looks on the verge of tears herself. The widow's face is black with congealed blood, crusted with the plaster dust that covers her hair and clothes. Tears run over tiny splinters of glass embedded in her cheeks. The face is lost in the dancing darkness, as bodies press around them. Men, women, children, dragging their lives in blankets and bedspreads, loaded on to bikes and wheelbarrows, all going but nobody knows where. As they walk they hear rumours, bellowed through the din. The wardens are terrified, staggered, panicking. They need to talk, to anyone. 'Don't go near the Old Kent Road, the gas works have got it.' 'No direct hits, thank bloody God.' Two kids buried in a shelter on Green Hundred Road, with their mum and dad. Family called Lucas killed in their beds on Sandgate Street, parents and three girls. Nunhead Lane took a hit. The sirens are going again as they reach Bert's house, where his mother is standing on the front step, turning a tea towel over and over in her hands like a twisted dolly. As the two women embrace in tears he looks away, up and to the south where the searchlights sway. 'They're coming again.' Vi has one hand buried in the hair at the back of his mother's neck, the other on her churning stomach. She is weeping for her baby.

The unborn child survived and became my father. The rest of it is true to what I have read and heard. I have read and heard a great deal these last months, including many things not spoken of before, and some things that should have remained unspoken. The fate of his family during that war, and just after it, determined so much of who my father was and so many of the burdens that he carried, but the stories were never told. In the end, when you have read and listened and asked the questions that are not welcome and tried to understand the limited, hesitant answers, what else can you do but imagine? Fragments of memory and half-truth lay around the family like debris. The ruin is cold, the smoke has cleared, the flash has long faded. All we have left is the damage done. Is it best forgotten? Perhaps, if you can. But sometimes you can't, because there is something in the debris waiting to explode.

7

'When's the baby due?'

'Next year. Spring.'

There seem to be babies everywhere: in prams, on shoulders, wrapped up in blankets, strapped to backs, in all these crowds. The streets are so full the truck can only move a few feet at a time, growling, hissing with its brakes, threatening a way through. Everyone's trying to leave, to get to their relatives out of town or down to the hop-picking fields. Even the ones who have nowhere to go are walking away from the burning fires and broken streets, with all they can carry or drag. Horses, cars, barrows, anything with a wheel or a broad back is on the road and in the way of the army truck that should be carrying Bert out of London.

He was awake as the dawn came, standing in the doorway of his mother's house and listening to the rain fall on all the broken things: the glass, the tiles, the bricks, the wood, the skin and bones. A calming sound after the engines and the bombs. 'You've got to go back,' his brother said, and Bert knew that he was right. He had to go back to the guns even if it was all over, even if they had no chance.

Vi had fallen asleep as the day came but he woke her and told her what she already knew. War makes people good at goodbyes. The door was closed and he was gone before she pulled the blanket back over her head.

At the local barracks they put him on a truck heading for Kent, because all the railways had been bombed out. They haven't got far, in all the confusion.

'What do you want, a boy or a girl?'

He's taking a lot of interest, the Welsh soldier sitting in the shadows on the other side of the flat bed of the truck. Keeping his eyes on Bert, sucking on a Woodbine, asking questions. Just being friendly. The words come rattling out of him thirteen to the dozen, shaken out by fear and weariness like tacks on to a table, but they bounce off Bert again, not getting through.

'Bet it's a boy. Hope so, eh? Be great for you.'

'Yeah.' Something like a smile twitches on his face. 'Yeah, be great. Woah.'

The truck lurches forward as the driver puts his foot down, emerging from the crowds to climb Denmark Hill. From the top they can see the thick, sickly smoke still hanging over the city, and the flicker of fires unquenched.

'This is a mess,' says Bert. His travelling companion nods.

'Heard about the Elephant? The gates were locked but there were so many people trying to get in they broke them down.'

The storming of the Elephant & Castle tube station by people desperate for shelter has been repeated all over the underground. There are already queues for places to sit under damp old railway arches, under the protection of sandbags and Victorian bricks. Those who have chosen to stay at home have no gas or electricity, the telephones are silent, and there is no milk or bread in the shops. In alleyways and pub snugs, money is already being exchanged for the leather wallets, driving licences and ration books of the dead, filleted from their bodies in the smoky darkness as rescuers call out for more hands. Bombed-out houses had been stripped of their valuables before the sun came up; but, then, who was to say whether the owner of a brass candlestick left miraculously intact in the rubble was lying on a slab, or a hospital bed, or trudging out of town with the rest?

As the truck crawls through south London it passes countless crowds heading in the same direction, who will reach the suburbs by nightfall with rumours that the city has been destroyed. Out in the countryside, in a copse by the road, the truck is waved down by a group of women still filthy from the raids, their faces streaked by rain and tears. Their children are huddled under trees. The coach driver who brought them there from a rest centre in Bermondsey hasn't a clue what to do next.

'Those were the orders,' he tells the sergeant riding in the front of Bert's truck. 'Bring them here. That's it. Then go back and get some more. But I can't leave the poor beggars out in the rain like this, they're starving.'

The jowly driver in his stuffed and stained white shirt throws out an arm towards the forty or so refugees, enough to indicate their predicament, but it is the listless gesture of a man who thinks there is nothing he can do. Someone should have met them but some of his fellow drivers don't know the countryside and with all the road signs removed or painted out it is easy to get lost.

'There's bloody massive craters in the road back there,' he says, 'and floods where the water mains have burst, and then you go round a corner and some idiot's blocking the way but he hasn't got a reason. I heard other blokes have been cancelled or sent to the wrong places and nobody knows why. Chaos, that's what it is.'

'Bedlam, brother,' says the soldier in the shadows, leaning forward now so Bert can see the dark cherry markings of the medical corps on one sleeve. They have both been listening to the driver through the canvas canopy of their own truck, leaning against crates stamped with big red crosses.

'London will become one vast raving Bedlam.' The medic speaks quietly, in low tones, his accent thickening. 'The hospitals will be stormed. Traffic will cease, the homeless will shriek for help. The city will be in pandemonium.'

Bert hears him properly for the first time, assuming for a moment that these unsettling words are from the Bible. They are not.

'The government will be swept away by an avalanche of terror and grasp the enemy's terms like a drowning man after a straw,' says the medic, relishing the final words of his quote. 'He knew what he was talking about.'

'Who?'

'Fuller. General. Invented the blitzkrieg that is going to have Adolf marching through here before we know it.'

'Don't sound German.'

'No, one of ours, although you'd hardly think so. They've locked him up for being a sympathizer, just because he thought we should have done a deal. Been proved right now though, so he has. We've had it.'

Bert nods. He's looking at a boy who is holding on to his mother's skirt, his knuckles white through the grime. The engine roars, the truck turns, sliding over muddy tracks until it grips the road again, leaving the boy and his mother to fade into the light and dark of the forest. Night is coming.

'You got a girl, Taff?'

'I have, gunner. At least I hope so, you know. Doesn't want to marry me. I miss her. You?'

'No, thanks mate. I'm already married.'

They both smile, too tired and overwhelmed to do any more. Bert leans back against his kitbag, spreading his legs wider to balance against the jolting truck, and closes his eyes.

'I hope it is a boy.'

★

It was. Arthur was born in March 1941. The birthrate that year was the lowest ever recorded in England, to nobody's surprise. All the babies conceived in a hurry after the declaration of war had been born by then, and most of the young men who might have become fathers were away. The charming Americans who would take their places in so many beds had yet to arrive. Bert had been evacuated from France in the summer of 1940 and waited in various artillery camps as the country braced itself for invasion.

Vi was twenty-five, a bit old to be having her first child. She stayed close to her parents for as long as possible before taking the government up on its offer to get pregnant women out of the city. Her sister Min was already down in the West Country, so she arranged digs with a couple in Musbury, a little village near Axminster which had a church, a pub, a skittles alley and the ruins of the house where Francis Drake once lived. It must have been hard to adjust to the place, however hospitable the family; and many were not at all welcoming to women like Vi.

'Slatternly malodorous tatterdemalions,' they were called by one academic who wrote to the *Spectator* magazine to complain about the city girls who had invaded the countryside, 'trailing children to match'. James Joyce used this rare word in *Ulysses* to describe Florry Talbot, 'a blond feeble goosefat whore in a tatterdemalion gown'.

Maybe they were malodorous to country noses. Some evacuees did come from tenements where baths were a rare luxury and the outside toilets were communal. The few clothes they had were indeed ragged, their shoes in pieces and their skin and scalps diseased. The bugs that hitched a ride on some of them took up residence in their new billets, infesting the wallpaper and bedding. They were easily judged by those who had never seen their natural environment, the close-packed city streets where the women had grown up trying to ignore the poverty and squalor around them or to overcome it by living on their wits and forming alliances with the neighbours.

'A Victim' wrote to the magazine claiming there was a 'Nazi-style conspiracy of lies' to cover up the hardships being inflicted on innocent people in safe areas who had to bear these awful invaders. The authorities were 'thrusting filthy women and children into the homes of decent cleanly people'. Country churches complained, too: a congregational journal asked why 'decent homes and furniture' had to be spoiled along with 'the corruption of speech and moral standards of our own children'.

The government had created this country class war by choosing to evacuate the poorest people first. Officially, this was because they lived in places that were most likely to be bombed and could not afford to get themselves out of the way. But there was another reason: the 'foreign, Jewish and poor elements' of London were thought to be 'the classes of person most likely to be driven mad with fright'. When the bombs dropped they were expected to panic, go insane with fear, then start looting the homes of the relatively rich. Far safer, then, to have them in the sticks, however much the farmers and their wives complained.

And they did. *The Times* and *Telegraph* printed furious letters which blamed evacuation for the breakdown of traditional country life, ruining good schools and weakening trade. The children of the poor were 'stunted, misshapen creatures, only capable of understanding the very simplest language and quite incapable of thought, moved by impulses at best sentimental, at worst brutal'. War had lifted a flat stone and these 'pale, wriggling things' had been brought out into the light. They should be taken away from their parents and into care. All of them.

Nine mothers in ten did not stick around to endure this abuse. They went back home instead, to take their chances among friends and family. Most of the original evacuees had returned to London by the time Vi went down to Devon to have her baby, and she was back before he was a year old. The Germans had started attacking Exeter and Plymouth, so the West Country no longer seemed such a safe place. My father had spent his first few months on earth living by a river in glorious countryside, but he would grow up next to a canal, hearing street hawkers, trolley cars and bombs.

8

'Listen . . .'

A snowy hiss swallowed my father's voice as I reached out of the bath for a towel to dry my hands. The cordless receiver was low on batteries.

'We don't have to go if you don't want,' he said. 'It's fine. I've got stuff to get on with.'

I understood. He was nervous. No good ever came of a telephone ringing that early, in the hours before daylight eases panic.

'Would you rather not?'

'No. I'm not saying that. It's up to you, son.'

'I took the day off. Let's go.'

'Right. Sure.'

There was a pause.

'Give me an hour,' he said.

I went under, lying back until only my nostrils and eyebrows were above the water. It's a little boy's game, lurking beneath the surface like a river predator, barely visible. Deadly. Except a crocodile doesn't need to splay its feet against the wall and thrust its hips into the air, all rolling wet flesh and sodden genitalia.

'He didn't sleep very well,' my mother said when she called a few minutes later. 'This is stirring things up he would rather not think about, you know?'

I did. I hoped it would do him good. That was what I told myself. Otherwise it seemed cruel to insist that he keep his promise and take me to the place where he had lived as a child. He had not been back for forty years, maybe more.

'He's fine,' said Mum. 'I'll make sure he comes.'

So we drove south. That was a shock in itself. If you had asked me where I was from I would have said east London, north of the river. That's where I was born. It's not much of a cultural identity but people who are born in big cities have to make or take what they can. Those of us who are from nowhere else do not have the constrictions of small town life to kick against, but we can also feel the lack of strong traditions to define and comfort us. The film director John Boorman grew up in suburbs like mine, colonized by men and women who had fled from the city and thrown off their pasts: 'They were strangers to themselves and they had this kind of foolish look about them of people who don't know what to do or how to behave. And I supposed that sense of not belonging to anything is what creates that sense of alienation.' So we their children borrow identities, becoming gangstas or plastic paddies; or we fall back on old London divisions, the simplest of which is provided by the river. You are from the north or from the south, and to cross over the water for more than just a visit is to enter another kind of city, another kind of tribe. North Londoners are sophisticated, cultural, metropolitan types who read books and like art. South Londoners are their ducking, diving, dodgy cousins from lower down the tree of life and the wrong side of the river. That is what I would have said, before we drove through the Rotherhithe tunnel and into what for me was the unknown. For him it was a trip into the past, to see things again before the tumour in his eye made him blind. They could burn it away with a laser, and do the same again if it came back, but eventually there would be no more eye to burn.

'Bloody hell,' said Dad, swerving the car and only just missing a bus. 'Edwardes, the bicycle shop. I bought my first bike from there!'

We were following the Walworth Road away from the Elephant and up to the Green he said, but I didn't have a clue what he was talking about. Nothing I saw meant anything to me as we stopped and started through the traffic, his head turning so fast from one side to the other it could have flown off.

'All I remember about the first place we lived was the big steps I would sit on with some Irish friends of Mum's. Sitting there and picking me nose.'

The road was so busy we couldn't stop, or he didn't want to, so I caught just a glimpse of a large, cream-coloured terraced house on Champion Hill. 'The shelter was a table with a wire mesh underneath it where you hid away in case the bombs came. The basement room we had was tiny, and there was damp running down the walls. You looked up to the people as they walked past.'

Vi brought him to the flat when she came back from Devon.

'We left again in a hurry in 1947. We were thrown out. None of me mum's family wanted to know. We were the black sheep.'

Why? I tried to make the question casual. He kept his eyes on the road.

'Not now. I'm driving.'

9

Sketches of battle fade in the blue sky. London is quiet again, for now, and there are children playing on Denmark Hill: girls skipping, boys kicking tennis balls and Arthur Moreton, just four years old, running in circles in the playground with his arms wide, shouting, 'Ack, ack ack!' The teacher is smiling and swinging her big hand bell to summon her charges back to class when the ground explodes. A rattling sound, the devil with a smoker's cough, and grit in her eyes as shells bite into the tarmac and children shriek. A huge shadow passes between the school and the sun and is gone. A stray fighter, lost and scared, heading for home at a hellish speed low across the city, firing in blind panic at anything that moves on the ground: a coal cart, a gun swinging, children in the playground. As the thunder of his engine fades, the boys and girls and teachers are in tears. Under the apple tree a boy with ginger hair kneels with hands over his face. There is blood on them. A girl clings to the railings, her fingers white around the iron. The gate swings open and Arthur is gone – out and running, down the hill, through the cemetery, breathless and blinded by tears. Wordless, thoughtless, running and running, stumbling and dragging his feet through the crowds, across roads under the hooves of horses, kicking up the gravel, running. Running home. Hammering his little fists against the door.

'Mummy! Mum!'

There is no answer. She's not at home.

*

'I don't know where she was,' he said, fifty-six years later. 'At work I suppose, or whatever ducking and diving she was doing that day.'

We were sitting on a bench in a park, looking at a triangle of dusty grass enclosed by iron railings and the back wall of the Hunnex bubble-wrap factory. The house where he once lived had been pulled down and its rubble mixed with the thousand other bombed-out, derelict, exhausted homes that were used to fill in the old canal when it was drained of water. The straight course of the towpath, from the docks by the river to the basins where the barges loaded and turned, had almost been erased by the sandpaper rub of time and rebuilding; but it was preserved for a mile or so as a tarmac path. Instead of tenements and warehouses on either side there were now windswept playing fields that opened up under a big sky. A jet came low overhead, showing its tail like a skunk, leaving a slick trail hanging in the air as it began the approach to Heathrow. Then another, close behind, dark in the sky like a bomber.

'Tarot, leave that!'

A huge, tawny Great Dane hung its head. The crow it had been worrying flew away, shrugging out of the jagged shadows cast by the roof of the factory and over the shimmering peak of a chestnut tree. The dog padded over to a slight woman on the path, whose lined face was old enough to have known the alleys and outside lavvies when they were still there. A turquoise headscarf almost covered her eyes, but if she registered us sitting on our bench at the edge of the park, what did she see? Not a father and son, necessarily. I am blond; his dark hair is flecked with grey. I was clean-shaven, his beard was clipped short that day but it is sometimes long and it has always been there, since before I was born. He is less than six feet tall, I am more than that. He wears glasses all the time, I leave mine at home. And yet, of course, there are more similarities between us than it would be comfortable to admit. We were both wearing a fleece and jeans that day. Our upper lips curl into beaks. We have the same forlorn eyes, although his are dying. I have the comfortable tummy he had at thirty, before it solidified into an immovable spread. My fingers used to be long and thin; but they thickened, and now seem more like his every time I look. How did that happen?

We were close together, half turned towards each other but not touching. My left arm reached out along the wooden slat of the back as he leaned forward, hands clasped, head slightly bowed. Our intimacy was just visible, to those who cared to read the secret, subtle signs sent out by these allegedly insensible male bodies. We were used to being physically close more often than friends, but not like lovers. Two people who needed to be near to each other, but could hardly stand it.

'We had two rooms here. One to sleep, one to eat.'

The house was old even then, and crumbling; long before Victorian was chic again, long after the hypnotic hiss of the gas lights should have been silenced.

'I remember having to get the mantles. I used to muck it up. The mantle was like a net that went around the gas flame and glowed. It warmed up; that's how you got your light. Sometimes when it was really cold we took the mantle off so there was just the raw gas flame, and a little heat.'

There were three floors, he said, sticking to the facts; mustering strength. The rent was cheapest on the middle floor, because you suffered the noise from above and below, and annoyed both sets of neighbours. They lived closely, sharing a washing basin and a small stove on the landing.

'I fell in love for the first time with the girl from the family below. I was only about six or seven.'

When I was that age I used to hang around outside the flat below ours, hoping Samantha would pass by, going out or coming in. She had a birthday party once, and I wasn't invited. So I sat on the wall, in view of her kitchen window, kicking the concrete with the heels of wellington boots. Can't remember why I was wearing those, only that they made my feet feel stupid when Sam's mum eventually came to the door and asked if I would like to join the party. I nodded. There was a fruit machine in their front room, which was astonishing and exciting, and we played musical statues to the song 'Oranges And Lemons'. I have not thought about that party since I was a child and yet I remember it now with clarity. My father sat on the park bench and remembered the brown-eyed girl from the Romany family downstairs.

'They were called gipsies in them days. They would have been out on the road but during the war they got used to being domesticated and looking for work.'

Vi was employed in a Lyons Corner House up in the West End during the day, and as an usherette next door at the Coronet picture house in the evening, guiding customers through the dark with a torch. At night, when she had kissed him on the lips, ruffled his hair and gone downstairs, back to work, Arthur lay awake and listened for the scratching.

He's asleep, snoring just a little, fooled into slumber by the warmth at last. A five-year-old boy with his mother's tired and twitching eyes, closed for a while; and next to him, in the same bed, under the loose twisting of grey sheets, mothy blankets and coats, his younger brother Les, who is nearly four. Ice crystals glitter among the woollen strands of the soldier's old greatcoat that covers them. The night is unusually quiet: snow falling outside deadens every sound and the tap on the landing has stopped dripping because the pipes are frozen. The boys are exhausted; they've been playing hard, throwing snowballs in the churchyard and hiding in the ruins of the canal keeper's cottage across the way. They miss their old playgrounds on Denmark Hill: the water tanks the size of bungalows and the twisted, blackened frame of a fighter that was never moved after it came down burning and was stripped like a beast to the bones by boys hungry for souvenirs. The canal is a consolation though; you can jump from barge to passing barge or shoot the tumbling rats with air gun pellets or stones from a sling. They make a thin sound like an old man sucking his teeth, and scrabble on the stones; and those are the noises Arthur would hear, faintly, if he were awake now. A rat is in the room, skittering on the damp floorboards, sniffing the strong scent of the boys. The rest of its pack is making the usual dusk run through the tangle of weeds and ruins at the back of the house, from the canal side to a peanut butter factory where nut husks and sacking await; but this rodent has been tempted by the stale waft of decaying food. It is up on the bed, and under the clothes, burrowing for warmth; nuzzling an ankle, whistling its breath, tail snaking in the dark, claws catching on the bed sheet. Arthur shrugs in his sleep and stretches a leg, curling the other as if to kick a ball, trapping the rat in the hot space behind his knee. It squeals for fear and he wakes, unsure why, turning again, releasing the rodent – which claws its way along his bare calf and thigh, fighting up through the blankets, twisting one way then another, rattling the air with high-pitched sounds. Arthur yelps as the rat erupts from the blankets in the dark, its teeth and eyes shining, running over the terrified boy's face and flying for freedom, landing sideways on the floor with a thud and clattering out on to the landing.

'Hey!' calls a voice, muffled by the ceiling. 'Shut it, cantcha?'

Arthur's out of the bed, reaching for something, anything, and throwing a picture frame across the room after the vanished animal, so the glass flashes and splinters in the dark. Les is hysterical, flailing around hitting out at imaginary rodents all over the bed.

'Stop it, stupid,' says Arthur, old beyond his age. 'Come on.'

He pulls his brother by the collar of the shirt he is wearing in bed, and has been wearing all day, and the day before that, and leads him in the dark down the stairs at speed, two at a time, out on to the snow. The cold burns the skin of the two young boys as if they were naked. The verger in the churchyard across the road sees them, hurrying and snivelling, one in great distress, the other screwing up his face so as not to cry; and he looks away, and closes the big oak door behind him. The mad eyes of a slavering beast stare down at the children from the one poster window at the Coronet, caught in the whitening light as Arthur pulls open the door. *The Wolf Man*, starring Lon Chaney. Night monster with the bloodlust of a savage beast.

'Oh, sweethearts,' says Vi, gathering the two shivering boys close to her. 'What is it? Come here. It's OK, Mummy's got you.'

I knew what the memory of those rats did to him. I had seen it before: the sudden silence, the glistening eyes, the tiny shudders of a body trying to shrug off a fear that refused to be eaten away by the years. The moment usually passed quickly, but not that time, as we sat on the bench. *The Wolf Man* was the first film he remembered seeing, sitting in the back row of the small, warm cinema, watching horror in sepia with the rat still in his eyes. Sirens complained and a bus braked in the street behind our backs. In the long wordless moment that followed I began to sense, for the first time, the pain and difficulty of what he was trying to do, out in the park in the sunshine.

'How can I put it? My mother was not the cleanest of people in the world. My mother was not the most honest of persons in the world.'

The sky was so blue. I made a little noise of assent, encouragement.

'Everywhere she went, and every house she had, turned into a pit. You see television programmes now where they go into the dirtiest, most horrible houses and clear them out. It was like that.'

Whenever he leaves crumbs on the work surface or a buttery knife on the table, or a smear of Marmite on the white Formica in the kitchen of their bungalow, my mother tuts and cleans. She's easygoing, not house proud at all, but there are standards. He was mumbling something.

'Unbelievably bad. There would be one room, with a little butler sink in the corner, and she did all the cooking in there. Instead of throwing things away . . .'

I wanted to put my arm around his shoulders, place a finger on his lips and tell him there was no need. That everything was fine. Let it go. But I couldn't. I needed to know. Keep talking, I thought. Keep going. Each word diminished him, like breath from a balloon.

'You've seen on the telly, when they're talking about the NSPCC or something, the classic picture of a kid in a dirty old vest, snotty nose, really filthy, holding a teddy bear? That was us.'

Those images usually inferred the child had been abused, I said slowly, unsure of myself and afraid of what we were getting into.

'We were never abused. Not at all. The exact opposite: we had the most love in our house anyone can imagine.'

He smiled but it faded.

'The bed would be alive with bed bugs. The wallpaper, they lived in the wallpaper, because the paste you used was yeast-based. So the bugs would be writhing in there. They would be in the bed because you didn't clean it out very often, and we're kids so we wet the bed. If you can imagine, a kid sitting next to you at school . . . he probably hasn't had a wash for a week, and he's got the same pants and vest on that he's slept in for the last three days, and his shirt has probably never been washed, because his mum didn't believe in washing them; there's nits coming out of his hair and he stinks. And he's got a squint in both eyes.'

He glanced back at me over his shoulder.

'You wouldn't want to play with him, would you?'

I had seen that half-smile before, in hospital. It was apologetic. Sorry for the mess. Resigned to embarrassment. All words leading to the one I do not want to write: humiliated. He smiled like a man who was having his head kicked in. Waiting for the next boot to swing. I looked away.

The adult bed bug is a flat insect with an oval body about a quarter of an inch long, and no wings. The female lays eggs at a rate of three or four a day, in the seams and folds of mattresses and sheets. The nymphs that emerge from the eggs are colourless, but begin feeding as soon as the light is dim and there are humans close by. They pierce the skin with long, sharp beaks and suck blood, which causes them to become reddish brown and swollen. Their feeding causes welts and red rashes on the skin of the human donor, which can become infected if there are many bites and they are left untreated. The bugs hide during the day but blood spots and smears of insect faeces can be seen on pillowcases and sheets. When a room becomes heavily infested they can be found in large numbers behind window and door frames, curtains and upholstery, and between loose wallpaper and the wall. The odour is distinctive.

'Can you skate?'

Arthur doesn't answer. He's playing tippy cat on the towpath, flipping one broken fragment of soap box into the air with another, trying to ignore the big boys. He likes to be down by the water, reading the names of places on the sides of the barges, daydreaming of riding them to the big river and then to the sea and to the wider world.

'Oi, moron! Can you skate?'

No answer. A boy with grease on his trousers picks up one of the half-planks and throws it down on to the canal, where it bounces and spins on the ice. The boats that drop their sails to fetch salt and bottles of ginger beer from the factories over the way can't get down this far now the water has frozen right over. The winter of early 1947 is the worst anyone can remember. The snow started falling on a Thursday night in late January, and within a couple of days the whole country was covered. The drifts are fifteen feet deep in the North, coal is frozen in the mines, the roads are impassable, the railways have stopped, the ports are sealed by ice. There is nothing to heat or power offices or factories so a million workers have been laid off. They've got no money to buy food, which was rationed anyway and is now even scarcer, and nothing to keep them warm at home.

The adults wonder if they have not suffered enough without this, and now the novelty has worn off their children are beginning to complain too, and falling ill. The wind chills them, the sun has vanished and the temperature never goes above zero. The cold, clean edge to the air since the chimneys stopped smoking is unfamiliar and harsh in the throat. In summer children swim, and drown, in the canal; but now they dare each other to step on to the slippery sheets that groan and crack as you shift weight. Three lads of about eleven or twelve have been arguing about whether it is safe to go out there, and now they want to settle the dispute by sending Arthur.

'Sod off! No bleedin' way.'

So they grab the little, skinny, squinty, smelly boy, a shoulder each and by the legs, and heave him out as far as they can, which is not far but far enough. His spine judders as his bony arse smashes through the surface and the bitter, bitter water runs up his back. He's thrashing about, kicking hard into the black folds under the ice but his legs are going numb now and he's tiring quickly. The boys have run away. He can't get a grip on the ice to pull himself up and it keeps breaking in his raw hands.

'Jesus!'

A man struggling along the snowy path sees something flailing in the shadow by the edge of the water and realizes it is a child.

'Hang on, son!'

He kneels in the snow, then lays on his stomach, spreading his legs wide out and soaking his black flannels, scuffing his shoes.

'Here!'

Arthur puts out his arms and feels the man's hands grab his left wrist, pulling him up. The ice cuts into his stomach, and his shoulder twists with a sharp pain but he's out, on the side, shaking with cold, blue in the lips, being held in a bear hug under a mackintosh and dragged with trailing feet up the slope, away from the canal, to the only warm place the man can think of.

'He brought me here,' my father said as we crossed Wells Way towards a red-brick building. 'Took me down to the boiler room for the public baths. All the heat coming out, warming me up, I remember to this day thinking, "This is heaven. This is where I want to be." And they gave me strong coffee.'

It was Camp coffee, made from the liquid in a bottle. I used to see it on the shelf in my grandmother's kitchen, but I never dared taste it. For Dad the sickly aroma of it made thick with sugar to treat a little boy's shock had fused with the memory of the cold and the pain.

'Even now Camp coffee makes me feel physically sick.'

A pair of mermaids watched us approach, each carved in Portland stone above the entrance to the old wash house. A plaque on the wall said it was opened in July 1901, along with a public library that was paid for by, and unsurprisingly named after, the philanthropist John Passmore Edwards. It was easy to imagine men and women shaking off the snow and entering the building by their separate entrances, glad of the rare chance to thaw out in that bone-rattling winter of 1947. They paid a penny a bath, and walked long, narrow lanes full of steam with grunts, splashes and contented sighs coming from behind cubicle doors. 'Drop more hot in number one,' someone would shout, then the bathkeeper took out his key to turn one of the big taps in the corridor.

'Until I was nineteen I had all my baths in here,' said Dad. 'Once a week. If we were good.'

We walked north along Wells Way, away from the baths and the site of the old house, making the short journey they made when the family moved from number fifty-eight to twenty-one. We passed grass and trees and gardens, but back then it was part of a terrace surrounded by ruins like a tooth in a rotten gum. The houses across the road had been destroyed by bombs and were still rubble; but the Moretons had electricity for the first time and a lot more space. They needed it, because a third boy had been born, Christopher.

There was a living room at the front of the flat with a table and a sofa, then a main bedroom and at the back the little kitchen with the butler sink that still made him shiver. 'Nobody except me and her and Les was ever allowed in there, no way.' There was no toilet. They had to go in a bucket then take it downstairs, through the home of the people who lived underneath them, and into the garden. 'We'd say, "Can we come down Mrs Brown to bring the slops through?" If she wanted to be nasty she would say, "No." Then we'd be on Queer Street. We used to have a lot of rows and arguments with them, so they said no a lot.'

So the bucket festered. Vi kept it in the little kitchen, with the rotting food and unwashed plates. The two older boys slept in the next room, divided from the other by a wooden wall.

'The smell was so bad that every so often the health people would come and try and clean it out. If I had a friend up we used to stay in the front. There was no evidence of the back, only the smell. You couldn't describe that. I'm not going to describe it. It's not relevant. I'll start dreaming about it.'

On the corner where we stood, waiting for the lights to change, there was a café where Vi went to buy the boys beef dripping and bread or cooked meat. He had always given the impression they ate well, I said.

'Yeah. You're getting into emotion now. It's difficult to describe, standing here on the street.'

Sometimes they refused to serve her. 'She used to get herself into terrible debt. She was never any different.' He was quiet, almost drowned out by the traffic; tired of talking and remembering. 'She went to prison a couple of times. We won't go into that now.'

Arthur the grown man, the grandfather, almost collapsed into his car, closed the door as if shutting out himself as a boy, and sighed deeply so that his shoulders fell and his body seemed to shrink.

'I know she was suffering from very bad depression. I know that now.'

His inheritance from her was a cheeky wit, a charm that worked on most people, an ability to hug his children, and the affliction that had nearly killed him at least twice: the savage melancholy that comes without warning. You can be walking at ease in the sunshine, then suddenly become immobilized by unsourceable grief, unshakeable sadness, so the blood seems to drain from your legs and your stomach lurches. For no reason. These were the things she gave him; and that he passed on to me.

'I don't love her . . .' He shook his head, and gripped the steering wheel. 'I didn't love her. I do now, funnily enough.'

10

I went back to Wells Way on my own, without Dad, a few days later. I wanted to be alone and quiet there, to see things you can't see when you're walking with another person, listening to every word and watching every movement for clues to the deeper meaning of the stories he is telling. I wanted to put my feet on the grass where his house had been and my hands on the bricks of the bath house, to see what I could feel. It was more than sentiment. Sometimes the colours and the textures, or the rub of the cement on fingers, or the shadows falling in a neglected corner, can offer up a sense of what has been lost. The spirit of a place does linger, and sometimes there may be more to it than that. As I walked I thought of a pub not far away that had been bombed during the war, then rebuilt. A dozen or so men and women were said to return after hours every night, when the pots had been washed and the new bar polished, to stand where they used to stand and sing the old songs:

'I'll be seeing you, in all the old familiar places . . .'

I did not know if the story was true, but if anywhere was going to have ghosts it was Burgess Park. Under the grass and the tarmac, close to the surface but just unseen, were the remains of old foundation stones, drains, fences and pipes that served and defined tight street after tight street, play corners and dens, crossroads and dark doorways, brawling sites and lovers' alleys, reduced to rubble and spread over with seed to deaden the sounds of the past. The Abercrombie Plan, conceived at the height of the war, proposed there should be four acres of open land for every thousand people living in this overcrowded part of London, and the Luftwaffe was helpful enough to clear a big hole in the tightly packed streets. It took decades for the plan to be implemented, and in the meantime the place was blighted. Nobody wanted to live in houses that were about to be knocked down, so businesses baled out and the shops closed. Before the ground was even levelled the council was building massive high-density estates to the north and south, excusing the hellish grey claustrophobia of these cheap concrete slabs with the promise of a park to play and breathe in. Nearly forty years after the war they finally joined together all the fragments of greenery and named the park after Mrs Jessie Burgess, the first Lady Mayor of Camberwell, who had lived no more than a hundred yards away from Vi and her boys. She was well known about the place during the war, Alderman Burgess, taking control, giving orders, running things, sorting out the mess where the bombs had been, fixing a cold eye on some poor man from the ministry and getting a wagon down there quickly to serve hot, sweet tea. But nobody who remembered her was likely to be out on the streets in the fading light now.

School search parties fanned out in ragged fashion across the playing fields, looking for distractions to slow their journeys home. It was not long since one of their fellow pupils, a ten-year-old boy called Damilola Taylor, had been found bloody and dying in a stairwell a few streets away. As his young and lively schoolmates ambled along they were passed by shadow people, men and women without light in their eyes walking dogs nobody could see and carrying shopping bags through the park, empty; not really going anywhere, but going there fast, heads down and determined. Three girls in uniform with their skirts hitched up to show bare legs jostled each other all the way across a pelican crossing with the little green man bleeping and two boys in a BMW calling out things only they could hear.

'No way, guy!' one of the schoolgirls shouted, turning her head away, towards her friends, giggling and nudging. They rolled along the pavement past the church of St George whose long doors seemed to have been built for a congregation of thin giants. Such a towering entrance demanded respect for the word of God, and a stubby gold cross with blunt ends sparkled in the dusk high above, promising the treasures of truth; but there were lace curtains in the windows and cars parked in the gardens by the old morgue. Visitors were not welcome since the church had been converted into 'prestigious apartments'. Trespassers would be prosecuted, not forgiven. Which was much the same when my father and his brothers were chased from the churchyard by the verger, who didn't want filthy urchins hanging around to spoil the place.

Christ stood watching. In the beginning his plinth had been white, until the gritty fumes of cars and factories rubbed it grey, and the sea-green of the copper statue ran into the stone in the rain like tears or blood. The Saviour was thin under his pockmarked robe and being eroded, fading away. 'For Those Who Served 1914–1918' said the inscription at his feet. So he had been there through it all: the bombs, the screaming, the moon turning red, the thousand times his name was called in the dark. Looking down. Watching a bench in a park where there used to be steps rising to my father's house.

In those days everybody knew the story and the statue. People would kiss their fingers and touch Christ's feet as they passed; but they stopped doing that, and he became a blackened curio, an interesting piece of street furniture, a mute reminder of things nobody wanted to remember. He shared his territory with other gods. The almshouses that had been an asylum became a base for the rangers who protected the new park, and a café surrounded by enchanted gardens: vines climbing frames in the Mediterranean corner, bamboo by a still pond in the Oriental, fleshy palms reaching out to represent Africa and the Carribean, and a star picked out in blue and white mosaic tiles around a pool in the Islamic garden. Summer was long gone and the beds had grown a little wild. 'TAKE CARE, sharp spines' said a sign, and there were others: 'Please be careful: poisonous plant.' They seemed comically overcautious, given the violence that had cleared the space for the park, and the hardiness of the people who had survived it. The café was closed. Notices on the garden fence that had been warped by sun and rain said nobody should interfere with the herbs but the herbalists.

'Plants can kill.'

There was parsley and thyme in the fields, and bluebells, when the men went to dig a straight trench for the Grand Surrey Canal. People would pull fish from it with their hands then, at the beginning of the nineteenth century, before the factories were put up and the water went bad. When it was closed in 1969 they pumped away four million gallons of water, revealing foul, stinking secrets: slimy prams, iron bed frames, even a safe and four communion chalices that had never been reported lost. A path was laid to follow the path of the filled-in canal, cutting through fields as the water once had, and an old iron bridge was left to rise out of the grass for no obvious reason. I walked down into the tunnel under Wells Way where the barge boys used to put their boots up on the wall to push their boats along, and I found white tiles painted with a mural. Graffiti had been sprayed over the mural but the outline of a map was still visible underneath, showing the boundaries of the houses on the street corner where my dad lived when he was small. I put my finger up to trace its lines over the cracked and dirty tiles. A man came jogging into the tunnel, shuffling, rolling his shoulders. His feet were as bare as his chest, but there were smudges all over his body, silver-grey like smoke, the colour of his long, dirty hair. There was no fat on him, he was lean and tanned. A big, odd black box like an old-fashioned mobile phone was attached to his belt. He held it with one hand as he ran, limping, shuffling. There was not a word between us, not a sound but his breathing echoing in the tunnel; no stopping, only running, as though his house had just been bombed.

The men resemble living ghosts. Burning limestone in the kilns by the canal covers each one of them in a fine white powder from bootcap to crown, lime sticking to sweat and filling creases of cloth and skin. As they drift out of Burtt & Sons at the end of another dusty week in the summer of 1948 some are walking Wells Way to Ashford's laundry, to spend a little of their money on a clean set of clothes and to flirt with the women who work there. You get a better class of girl at Ashford's, the employer of choice since the Watkins bible factory burned down and ashes with scripture on them fluttered down from heaven. The ruins of the factory are still standing. The war has been over for three years, but many of the bombsites have yet to be properly searched and demolished. They are the playgrounds of children like the seven-year-old who pulls himself free of a gap in a fence and skips through the ghostly crowd against the drift, throwing little tubes of brassy metal up into the air and catching them as he goes.

'Come here, son,' says a policeman standing in his way. 'What have you got?'

Arthur holds out his arm, stretching upwards towards the man's face, and unclenches his fist. The policeman sees the matted hair, the shirt that used to be white, the shorts with the seams torn at the pockets, and socks bunched up at the ankles above shoes with soles that flap like a pair of loose jaws. He sees the welts and rashes on the child's legs and wrists, from bed bug bites. He sees the scabby knuckles, the chipped fingernails with enough dirt in them for a vegetable patch, and the fingers uncurling to reveal three cannon shells.

'Where did you get those?'

No answer. The boy looks up at him, unblinking.

'Be careful, eh?' says the policeman, surprisingly gently, when the shells are in his shoulder bag. 'If you find anything else like that give it to me, will you? Or your da. Your da's around, is he not?'

The boy says nothing.

'Fair enough, son. Go on, get out of it. But be careful . . .'

His voice rises as the child turns to flee, running with a stumble to a big black pram with high sides. The chrome trim has all been stripped off. There is a pile of coal in it where a baby should be. The policeman has seen this boy before, wolfing down bubble and squeak in the café like it was his last or first meal, and outside the Coronet badgering people to take him in to see a picture. He's seen him pushing that pram before too, with a baby in it and his younger brother by his side, up at the playground on Camberwell Green. Arthur may be young but he knows the story of what happened there, as does every child who goes to the swings. Sid and Lizzie Wright danced together in the pub across the road on the night their son Sidney got married in

September 1940. The party was good and their five daughters were with them: Dot and Mary, both eighteen, danced with boys; Elsie, only just a teenager, sat shyly in the corner and watched; Joyce the ten-year-old was by her side, as always. The youngest, June, was eight. She ran in and out of the pub all night, making mischief. They had a fine time until the sirens sounded. Some people made straight for home, but the Wrights went down into the underground shelter on the Green. The whole family was in there when a mine landed on the roof and killed them all. Emma Ross and her boy Stan died too, and old Mrs Nadel from Church Street, and Norah Flaherty, aged nineteen. All gone, just like that.

Most shelters were a scandal: cold and damp, no air in them, and the worst of it was they were death traps. Somebody at the ministry got his sums wrong, or a crooked builder thought he could make some money on the deal, and the concrete mix was all wrong. The underground shelters like the one on the Green were slightly better but caved in just the same under a direct hit. There is no memorial and never will be, because if there was a memorial at every place where a resident of Camberwell lost their life the streets would be jammed with them. Death was always imminent here during the war, and tragedy commonplace. So there is just the park where Arthur is left in the morning with his brothers while Mum goes off to one of her jobs. She's always in trouble with the tallymen, but so many around here are. One week you fall a bit short for the rent or food for the babies so you pawn a coat, but then you need a coat so you borrow to get it back or buy one on tick, and soon there is no way of breaking the cycle. When the heavy-handed lads come knocking all you can do is pretend to be out. Not that they ever take silence for an answer.

'Shove off! Bleedin' pests, I'll have you on a meat hook!'

A butcher flails around with a broom, chasing wild cats from the door of his shop. They're everywhere these days, picking through the rubble, stalking rats and mounting raids for food from sawdust shop floors. Two ladies tut and shake their heads in mock disgust. The butcher is not a man of fine manners, but then some of his customers have not forgotten the sight of human bodies on his cold white marble slabs, on the night of the worst bombing when they laid out the dead and dying wherever there was space. The shops had good flat surfaces. When the cleaver comes flashing down there are still folk who see the glassy eye of a corpse, blackened by smoke and blood. For the man behind the counter in the chippy, the deathly pale flesh of uncooked cod is a reminder of white skin showing through soot as a young widow's tears washed her husband's cheek. The body was curled up like a baby after the blast but the wardens straightened it on the preparation surface in the darkened shop before they let her see him. She brushed the glass out of the dead man's hair with her fingers. Their two faces reflected in the curved metal of the fryer

As Arthur walks down Wells Way the Kelleher twins barge one another at the shoulders to be first into the café, with their mother close behind. Their father came this way on the day they were born, elated but dazed. He went to the barber for a shave before going to the hospital for the first time. That was a direct hit too, a V1 out of nowhere hit the roof of the shop. Kelleher was killed in an instant. He never did get to see those lads, nor they him.

The gears of a Dennis lorry clash and the engine complains as it turns the corner, loaded with tea chests intended for Jonathan Hunnex and Sons. They're fetched from tea ware-houses and brought down to the packaging factory until removal firms want to use them. Eight of the nine Hunnex children were married in St George's church, just opposite the business, and the family lived very close by in Parkhouse Street. Their big Victorian house must have been very impressive when they moved in just before the First War; but it suffered like the rest when the Blitz came. Freddie Huddleston, who had married Elsie Hunnex, was stripped to the waist for a wash at a basin on the first floor when a bomb blew the front of the house off. He climbed down the faceless building on a ladder, bare-chested and filthy, amazed to be alive. Olive Hunnex was in there too, the ninth child. She survived to marry a GI.

Arthur disappears into 21 Wells Way just before two men arrive. The tall one in a grey mac and trilby has a sour face like an undertaker whose cat has just died, while the human billiard ball next to him is wearing a tired brown suit that looks stuffed with padding. Mrs Brown from the ground floor listens to them, nodding, before pointing upstairs. The tall one stands aside to let his more substantial accomplice enter first.

'Come on Mrs M, enough's enough,' he calls into the hallway.

The shadows are disturbed, then comes a muffled bellow like the cry of a bear caught in a trap. The bailiff stumbles backwards out into the sunshine, hands up to his head with a child on his shoulders. The boy just jumped on him from the first floor landing and now has his legs wrapped around the thick neck, filthy fingernails digging deep into the sweaty bald scalp.

'You leave her alone!' screams the child, spittle landing all over the shiny head. 'Leave my mum alone! Garn!'

The bailiff staggers down the path, shaking his shoulders to get free of his avenging angel, but the child won't let go. Instead he kicks his legs and raises a hand behind him, holding on with the other.

'Wooh!'

The boy rides the debt collector like a bucking bronco, a sight that makes even Mrs Brown smile. She'll get a mouthful later though, for opening the door.

'You should sort that boy out,' she calls to the policeman. 'He's a menace, he is. They all are.'

The boy lets go his grip, slides down the bailiff's back and runs upstairs to the cover of his mother's apron, but he is in no danger of being arrested. Difficult as the Moretons must be to live with, they are not often the concern of the law – and certainly not when they jump on the heads of bruisers whose methods of collecting payment can be clumsy at times.

'Not one for me, I'm afraid,' says the constable when the front yard has cleared. 'Did you see his old fella at all?'

'Ha!' Mrs Brown makes a high-pitched snorting noise, shakes her head a little on a stiff neck, and goes back to beating a carpet.

And there is the mystery. As I walked back through the park more than fifty years later, imagining the houses and factories as they had once been and seeing the people I had read about in the local records come to life in my mind, I realized that none of Dad's stories about the years just after the war included any reference to his own father. He spoke warmly of his mother, who for all her troubles never stopped trying to look after the boys as best she could. The bond that developed between them during the bombing, the burning, the hungry days and all the mess of their survival, was never broken by misfortune or death. Bert, on the other hand, was missing from all those memories. Surely he was there in real life?

'No,' said Dad next time I saw him. 'No, he wasn't there.' The subject made him talk very quietly, and carefully. I had asked the question casually, not realizing how painful he found the answer. A secret had been uncovered. We were about to get out of a car, but he stayed in his seat not speaking for a moment. The windows were closed.

'He didn't come home from Germany for a long while. I don't know why.' He looked over his shoulder at the back seat as though to be sure nobody was listening. 'And then when he did come back he didn't want to stay with us. I remember a huge great row and him walking out. Coming back and leaving again on the same day.'

His eyes glistened.

'You think, hang on, everybody else's dad is home. Doesn't he love us? What have we done?'

11

Maybe they had not done anything at all. Maybe the war had been so terrible for Grandad that he could not handle the return to normal life. Maybe he was so scarred by what he had seen and done that it was almost impossible to re-adjust. There must have been many others who had gone through the same thing. Still, I could not understand why my father had kept silent about his childhood all this time. They were poor, their house was a tip, the memories were painful and difficult to express, but there had to be more to it than poverty and squalor that were accidents of time and place. Dad often made a joke about his humble beginnings – as a sometime socialist and emigrant to the suburbs, these little wisecracks were useful in displaying his working-class credentials and expressing gratitude for what he had. The grim truth behind them also provided some explanation for the fearful drive I saw in him: the fear of falling back and living like that again was part of what had compelled him to seek promotions he could barely cope with and houses he could only just afford, always trying to get out and away from the city to a place of safety, a state in which his family would be comfortable, not hungry, and never have to suffer as he had. I understood his long hours at work as a product of that compulsion; and the long hours in the council chamber as an expression of the responsibility he felt for the people he was working so hard to leave behind. He too was a good man, trying to do his best by his family, and his achievements were impressive. The scars of his childhood drove him to achieve things that would have seemed almost impossible back then, and I was proud of him. He had nothing to be ashamed of, so why the silence?

Those years after the war were supposed to be a time of celebration, of reunions, of bright hopes and determined rebuilding. Bert was not there.

'I lost any respect or love for my father at a fairly early age,' Dad told me, in language that reflected the counselling he had been through during his depression. 'The long-term emotional damage he did was not really apparent until I got married and you came along. But then I accepted responsibility for my family, which is more than he did. The experiences I had as a child helped me come to terms with it, to realize what was right and what needed to be done.'

We both thought of York Lodge when he said that. It must have been so hard for him to hear his grown-up son talk about feeling abandoned because he had been sent away to a hospital by the sea for six months at the age of eight. I had never really felt at home again after that, not for years; but the queasy rootlessness, the homesickness without knowing where home was, the inability to settle, must all have been only a faint echo of what he had felt all his life. Knowing that made it easier to bear no grudges. My parents had felt distraught at having to be separated from their little boy but it was done on the best medical advice available to them. I worked that one out for myself, eventually.

'The weird thing is that when your mum and I started going together she thought I was lucky because my family always showed love and they weren't afraid of cuddling. I never saw it that way. I knew we would fight to look after each other, so yes the family was important. But not love.'

There was something missing at the centre of his family

life and he blamed his dad. 'The long-term damage has been inside the head. Emotional and psychiatric. What people have seen over the years is probably not the real me. It has made me prone to depression, prone to never knowing when to give up. I would go and cry in private.'

He said all this, but still would not tell me what had happened. Perhaps he couldn't. The words just didn't seem to come. Don't ask me, he was saying. Ask him. Go to your grandfather and put the questions his own son cannot get out. 'What happened?' 'Why would you never talk about it?' And, most of all: 'Where were you?'

Ash on an old man's sleeve
Is all the ash the burnt roses leave.
Dust in the air suspended
Marks the place where a story ended.

T. S. Eliot, *Little Gidding*

12

Grandad Drums tried to swim every day, even at eighty-four. I found him at the local pool, down to his underpants in the changing room. The nails on his feet had twisted like yellow claws. His skin was shiny, leathery, sunblasted, with white hairs bushy on his chest. They burst from his nose, untamed. Old man hairs. I watched him for a moment, unseen.

'Grandad?'

No reaction. Then a look up, straight at me, bemused. It took him a second.

'All right, mate? Didn't know you came here.'

'Not often,' I said. 'Just today, with Jake.'

'Oh, the boy. Is he all right then?'

'Fine,' I said. 'Swimming with his mum.'

'It's good for him, mate. Keeps the lungs going. You should do it every day.'

He was smiling, chuckling. Wheezy, but better than I'd seen him in a while. His eyes were bright and beady now the cataracts had been removed. Bert folded his clothes as we spoke, and introduced me to his mates: a big man with bags under his chin and a heavy belly, who called me son, and a wiry fellow called Lionel who twisted his towel as he spoke. Both had retired from the Post Office but still came here to swim with their old pals.

'We know Bert,' said the big man. 'Never misses a day.'

I looked around, but Grandad was gone; off for his swim without saying goodbye. Afterwards, when I had dried and changed, I climbed up to the public gallery and sat in a row of empty wooden fold-down seats, watching him move through the water below me, in the intermediate lane. Light flooding through wide, high windows splashed in the water around him, and skittered off his bald head. Did he know I was there? I found myself hoping for a smile, a wave, even a look. Was there a way to connect with him? Our conversation had reminded me of the way he reacted five years earlier when Jacob was born. Or rather failed to react. His first son's first grandson was just another child of many, and although he was pleased enough when we saw him at family gatherings he did not come to visit. Bert had thirteen brothers and sisters that lived. Perhaps half a dozen more were conceived and died, at birth or soon afterwards. Then his five children gave him twenty-one grandchildren. I don't know how many great-grandchildren there were. His world was a busy place, full of faces. Another one was welcome, but what was it to do with him, really?

He was called Grandad Drums because of the old kit in his bedroom, with its dull brass cymbals and battered snare. Sometimes, after school, I would go round and smash away with the drumsticks and nobody ever told me to be quiet for the sake of the neighbours. Or I sat at the electronic organ as he tried to show me scales. Those evenings were always the same: we would pretend it was a proper lesson, then he would get bored and go off, for a cup of sweet tea or sit down to read his copy of the *War Cry* through a magnifying glass. I would improvise, making the organ bellow and shriek, setting its tinny drum machine to the fastest speed, gradually picking out a manic tune. He never complained. Then he would let me sit beside him on the stool as he played 'What A Friend We Have In Jesus', slowly but with a little swing. It was warm in the front room, with the bar fire on. The plastic señorita dancing flamenco on top of the black and white television may even have felt at home. She must have been a gift from someone because the furthest Nanny or Grandad had ever been on holiday was the Channel Islands, a great adventure of a trip to see their son Chris when he was the Salvation Army captain on Alderney. They were proud of him. The rest of the house was dark and cold and it stank. Stale bread, fat gone cold on the oven, unwashed pans. The toilet was indoors but you didn't hang around in there, nor look down at the bowl. There were false teeth in a jar by the bath every night, next to a packet of baking soda. The wallpaper was peeling, the roof was leaking, the sheets were damp, but I loved to stay there anyway. To lie in uncle David's old room, under a psychedelic poster of a flower-strewn beauty and a mushroom cloud, and listen to Radio 2 as it came on with the alarm at four in the morning. Grandad was usually awake before then. The scent of eggs and bacon came up the stairs, followed later by the rattle of his big green bike going out into the dewy morning.

When Nanny died the house was thoroughly cleaned and redecorated. Grandad lay in the garden more often and for longer, on the sun bed by the rusty salt-green swing that had always been there. He pulled down the Anderson shelter, the corrugated iron shell that was stuffed with rubbish, and put a flower bed in its place. Two decades later I watched him in secret as he moved through the crowded pool at his own pace. Slow, steady, his eyes set on a fixed point, arms arcing through the water in the breast stroke. Economy and poise. Nothing disturbed him. I did not call out.

I'm being unfair. He sent birthday cards with banknotes that fluttered from them, which was generous, and he did come to our house one Christmas Day. That was the first time I ever heard him talk about being in the army. The real army, that is – he was always banging on about the Salvation Army. After lunch that time he sat up at our piano and began to play a few chords. My son Jacob, who was two years old and had been trying to get the measure of the strange old man with the mahogany skin and wheezy breath, suddenly ran to stand between his legs, between the piano stool and the keyboard. The instrument was usually his domain, and if anybody was going to make a noise on it then Jake would be joining in. Grandad laughed and began to sing.

'A soldier was kissing his mother goodbye, was kissing his mother goodbye.'

He sang heartily, absurdly, like a music-hall performer on an off-day, and Jacob giggled. They were pals for the rest of the afternoon. Later, when Grandad was tired and breathless in an armchair, I took him a mug of tea. Over the years I had got used to him sitting in the corner at gatherings like this, watching the young ones and saying nothing, but this time was different. 'He's a bright little one, isn't he, your boy? Knows how to pick out a note with a finger. You should encourage that.' I nodded. 'We used to sing that song in Germany, when I was with the Royal Welch Fusiliers. They were lovely fellas, some of them. You get a feeling when you're close together like that, digging your camp and keeping the guns clean.'

Did you see much fighting? I asked. We always ask that, we who have never been under fire and never really been frightened. His answer was evasive, and gentle. 'No, not much. Not at all.' Then he shut up. He sat and watched, while we played charades.

★

Fish and chips were the family sacrament. On the way home from school Vi's boys would jump off the tram and scoot to a chip shop run by their auntie, where they would be fed without question or charge. Battered fish and fried potatoes were the host around which the family gathered as it grew over the years, out on the promenade at Leysdown or Clacton-on-Sea or Southend, or some other seaside bank holiday town that was not too far from London. Everybody eats fish and chips, of course they do, but listening to my father's stories I realized this quick and relatively cheap meal had become something more symbolic for us. It was the gift of choice, the thing you brought when visiting to express your contentment at being together. In his old age it was understood that if you went to see Grandad at a mealtime you took a packet with you, wrapped in white paper, warming the inside of your arm as you carried it with the juices in your mouth running at the sweet golden scent that was always far better than the actual taste of the chips.

Not that I visited him very often. He didn't live much more than a mile away, in the next suburb to ours around the North Circular, on the edge of Essex and east London. I told myself it was because he was never in, always swimming or walking in the park. He didn't hear the phone when it rang anyway, because he was getting deaf, or having his nap, or stretched out on a camp bed in the garden again. The truth was that time just slipped by and I was always too busy to nip over. Sometimes I thought, 'What if he died?' I would have felt desperately sorry not to have seen him for so long, not to have had one last encounter. But that's not much of a basis for a relationship. He kept on going, chalking off the years, and not much changed. Until, of course, I wanted something. After the visit to Camberwell I needed information, longed to hear stories. To get around the awkwardness at just turning up on his doorstep for the first time in years I asked Dad to come with me, and we took cod and chips from the Cranbrook Fish Bar.

We sat in the back room with the aluminium french windows that would have overlooked the garden, if the net curtains had not been closed as always. Up against them was a big, long, dark-wood table, a reproduction cherry wood. A white tablecloth with orange borders had been spread over half of it, leaving polished wood exposed for the other half. Places had been set, with mats, knives and forks, not laid out but at ease on the table. Slices of white bread, cut in half, were high in piles on blue and white Chinese-patterned plates, and a carton of Butterlicious spread was already open on the table, the lid removed, the gold foil still halfway across.

'You don't drink tea, do you?' he teased. While he was in the kitchen waiting for the kettle to boil I unwrapped the portions of cod and chips and put them on the plates, wrappers open. We ate with our fingers, despite the cutlery. The tea was strong and sweet, drunk from thin china cups with a blue floral design, although much of it had been spilled on to the saucer by his unsteady hand. Jazz came from a silver and blue cassette player perched on a heavy but redundant wooden speaker cabinet with a gold cloth front. He turned off the music when we started talking.

I remembered watching some Wagnerian opera in that room, on a black and white television, in the dark. Must have been getting on for twenty-five years ago, when Nanny was still alive. I remember the strange smell. The small, standing-room-only kitchen was an awful place then: dirty, stagnant water, old cloths that looked like they had washed the floor, congealed fat. I didn't like to eat there. My throat tightened at the memory of it, although he kept the place clean enough on his own. The house was very cold and Bert was wearing a woollen bobble hat with his sweater and tracksuit bottoms. He was in a strange mood, talking about a television programme that had frightened him with its re-creations of battle.

'When you get older it all comes back to you,' he said. 'Some old people now, they still have nightmares.'

He didn't say much else at all, just talked about digging trenches and praying, but it was a little more personal, and vulnerable, than either my father or I had heard before. That makes us sound like emotional vampires, dependent on extracting the emotional blood from Grandad for our future survival. Sometimes I worry that is true. The facts of Bert's life as a soldier, as known to his four sons and one daughter, were these: he went to France as an artillery gunner with the British Expeditionary Force, but was left behind as his unit retreated from a sudden enemy attack; he made it back across the Channel on an old coal barge, and was sent to fire guns into the night sky over London during the Blitz; he chased the burning tails of doodlebugs with his sights, then took up a rifle again to join the conquest of Holland and Germany. He was changed by the war but would never talk about how or why. He thought that was not important. The family did not need to know what he had seen.

'My mum had seven boys in the army,' he said. 'Don was a firewatcher. He did a lot of good, used to pick you up. Very good to me, used to take me to church.'

'He was a sensitive man,' said my dad, biting a gherkin. 'Very sallow.'

'He had diabetes I should think. They wouldn't have him in the army. Then we lost our mum. That must have been a shock to him. He didn't have anywhere to go. He used to go to see my wife a lot during the war. She was like a sister, like a mum to him. He used to love Vi, really, and Vi used to think a lot of him. I used to love him, he used to come and take me into London to the theatre. We were in the Palladium one night and the bloke said, "'Scuse me people but there's a raid on. If you want to get to the back you can." Nobody moved. You could hear the guns going on outside, the bombs dropping, but they still carried on. Those blokes singing "Underneath The Arches". The Crazy Gang, they was. Don was there.'

What happened to him, I asked. My father watched his father's face.

'They found him in the canal,' said Grandad. 'They don't know if he jumped in or fell. I reckon myself he was on his way to Vi's. He'd lost his mum. It was a rather foggy night, and he ended up in the canal. I reckon he was too sensible to drown himself.'

'There was another brother who I'm told was a bit of a villain.'

'Oh, Lionel. You had to keep out of his way with money. Whatever he played he would beat you – draughts, whatever. Sometimes he'd come home with loads of notes he'd won gambling. He'd give my mum £50. "Put it on so-and-so." Mum was a big gambler too. In those days you had to put it on with the street bloke, cos it was illegal to gamble. There would be a lookout, a bloke with one leg. Lionel got into gambling in a big way. He had a big house in Catford. Charlie told me he lost it, gambling. That was his way. One day I was at work, just getting ready to go out on a round, somebody came up and said, "There's your brother outside wanting to see you." He said to me, "Bert, I'm a bit stuck, can you lend me so-and-so?" I said no. He went right down. I said, "Look, here's half a crown, get yourself a drink." I wouldn't give him no more.'

Lionel had a good war, and became an officer. It did not change him.

'Another time a chap knocked at my door. He said, "What about that money you owe me? That cheque you give me the other day bounced." He was a Salvationist with a shop at Nunhead, and he had taken Lionel for me.'

Dad could not contain himself. The talk was flowing, so he asked the question that had been welling up inside him a long time, never articulated.

'What I could never understand was, at the end of the war, when other kids' dads were at home, and you weren't at home . . .'

I could not look at Dad then. He was four years old when the war ended, the same age as my son. In that cold and gloomy room, stumbling over those words, he was four again.

Grandad changed the subject.

13

It was Dad's idea to go to the Imperial War Museum, but when we got there he could not go in. 'Let's just have a drop of tea,' he said, so we sat on another bench by the refreshment stall at the entrance to the museum grounds and drank from polystyrene cups. I thought he just wanted to enjoy the sunshine for a moment, because the drive had been long and bad-tempered, so I watched school children swarm off their coach and through the gates to where the two giant barrels of a naval gun held them to attention. We would find ourselves in the dark with a dozen of them later, waiting for the start of a show that recreated a night in a shelter during the Blitz. They would giggle and whisper wisecracks as we waited, but file out silently afterwards, shocked and frightened by what they had seen and heard. That was to come, but first I had to persuade Dad actually to go up the steps and into the building.

'I'm not sure I can. This is difficult.'

'What's the problem?'

'I haven't been here in a very long time. It's exactly the same.'

'Well, it would be. From the outside, anyway.'

'Yeah, all right. Bear with me, will you?'

The dregs of our tea went cold. A young couple walked past, sat by a gleaming metal peace sculpture and canoodled their lunch breaks away, then left.

'This place was so important to me when I was a boy,'

said Dad at last. 'I didn't get much out of school, I used to go up to One Tree Hill to look at the city and imagine what it had been like at the time of Boadicea. I wouldn't be playing cowboys and indians, it would be Romans and Britons. I didn't learn that from school. God knows where I got it from, but I was definitely more interested in reading and finding out for myself than going to lessons. In winter I needed to keep warm and off the streets so I came here. It wasn't far. I knew I could get in for nothing and the guy from the school board wasn't going to find me. I ended up in the library, where the man and the lady would talk to me. I would go up there stinking like a ragamuffin and they would make me wash my hands before I opened a book, but they were interested in what I thought. They would give me a cup of coffee. You needed a ticket to get into the library, and you needed to be working on a project to get a ticket, so I kept on inventing projects. I could look through all these pretty books and learn about things. It taught me to respect books. It taught me to want to know more. It taught me logic. And it taught me how to bull-shit. I gave them what they wanted, and they gave me what I wanted.'

There was one particular exhibit he wanted to see: a painting of a line of men blinded by a gas attack, with bandages on their eyes and hands on each other's shoulders for guidance. 'This is how my uncle died, or so they told me, in the First World War. I would come and sit here and look at it for hours, imagining what had happened.'

We looked closely at the picture and noticed tiny figures of men playing football among the trenches and barbed wire, and flecks of paint that represented biplanes in the sky. He didn't want to talk, though. I left him alone for a while.

The painting was enormous, and as he sat there in front of it my dad looked very small.

Some fathers never came home, of course, because they lay buried in a corner of a foreign field or could not find a way back to their families for other reasons. I once spoke to the son of a GI, who had never met his father. He was born in 1945 to a teenager from County Antrim and a sergeant in the US Army Air Corps. The couple wanted to go to live in America but her grandmother would not give permission so the military could not allow it. The boy knew nothing of his dad because when he was a year old a new man came into his mother's life, and all the photographs and letters from the GI were destroyed. He tried to trace the sergeant but even the old members of his squadron did not know where he was. One of them did give the son a picture, however. At the age of fifty-four he saw his father's face for the first time. He continued to search, with half an address. 'The longing never goes away,' he told me. 'I feel I will not be allowed to grow up and become myself until I shake my dad's hand or put flowers on his grave.'

The library had been moved, away from the dark-panelled rooms of his memory, but you still needed a reason to be there. I had left my coat and bag at the security desk and waited for a librarian to escort me past the field guns and tanks, under the Spitfire suspended from a high-vaulted ceiling, through the electronic gates, into the lift and up an iron spiral staircase to the reading room. A dozen men and women, mostly elderly, sat on green leather chairs making notes from documents that were older than themselves. Nobody spoke, there was only the hum of an air-conditioning unit and the soft burr of pencil on paper. I had gone back to try to understand something of the experience of coming home after the war. If Grandad would talk to me, when I got him on his own, then I wanted to be ready. If he would not, then I thought I might get clues to what he had been through by reading about the experiences of others. Reading through letters and diaries, and old magazines, and the newsletters of veteran societies, and books that recalled the period, I began to see that Bert was just one of many who struggled to cope with their return.

'Nothing was the same and no one understood. What was I seeking? I had not the slightest idea.' The words of a former prisoner of war were written in pencil, in a loping hand, into a lined exercise book, a long time ago; and I found them in the archive. 'I was like a ship at sea, tossing out of control with no anchorage. The only security was round the bar, at the pub. I removed the tensions and inhibitions with an increase in the alcoholic content.'

The author wrote like the doctor he would become, slowly and with a great deal of effort, during a process of readjustment that took years. He helped himself by publishing a memoir, whose pseudonym caught my eye in the computer database that recorded the contents of thousands of deep-filled cardboard boxes in the back rooms of the museum. I read the original, unedited version, the pages of which had not been turned since they were left to gather dust in the dark. They rested on another volume, this time bound in black leather and embossed on the top right-hand corner with what I was shocked to discover was a swastika. The photographs inside were of a POW camp somewhere in Germany, although how the prisoner managed to take and keep pictures of such a place I don't know. After close confinement it was hard for him to be free in England again.

'I was alone in the world. I had had company for three years, and apart from that had never had to make a decision. But now I was in the great wide world as an individual. The thought frightened me.'

He could not sleep, but tossed and turned at night and was pursued by nightmares. 'I disliked being alone. I had lost my self-confidence. I wanted to turn back and hide myself amid the crowd.' He found it hard to talk to anyone about anything, but women rendered the traumatized pilot mute. 'The sight of the opposite sex after such a long time unnerved me. I had no topic of conversation. I could not just look dumb. I retreated to the bar, but the smell, after a big meal, nauseated me. I was not going to fit into this life, the one I had enjoyed.'

The divorce rate rose by nearly 400 per cent in the ten years after 1939, as the fighters and those they had left behind to survive on the home front decided they had changed too much to be reconciled to the old life. 'The suffering and death I have seen have entirely altered my values,' said a soldier at his post in 1945, overheard by one of the anonymous researchers of the Mass Observation project. 'I shall never go back to my old life of security and comfort, thinking only of a safe job and going to dances. I have lost all ideas of that kind. I may be a monk, or a tramp.' He sounded the melodramatic type, but there were very many who found it hard to cope with peace because of what they had seen. War Office papers warned of 'hopelessness, impotent anger, and despair' and 'depression sometimes to the extent of suicide'. The notoriously tough-minded politician Enoch Powell broke down and wept on live radio half a century later when he talked about the guilt he still felt so deeply at having survived while people he admired and loved had been killed.

Few men could put it into words like Powell, but their actions were eloquent. There was the former prisoner of war who had become so used to guarding his few personal possessions in the camp that when he came back, emaciated and weak, he would not allow anyone else to touch his clothes, his books or his knife and fork. He never changed. Another prisoner sat staring into space for hours, and woke up screaming German in the night. A third, who had suffered Japanese cruelty, would leap out of bed and make for the sniper he thought was firing at him from the wardrobe. Then there was the man who could not pass a bakery without buying a cake and cramming it in his mouth, crumbs showering his chest, tastebuds singing at the sensation of a sweetness he had believed he would never experience again. Or the infantryman who had slept on the ground for so long he could not stand the new bed and mattress his wife had bought for his homecoming. Night after night he rolled out of bed and lay on the floor instead.

What if you were better at war than peace? An East Anglian priest called Peter Owen Jones wrote about meeting veterans in their old age, and burying them. Sometimes an old comrade-in-arms would turn up at a funeral, someone who had shared experiences with the deceased that his widow and his family could hardly begin to understand. 'We're in fashionable denial about war; it's clearly potentially very exciting to gamble with death, must set your synapses on fire. It's not for everyone – we're not all born soldiers – but there are undoubtedly some people that are good at it. No wonder they don't talk about it. The shock of coming home for some of them after the Second World War, the ordinariness of it, must have been desperately hard to come to terms with, to have done things that on a normal day you would have been hanged for, to sit on sofas in painted rooms holding tea cups having bayoneted other young men to death must have created an awful inner loneliness. I've buried killers. Their wives, their children, all say the same thing: he never talked about it.'

Sometimes their families did. Margaret Wadsworth, a contributor to a book called *When Daddy Came Home*, described what it was like for her father and others in 1945. 'They came home in various moods. Some so weary they could hardly think straight, some so bitter and disillusioned it was almost like brain damage. Some came home cheerful, hopeful and raring to get back into civvy street. Actually they were the ones who suffered most. Civvy street, as they knew it, no longer existed. Civvy street was beaten into the ground by fear, shortages and sheer weariness. We put flags up for them, we had parties for them, but the boys that came back were not the boys who went away. They were men. Different men with different ideas, and they found us different too. The shy young girls they left behind became women, strong useful women with harder hearts and harder hands capable of doing jobs that men never dreamed women could do. Some of us were mothers, and the babies did not know their fathers and the fathers did not know their babies. There was jealousy on both sides. The children who had Mum to themselves had to share her with a man who was almost a stranger. A man who dreamed of lying in his own bed with his wife would have to fight a furious little son or daughter who thought they had a right to be there too.'

There were many similar tales in the war museum library and archives. Avril Middleton was six years old before she met her father, a Royal Marine. 'I was forced to be a "substitute husband" for my mother as my father refused to take responsibility for anything, either financial or personal. He should never have married and should have stayed in the

Navy. He was excellent as a leader, being dropped behind enemy lines to set up resistance cells, winning medals and being a hero. It was the everyday life he could not handle.' The wife of a former officer had to follow his exact orders, barked as though he were still in command of a platoon. 'We became quite afraid of him and all the aggression within him. It really had a devastating effect on our lives, as my little girl and I had been so close because of all the trauma of bombing, air raid shelters, and so on. We both resented this man who dominated our otherwise close and loving relationship. It did something to all of us so that we were never able to get back on the same level as each other ever again.'

A girl who had bent to kiss the framed photograph of her smiling father every night of the war ran screaming from the gaunt, emaciated man who held his arms open in the doorway, and she yelled, 'He's not my daddy!' A boy of my father's age, living near them at the Elephant & Castle, returned from school to find his dad was back and found him strange and frightening. 'He was scared of him at first, more or less,' remembered his mother. 'Like most children at that time I don't think he ever got over it, not really. The first five years of a child's life are the most important.' A boy hated being told off by a man who had never been around. 'Mum tells us what to do,' he said, and he kept asking, 'When are you going away again?'

Children who had shared their mother's bed, offering mutual comfort during bombing raids, resented being thrown out of it. A woman was forty-seven before she felt able to go to her elderly parents and tell them she had something to say, to get it off her chest. They listened in silence as their daughter said she felt in the way whenever she was with them, and that this awful sense of isolation at being unwelcome had been there since childhood; but that when she left them she felt lonely and desolate. Her elderly mother began to cry as she heard this. Her father said nothing. The feelings, the daughter said, went all the way back to the war. While the fighting was going on she had a relationship with her mother that was close and loving. Then Daddy came home and Mummy changed. 'She always seemed to be afraid of showing her love for me and of course he found it very difficult to love me,' she wrote. 'What I'm trying to tell you is that I loved and adored them both; but that the repercussions of the war can last forty to fifty years.'

Germaine Greer wrote about her own upbringing in *Daddy We Hardly Knew You* and described scenes that also occurred in untold numbers of homes across Britain and the world. Having been far from home and out of touch for years, Australian servicemen returned and endeavoured to pick up their former lives, aware that their children were questioning the presence of a strange man in their mother's bed. 'There was no way these damaged men could explain their incapacity for normal emotional experience except by complaining, and they would not complain. But their children must.'

I read those words and thought of my dad on that wretched bench, slowly prising words out of himself that nobody had ever heard before, admitting things he would rather were not there, reviving memories that would rise up and sting him. I thought about the silence of my grandfather, the man I had always assumed was some kind of hero. My theory, for the moment, was that when heroes suffered so much for their survival it was inevitable their families would suffer too; but there were so many unanswered questions. Was my grandfather actually a hero? I was beginning to doubt it. Why did he not go home when he should have done? And if I went to see him on my own, would he talk?

14

> All your anxiety, all your care,
> Bring to the Mercy Seat, leave it there.
> From the *Salvation Army Chorus Book*

The outside door was locked for once, and the doorbell, a button set in a brass circle, did not seem to work, so I rapped on the glass with my knuckles. Nothing. Perhaps he wasn't in. There had been no point in calling him on the telephone beforehand because he was too deaf to hear the ring. Then I saw him moving in the kitchen and rapped again. This time he came, squinting out through the glass in the heavy door, and seeing that it was me he gave a thumbs up. The varnish on the porch was still sticky. He refreshed it every year, still using the same wrong stuff he had used for two decades, so that anyone who brushed against the door frame stuck to it like a fly to a paper. You had to watch your step too, so as not to tread on the name plate that had been carved from a piece of wood but never nailed to the door: 'Vi-Bert.'

This time we sat upstairs, in the big room where he used to sleep when Vi was alive. It had become the music room, with one of his two electronic organs, and an old acoustic guitar that still had the same flowery strap one of my cousins put on it in her hippy days. The strings did not seem to have been changed since then either, and were untunable. As usual the drum kit was set out ready to be played: bass drum, snare and cymbal, set low as for a jazz band or a regimental dance. The skins were dead and grey, almost transparent in parts from years of being tapped and rat-tat-tatted, and the bluey-green metallic finish on the drums themselves had lost its sheen. Jacob had been thumping on them a few days earlier, in the company of his great-grandad and his cousin Rebecca. 'He was good in the end, your boy, got a good bit of control instead of just bashing away.'

While he was downstairs I started up the organ, a wooden box the size of a sideboard, and selected a nice cheesy bossa nova rhythm that popped and clicked. I could busk with two-finger chords on the left hand and the right playing some kind of melody, but it was only a practised, habitual version of the tricks he had taught me more than twenty years before, on the same instrument. I felt a tug of regret at not having taken it more seriously. Then I slid on to the stool behind the snare drum and tried to follow the rhythm of a record like I used to when I was a kid. Back then I brought my own: the last one was the twelve inch of 'Planet Earth', the debut single by Duran Duran, which shows how long ago it was. This time a crackly Slim Whitman was coming from the gramophone player, a fine piece of furniture that was even bigger than the organ.

'You know these songs, dontcha?' he said, coming up with two cups of tea on a tray. I nodded, humming along to 'I'll Remember You'.

'You're getting old,' cackled the eighty-four-year-old.

'Sure am,' I said. 'But I'll never catch you up.'

'Those things are rubbish, really,' he said, waving a dismissive hand at a silver plastic CD player sitting on top of its much more substantial predecessor. 'They break on you. I've had the other one for fifty years. Got it second hand. Nothing wrong with it, is there?'

'Doesn't seem to be.'

The house was warm. The sun was out, the curtains drawn and the central heating filling the room like invisible cotton wool. Grandad was wearing a blue woollen sweater, and just visible under it was a white shirt with a collar that was badly frayed along the top edge. He had those baggy black tracksuit bottoms on again, with the drawstrings dangling. And on his feet, surprisingly, were flip-flops. Black and fluorescent pink, with the words Canary Islands written across the strap. One foot was worryingly purple, the other bound in a soiled yellow bandage and support stocking.

'Me leg swelled up. Been like that for ages. I was treating it meself.'

That was until Rosemary, his daughter and youngest child, came round and didn't like the look of it.

'I was just in me pants, so she saw it. She said, "How long's it been like that?"' There was a black hole in his smile where two of the teeth on his false set had come out. His smile was self-contained, as though he was looking inside himself. I knew something cheeky was coming. 'Then she said, "Where's your penis gone?"' He chuckled. 'I said, "That's gawn a long time ago."'

Rosemary called for the emergency doctor – 'a black man' – who bandaged him. 'Did a good job an' all, you know?' A nurse visited twice a week, giving him medicine to 'purify my insides' and thin his blood. There would be no swimming for a while.

His hands were also purpled, the veins sticking out, the nails crumbly and wild yellow. He seemed to be shrinking. His silver hair had been cropped close again, with black growths around the nape and bushy black hairs in his ears. His eyes were milky, glassy. Once we had sat down in a couple of white plastic garden chairs, with a chocolate chip cookie and a cup of tea each, he started to talk. He knew I had come for stories, and he was ready to give them. Yes, he had kept them to himself for a long time, but I wondered whether anyone had ever asked him to talk.

'Did you tell your kids about the war?'

'Not a lot really. I don't suppose they were bothered about it.'

How wrong you are, I thought.

'Sometimes when you start talking about things you suffer more when you get older than when you're young,' he said. 'By bringing it all up you could have nightmares. That's why I don't listen to me wife.' He looked at the cassette player. 'I've got a tape of Vi's voice, but when I listen to it, that brings it all back. I expect my kids have nightmares.'

This was an unexpected admission. I didn't interrupt. 'They didn't have very good childhoods. Especially Arthur and Les. They was in a small flat, and the people who was in the flat with them weren't all that good. They wouldn't even let them use the toilets and things like that. They were brought up in a rough, dirty way, but they were good stickers.'

I had never heard him talk like this before, about these things, and I doubted that my father had. 'They were good children. It didn't spoil their characters. They got on with life. I know what it was like because I had a bad time when I was a kid. I was born into a poor family like they were. Partly mad, you know?'

His father was a heavy drinker who retired at forty because of consumption. While he was still working, young Bert would have to go down to his office in Nunhead to get what he called 'the Saturday penny', before it was spent in the pub. Sometimes he would be sent out later that night to find his father and bring him home, which meant cajoling the big drunken man on to unsteady feet.

'He could hardly walk home sometimes. I thought to myself, "I'm never going to get like this."'

That must have been part of the reason why Bert had become teetotal.

'I suppose it is. He used to come home after we'd all been put to bed and go out early. We never saw him.'

The strange echo in those words took me by surprise. A reminder of what I had said about my dad, and he about his. History was repeating itself, with variations.

Bert was the ninth of fourteen children, born above a shop in Nunhead Lane, Peckham, in 1918, the last year of the Great War. He left school at fourteen to work in a factory, a job arranged for him by his dad, but he was sacked on the first day. 'They didn't give me much to do, just clean all the tools, but I put them all in a bucket of oil and messed them up, didn't I? Didn't know any different. How could I?'

The school had not given him a good reference. 'Don't blame them. I was a dunce at school, an ignoramus. Could hardly read or write. It was only later the doctor told me I was not getting enough oxygen to me brain, that's why.'

He was crafty enough to make some money buying rags and off-cuts from the dressmakers, bundling them up into bags and selling them on to engineering firms that needed old cloths to clean the lathes with. And he fell in with a gang of lads who made money any way they could, sometimes on the sly.

'I only come from the slums,' he said. 'I was the dopiest one in the family. That's why I'm so thankful today. All this to me is a miracle. First thing I do in the morning is praise God.'

None of his family was religious, but Bert was in the uniform of the Salvation Army a long time before he was made to wear khaki. On Saturday nights the streets of Nunhead were always busy, and groups of churchgoers would stand on the corners singing and preaching. The minister at Rye Lane Baptist, a man called Danby, had a knack for speaking to young people, and at the age of no more than seven Bert would slip off out of the house to go and hear him.

'When you've got a big family your mum and dad don't care where you are as long as you're out the way. You can go and play in the canal if you want to.' He opened his arms out as if embracing the room. 'One time I was in a place where I had nothing.'

I knew what was coming. Whatever the subject of conversation, Grandad would get up into his pulpit sooner or later. Maybe it was because he had been more direct with me than usual, but the familiar riff sounded more honest this time, less like platitudes. He meant it. 'The night to me was so black, like a long tunnel. But when I look back there was some power within me. If I didn't have that power perhaps I would have committed suicide, I don't know.'

Who was he, this old man sucking tea from a saucer and speaking symbolically of the darkness? You can know someone all your life, listen to them snoring on the sofa, dribbling behind the toilet door, or humming to themselves as they make the tea, but they will always remain strange. As he spoke my mind was filling in the gaps, running the movie, slipping back and forth between the conversation we were having in this stuffy upstairs room in Stradbroke Grove in the present day and the corner of Dulwich Park in 1933.

*

This house was probably not here then. The late summer is so hot there are fires burning out in the fields on the edge of the forest. The evening breeze blows across the bowl of London, over the river and down to Dulwich Park, where it cools the boys in shirtsleeves and the girls in summer dresses as they sit on the lawns listening to the Salvation Army band. Bert is walking between the trees, scrubbed up and tanned with his hands in his pockets, whistling the melody the trumpets are playing. At fifteen he likes to stroll out on his own on a Sunday, away from the pandemonium of his crowded house, to enjoy the cool of the evening before going to the pictures at Goose Green. He'll meet his brothers and sisters at the cinema later. One of them will pay for admission then go right up the back to the toilets, and pass the ticket out through the window so the next one can bunk in.

I was listening to one of the open-airs there. A chap came up and asked me to go to the meeting.

The Sally Ann are out among the people with the big bass drum and the soft, beguiling tones of those silver instruments, smiling and sharing the joy in their hearts. It must be difficult when they're feeling down, and there are those among the corps who know what it is like to be hungry and have no way of getting money while they're out of work, but they put on their uniforms and go out anyway. Bert has heard the sound before and walked away, but this time he lingers. The music stops, the players relax and their circle loosens, widens, to include those around them. A man called Jack tells a story about how he was once so overcome with drink on his coal round he drove his horse into a wall. Then he sings, in a baritone as dark as his load: 'O the peace my saviour gives!'

'Will you come to the hall with us, brother, to hear the gospel?'

'Yeah. Why not? I will.'

It was cheaper than the pictures.

The young man hangs back as the band re-forms and marches, but although he walks on the pavement and not behind them on the road, his pace is the same. Any friend who happened to be passing might think he was hurrying to meet a girl outside the Sally Army hall. Not that Bert has ever been seen with a girl. He's a loner.

Everybody seemed so happy. Remember the greatest gift for a man is to be loved.

The captain is well spoken. The colour sergeant runs a shop. They both take care to shake the stranger's hand at the entrance to the corps, before the meeting begins. 'You are welcome here, it is always good to see new faces. Please, take a seat.'

They treated me properly. I was moved by the people . . .

The room is packed with men and women, most of them in the blue uniforms that look black in this gloom, with the day dying in the high windows and the sunbeams weakening as they fall across a golden star on the platform. Bert sits at the end of a row, right at the back, next to a small, elderly woman who smells of lavender.

She smiles, and hands him a Bible open at the right page. 'For God so loved the world, that he gave his only begotten Son that whosoever believeth in him should not perish, but have ever-lasting life.'

The words that will become so familiar to him go straight over his head this time. The preacher jabbers on for a long time, and Bert wishes he smoked, so he could duck out for a fag on the steps as several of the bandsmen do. He wonders what he is doing there, and when the meeting will finish, but he can't walk out after being welcomed like that. The singing comes as a relief: the words are simple and the tune is familiar as 'My Darling Clementine'.

'Come to Jesus, come to Jesus, come to Jesus just now . . .'

'This is the question that is being asked of you this evening,' says the captain to the congregation. 'Are you ready to be welcomed into the kingdom of God? Will you surrender yourself to the Lord's embrace?'

'He will save you, he will save you, he will save you just now . . .'

'The Lord is waiting for you. Perhaps you feel unprepared or unworthy. You may say that you are a sinner. So am I. We are all sinners, but Jesus calls us all. Salvation awaits. Will you answer his call? Come, if you will, to the Mercy Seat.'

Bert's heart pounds away and his scalp tingles.

'Flee to Jesus, flee to Jesus, flee to Jesus just now . . .'

A man rubs his palms against the lapels of his grey suit as he slides out of his seat, apologizing to those who give way, and walks down the aisle as though being led by the nose. He kneels on the bench they call the Mercy Seat, his shoulders shaking, and his hands in his face. But when he lifts his eyes and looks back at the rest of the hall, and seemingly straight at Bert, he is beaming.

I thought to myself, 'I'll have a basin of that.'

So Bert finds himself at the front, unable to say how he got there. This is not his epiphany, however. This is not the moment that will bind him to the Salvation Army for the rest of his life. That comes next. As the room empties, the lavender woman offers a hand, a gesture of respect from the type of person who would usually cross the road to avoid a low-born, penniless, graceless chancer like him.

There was an old lady at the door, a welcome sergeant they call them, she shook me by the hand. I was moved by the people. I was moved that somebody would come to shake hands with me, a bit of dirt really. Just a bit of dirt.

He was tearful at the memory of that moment almost seventy years later. *The greatest gift for a man is to be loved.* The welcome sergeant on that first Sunday invited him to come again, and to read the New Testament in the meantime.

'When I got home I said to my mum, "Mum, I been saved. Have we got a New Testament?" She said, "We must have one about somewhere."'

They found an old Bible at the back of a drawer.

'I said, "Mum, can I borrow your glasses?"'

He went to every meeting there was. Whatever the weather or the time of day, Bert would be there. Bandmaster Finch noticed this. Every band leader in the history of the world has been plagued by musicians who didn't turn up to rehearsals or meetings, so a keen teenager was a godsend. Never mind that he couldn't play anything and there was no way he could afford an instrument. 'He taught me how to play the drums. It was really interesting; you had to count your time. After a time he taught me to play a cornet. I said, "What do you want me to play a cornet for?" I wasn't good, mind you. He said, "You're always here." In the Army it don't take much to get in the band. You play a C scale and you're in.' Somebody's father died and Bert was given the uniform. He took his instrument home and polished it with care, and put a bit of his meagre earnings aside for the weekly 'cartridge' payment soldiers were expected to make to the Army. He stopped swearing, and going to the pictures, and hanging out with his old mates, because he was too busy with band practice and meetings. Bert had found a way to be different from the rest of his family, to rise above his surroundings. The people he met at the corps were very different from the villains, street thieves and petty dealers he had been mixing with. Or at least that was the story he told me, and the story he told on his streetcorner soapbox way back then. 'We used to have a lot of neighbours round where we lived, they'd all come out and see me in this big band. We used to go to different places and I was preaching, telling them what had happened to me. It changed my life. Rescued me, really. Without that I would be in prison, probably. Or dead. Or turned to drink like me dad and some of the others. My family said it was only a flash in the frying pan. Well, I'm still frying now.'

The book I had borrowed from him fell open in my hands at page thirty-eight. A paragraph was marked with three lines of blue ink running down the side of the words. 'The flower girl in *Pygmalion* behaved like a lady when she was treated like a lady,' it said. 'The converted though still semi-literate labourer, slowly spelling out his recently acquired copy of the New Testament: "Unto Him that loved us . . . and hath made us kings and priests unto God . . ." felt himself lifted to a station and clothed with a dignity he had never known before. A king and priest! Then he would behave like such, even though he still lived in a slum. The theological content of the phrase was doubtless not fully understood by him. But he sensed its practical implications. He was no longer a dogsbody – to be pushed around. He was dear to God. That fact was enough to set a man firmly on his feet. Nor was this truth to be dismissed as another variation of pie in the sky. A man's common sense told him that a faith which could not come to terms with the reality of death as well as life was not worthy of the name. This new calling invested his present life with a sense of worthwhileness.'

Those words were written by Frederick Coutts, who used to go to the same corps as my grandfather. He was a commissioner, one of the big guns at the international headquarters of the Salvation Army in Denmark Hill before the war, but would still walk down to the Dulwich corps on Sunday to play his part in meetings and open-airs like an ordinary soldier. Later he became General Coutts, worldwide leader of the movement, and wrote a book called *No Discharge in This War*. His tone in the book is a little condescending, but Band Sergeant Moreton was deaf to all that. He marked a paragraph for himself, as if to say, yes, this is the new truth. We are all priests and kings. Even me.

The bands don't seem to march any more. The Boys' Brigade must have run out of boys, and the Dagenham Girl Pipers, who have a very different sort of appeal, must be staying indoors or playing at showgrounds. Even the Sally Army bands that stand on street corners in the West End of London at Christmas time are much smaller than they were: quartets or trios rather than the battalions of old. I used to go to the Army with Grandad sometimes when I was a child, because I liked the music and my cousins would also be playing in the band. I walked behind them as they marched to the gardens in the park opposite their corps, and stood on the edge of the circle as they played hymns. The sound of those silver instruments had an irresistible melancholy. After listening to Grandad tire himself out with his testimony, I felt an urge to go back to the old place and hear that sound again, even though I knew it couldn't possibly be like the old days.

The sign on the wall of the Walthamstow corps said there

would be an open-air at 4.15 p.m., followed by a 'Salvation meeting'. The park opposite the hall was busy with people at the right time, but I could hear no band. There was a man with a red face and wild eyes staring at the roses from a bench, holding firm to a black and gold can of strong lager, and an acquaintance of his taking care over every footstep as though he might lose balance at any moment. A lad in a baseball cap banged on the wire of an aviary, panicking the birds into a silly frenzy of cheeping, and his friends told him to stop. A couple of families were having a picnic on the grass, buggies arranged around them like covered wagons circled for protection. There were no sweet songs of salvation here, among the bright flowers and lawns, just the giggles of toddlers running after pigeons, and the muttered intimacies of lovers lying like spoons in shady corners. And the whoosh and crump of skaters losing it at the top of a half pipe, falling on their arses so the tarmac burned a hole in Linkin Park T-shirts. And the holler of an ad-hoc team, as an improbably huge and fit teenager pushed up through flying elbows to hang in the air with a sudden stillness and drop a ball into a basket. A slightly built child of about ten was rolling on the ground and cursing in Urdu, having tackled his uncle from behind for a fluorescent yellow football and got a strain or a snapped tendon. He got a clip round the ear for his language too, as he lay there writhing in pain.

Is this what it feels like to be old, I wondered? Not because I had a few more years and pounds on me than I used to have when I played in this park, swung on those swings, bought a slush puppy from uncle Mick in the boarded-up café; but because it was changed, just a little but enough to be disorientating. The structure was still the same: the terraced houses built of those warm, sandy bricks, backing on to the fields, and the school way over in the corner of the park, and the willows that hung over the edges of the duckpond. There was no bandstand where it used to be, and a scented garden had been planted where once there was a store, but one change was more significant, and brought up feelings of confusion and guilt. It was that most of the skins were a different colour. I can't find a way to voice this that does not sound prejudiced or frightened, although I do not believe that I am either. The population has changed in the places where I grew up. That certainly does not alarm or disgust me, although I knew many people in the old days who felt that way, when it started to happen. At our school in the late seventies it was cool to be in the National Front even if your best friend was black. Mine was called Sunil and his parents came from Pakistan, so I didn't buy the NF line, even at twelve, but I knew those that did. Perhaps they changed their views as they got older; or they joined others on the journey out of London to quieter streets and private houses and whiter suburbs in Basildon and Billericay and those towns all the way to Southend where the racism is now unspoken but as real as the weather. As I walked through the park I almost felt guilty just for noticing the change, but it was a fact: most of the kids had once been white, now they were not. I wondered if that was a reason why the Salvation Army was no longer so visible. The Booths fought street battles for the right to testify in the open, but the world had changed.

The window of Sedgwicks sports shop was blinded by a metal shutter. Of course it was, on a Sunday afternoon. But I remembered the first time I saw it like that, in the very early eighties, when you could usually look in at Green Flash trainers and cricket whites any time, day or night. There were race riots in Brixton and Liverpool, and the threat of them in Walthamstow, so the shutters went up. I looked out from the back seat of the family car as we drove down Forest Road one Saturday and it was deserted. Coming towards us along the pavement, in four or five ranks, was an ad-hoc unit of skinheads with their brown Doc Martens polished and their braces jangling, looking for some open-air action of their own. They owned the streets that weekend. Thank God it didn't last.

There was nobody back at the hall, with fifteen minutes to go to the advertised starting time, so I idled by the window of the thrift shop, which had been decorated with little fluffy Easter chicks. It was Easter Sunday. A reasonable looking dark-wood dresser had been draped with a green scarf in sari material, and at its feet had been arranged a great deal of cream crockery printed with Japanese scenes. Every item was labelled with a raffle ticket rather than a price. They were against lotteries, so presumably you could haggle. Through toughened and dappled glass I could see a Scalextric set and a writing box with a broken hinge, waiting to go on display. The inscription on a foundation stone said it had been laid in 1912 for the United Methodist Church, School Hall & Institute. Now this three-storey building, which had false battlements and turrets on the corners, was home to the Salvation Army Pastoral Unit and a marriage guidance service run by Major Jurgens Booth, presumably some relation of the founders. I pressed the buzzer but got no answer. There really was nobody about. The dozen young Eastern European men who were stretched out in the formal gardens of the park across the way, passing around grass of their own, must have wondered what I was up to. The busy road between us was like a raging river as lorries and buses cut the afternoon strollers off from this grand structure that nobody ever seemed to notice. It looked like there wasn't going to be a meeting at five, since the main wooden doors were bolted. There was not a uniform in sight. I felt heavy and deflated, unexpectedly sad, thinking about the men and women my grandad used to come here to be with, to sit in that dusty wooden hall and talk about the glories of the gospel and sing songs that belonged to another century and another kind of world altogether. Were they all now too old to come? Did they sit and read the *War Cry* on a Sunday night, and watch *Songs of Praise* alone in their homes, each one alone, and hear timbrels rattling in their minds and see young women smiling in their black bonnets? Were their uniforms hanging in the wardrobe like his, pressed and mothballed? I wanted them to start turning up, all dressed the same and carrying instrument cases, apologizing for being late, happy to shake the hand of someone who was interested enough to arrive without notice. But there was nobody there, and no sign to say why. The sun went in and the breeze became a cold wind. The iron railings across the main entrance remained locked. 'No goods to be left here' said a hand-written sign above two bin bags slung over into the porch. I looked in through the window and saw only a darkened lobby, and my elbow brushed an empty Coke can off the ledge on to the pavement, where it rolled into the gutter. The alleyway led to a night shelter, but that was barred by an iron gate with a notice: 'No Dumping Anything'. Behind it was an upturned sofa, a half-smashed wardrobe and a twist of chrome that had been a pram.

I felt the urge for a stiffener, brought on by the memory of sitting outside a pub with my uncle in his uniform and his glass of lemonade and lime. There was a lovely girl at his corps on the Isle of Wight, where I used to go on holiday in my teens. I rang her up one time, on my last afternoon, and nervously blurted out what I had been trying to find the courage to say for a fortnight: 'D'you wanna go out for a drink or something?'

A drink? She had voluntarily signed the Articles of War, a statement of faith for every soldier, promising to 'abstain from alcoholic drink, tobacco, the non-medical use of addictive drugs, gambling, pornography, the occult and all else that could enslave the body or spirit'. This young lady, who cared enough about the Army to wear (and look gorgeous in) the uniform of the famously teetotal organization, and who never entered a public house except to sell the *War Cry*, just said softly: 'You really don't get it, do you?'

15

Bert met Violet under the Ferris wheel at a fair on Peckham Rye Common one Easter. He was on the arm of her best friend, a relationship that did not last long. 'She was too forward for me,' my grandfather said. 'We were at the pictures one time and she put my hand down her shirt, on to her breast. I didn't mind that, did I?' But he did. A shy boy whose raging hormones were being churned up still more in the heat of conversion, he couldn't quite handle it, so to speak. 'Vi wasn't like that. You kissed her but that was as far as it went. I liked that about her.'

Her father was the manager of a gentlemen's outfitters, and did not entirely approve of his daughter associating with a rag dealer. Mr Gennery was one of many who enjoyed Army meetings for the singing and the teaching but never joined up or wore a uniform, and he stopped going altogether after one of his sons died of consumption at the age of twenty-one. Vi was devastated but Bert was able to offer comfort, as he told her, because he knew how she felt.

'I lost four of my sisters, from diphtheria and so on. The last one, Marie, was about eight years old. I loved her. She used to come to me for a Saturday penny to buy ice cream. My mum stopped me one morning, when Marie was ill, and she said, "Before you go to work, go and say goodbye to your sister." So I did. She was in bed.'

Marie died later that day, while he was not in the house. 'Broke my heart. When the funeral came by everybody in the street stepped out of their houses to see it. They were like that when the children died. My mind went a bit for a while after that, I couldn't even remember my own name.'

Violet was serious, and quiet, and always smartly turned out, even when she was heaving dumbells in a hall with the Life-Saver Guards, a cross between the Salvation Army and the Girl Guides. She was short, her glasses were thick and they hid a squint, but she had an easy charm with most people. 'She wasn't pretty like the other one, but I didn't mind. She was an educated girl, very well spoken.'

The opposites were attracted to each other. She was a little shy of him, as some self-protective instinct made her draw back from his athletic eagerness and street savvy. Bert had no social graces, and made no apologies for that. An acute awareness of his place at the bottom of the pile was balanced by a strong, mostly unspoken, belief that he had just as much right to the chance of a living as anyone. He was used to finding his own path through life and defending it, in that big family of his. She was a couple of years older, and seemingly far more sophisticated, but she would let him protect her. He could not have known how sorely she would test his willingness to do that. 'She saw things in me I did not see myself,' he said. 'Looked up to me, or so I understand. When the men wanted me to become their band sergeant, responsible for their spiritual health, I didn't want to do it, couldn't see why they was asking. Vi said, "You've got to. You've got something in you they want."'

If Bert thought the girl he went to the park with every Sunday was too good for him, his father believed the opposite. He had heard from friends of the family that she had problems any potential suitor would find it hard to overcome: she found money easy to get, by charm or connivance, and hard to hold on to. So hard that she kept spending even when it was all gone. There were some at the Dulwich corps who prayed, fervently, that this young couple would part before she got him down the aisle. It looked like the war might provide an answer to their prayers when Bert was called up in July 1939, one of the twenty-one-year-olds who were conscripted as the Germans prepared to take Poland. The captain who had shaken his hand on that first Sunday cycled down to Nunhead to say goodbye to his eager young bandsman, and gave him a leather-bound copy of readings from the Bible selected by General Evangeline Booth, the seventy-three-year-old leader of their movement. She set sail for retirement in America soon after war was declared, by which time Bert was in basic training with the King's army down at Blandford in Dorset. Love is a strange thing, he said whenever anyone asked him about Vi. They might never have got married in the autumn of 1939 if it hadn't been for Hitler.

'What, *now*?'

'Yeah.'

'When?'

'Tomorrow, at the town hall. You need a special licence, costs a couple of quid, but I've got that off the army wages, haven't I?'

'You're mad, son.'

'Maybe, Dad. Maybe I am. But we're going to do it anyway, me and Vi, twelve o'clock tomorrow. A lot of blokes are doing the same, they said so.'

'As you will, son. As you will.'

'So he comes to me, his mother, quiet as you like, and I know something is up. He's got that look, you know, over the eyebrows like they get when they're little ones and they're thinking of doing something naughty. I should know that look by now, the house I've had. But anyway, I'm in the kitchen washing up the pans and the big man is down the pub, as usual, and Bert comes in. The girl is in the other room, keeping quiet.

"Mum," he says.

"Yes, Bert."

"Mum. Can I sleep with Vi tonight?"

Well, I mean, what do you say? "No way. Not under my roof. There may be a war on but you've got to have standards. Why should she get your army allowance, did she bring you up and pay for everything? No, she didn't." But you can't, can you? He's only here for a day and a night, travelled all the way up from Cornwall on a forty-eight-hour pass, and they're getting married in the morning. Ridiculous, isn't it? I can see why though. God love him, I can see why. There may not be long left. Don't get me started. So I said yes.

"Yes, you can. Only, one thing . . ."

"What's that?"

"Don't tell your dad."'

The wedding of Herbert Moreton and Violet Gennery had fewer witnesses than was usual, on account of its hurried nature. His father was too ill with his bad chest to come out of the house but his mother was there, standing under the grand stone façade of Camberwell Town Hall on a wet Saturday morning, holding a bouquet and wondering what on earth would become of her son. A couple of his brothers turned up, but nobody else. The ceremony was over quickly; haste was becoming a feature of this relationship. He had risen early that morning, so that they were both downstairs fully dressed and drinking tea when the old man woke up. The look on his face was a picture, but there was nothing he could say, whatever he suspected. Bert had stood by the window as the dawn broke and the birds started singing, and wondered, 'Is that all there is to it?' Vi was snoring then. He looked at himself in the shaving glass, searching for a difference, but found none. No marks of sin.

There was no music in the register office, but outside an accordion played for pennies. 'We'll Gather Lilacs In The Spring Again.' They had both taken the pledge, of course, so there was not even a retreat to the pub for a parting glass. His brother Norman shook his hand, his mother wiped a tear away, and turned her back as Vi tiptoed up to kiss her new husband. Then Bert hauled his kitbag on to his shoulder, tugged his battledress straight and walked away.

16

'That's how it was in those days,' Grandad told me, the third or fourth time I went to see him. He didn't seem to think it was odd that his grandson had started turning up once a week or so after an absence of years. Or at least he didn't say so, just put the kettle on, turned the music down and started talking, a little more freely every time. He couldn't go out so often now, with his bad leg, so he had time to spend chatting. Sex was less of a taboo subject for him than the war, and always had been. Even after a lifetime as a Salvationist he was still a salty old geezer who appreciated the sight of a firm behind and once greeted a new girlfriend of mine by saying 'your bum's not as big as the other one's'. *Carry On Girls* was in the pile of videos by his television, and *Dirty Dancing*.

'That's a good one. I know it's sexy but there's a good message, and some good dancing. All the young people. It's a good one to watch before you go to bed.'

Now he was out in the garden, hanging his smalls out to dry and telling me about the disappointment of his wedding night. 'To tell you the truth I didn't enjoy it really. I thought, "If that's what it's like I don't think I'll bother much, thanks." I think that's what made me not put myself out over women. Cos when the war really did start and you were fighting for places, the first thing the English soldiers was after was a bit of crumpet. They used to get it from the Germans for nothing, for a bar of soap.'

Grandad lifted a yellowing pair of long-johns from a

plastic bowl and hung them on a wire he had pulled across the old green swing we used to love. Lately he was back in the habit of soaking his underwear in the soapy water he had washed his body with that morning, as they were taught to do in the army. 'There wasn't many at the register office, really. They was all away somewhere, it was so sudden. It was quite a nice wedding, actually. You would have thought it was in a church.' He caught a bus into the West End, then a tram, and a few hours later he was sleeping on the floor at Olympia in Earl's Court with several thousand other soldiers, waiting to depart for France. 'That night we went to Tilbury Docks, got on a boat there. We landed at Cherbourg. I didn't know if I would be going back.'

He didn't have a clue what was going on, of course. Most squaddies don't. Split up into units, cut off from news of home or the wider conflict, reliant on their officers to tell them what they need to know, they become focused on each other and the immediate problems of surviving, and being prepared for action. Gunner Moreton had some vague idea that he was part of a big force crossing the Channel to put up a defence against the Germans but he couldn't have told anyone there would be close to three hundred thousand soldiers in France by Christmas. His Royal Artillery unit caught a train all the way to Reims, just south of the border with Belgium, where it was told to defend an airfield. The men levelled their site, dug trenches and built circular sandbag emplacements for each of the four heavy anti-aircraft guns grouped around a command post. They slept under canvas at first, dreaming of white sheets, then dug an underground mess and put bunks up in that damp, dark space. The parts for Nissen huts arrived and they built them for their officers, then somebody found a cowshed the men could use for a rest, kipping in the hayloft with the cattle mooing underneath. There were lots of drills, and occasionally they got to fire off a few shells, but mostly life was no more exciting than it had been down on the range in the West Country when they had shot at targets towed behind slow aeroplanes. Bert was bored and homesick.

'I was getting ready to come home on leave one time but the officer called me over and he said, "I've got some bad news for you, Moreton. Smith's mother has been taken very ill, and that means he gets priority, I'm afraid. Your leave is cancelled."'

Gunner Moreton was not happy. So he decided to bunk off.

'This is true. I went under the barbed wire around the camp when nobody was looking, and I ran off to the farmhouse to get changed, and I was thinking, "I've got to get home somehow." I was going to desert, you know? So I walked into Reims, which was a bit of a way, looking for the railway station, and I saw a big place we all called the Soldiers' Hall. You could get a cup of tea in there.' He walked in and heard the sound of English male voices singing a hymn in a side room. '"I Will Lead Thee Every Hour". The soldiers were standing in a circle, singing and praying. I went over and joined them. What choice did I have?'

After that his conscience would not allow him to keep running. 'I had a change of heart. I went back to the camp and nobody had even noticed I had gone.'

Still nothing was happening. One of the newspapers back home called it the Phoney War, another made a pun on the new German style of fighting and said it was a Sitskrieg. The French boasted about the Maginot Line, a hugely expensive series of concrete fortresses, underground bunkers and gun batteries along its border, and in any case nobody in Paris thought the enemy's panzers would ever be able to hack through the dense forests of the Ardennes, so that was a natural defence. The Prime Minister, Neville Chamberlain, visited one unit in December and told its commander: 'I don't think the Germans have any intention of attacking us, do you?'

The answer came in May and it was shocking. Norway fell to a lightning attack, and Chamberlain was forced to resign, hounded from the House of Commons by back-benchers waving papers and yelling 'Go! Go! Go!'. Winston Churchill, First Lord of the Admiralty and the one who had been saying loudest and longest that appeasement would not work, became the new Prime Minister. Bert was told about it, of course, and even heard a strange echo of Salvationism in the new leader's promise of 'blood, toil, tears and sweat'. But spring had come to the airfield and the flowers were bright. He gave thanks that all the action seemed to be happening far away.

17

The midnight shift is always the longest. Gunner Moreton is cold, damp and bored. He has been walking around his anti-aircraft position for what feels like hours, around and around in circles in the dark. The Germans are miles away. They won't be here tonight or any night soon, he thinks, looking up at the blank sky. No moon, no stars, no raids. But there are footsteps. Not before time. The mouth organ that has kept him company comes up to his lips, and he blows a little tune: 'Here Comes The Bride'. It's a joke. He expects a laugh. He gets the furious thoughts of his battery commander hissed into his ear. 'What the hell do you think you're doing with that instrument? The enemy will hear you all the way to Berlin. Damned fool.'

The klaxon begins to sound just before five in the morning, but nobody panics. Another bloody drill.

'Bit early, isn't it?'

'You'd think they'd have some consideration.'

'Better get your shirt on, Bert.'

Gunner Moreton is supposed to be fully dressed and ready for action. The detachment on duty through the night is allowed to rest, taking turns to be the man on guard, but you're not supposed to roll your tunic up and use it as a pillow. And you're certainly not meant to fall asleep. Bert eases himself off the short wooden bench built into a recess in the circular wall of sandbags around the gun, and feels for the lump of bread and butter pudding he hid in a corner last night, after swiping it from the cookhouse. Gone. The rats have had it. Other soldiers are rousing themselves around him, but the airfield is peaceful in the blue haze of morning. A few mechanics run out of hangars in the distance, towards their aircraft, but there's no need for haste. They've all done this before, countless times.

Then a faint whistle adds itself to the moan of the horn, sharper and growing louder, into a scream. The cookhouse shed dissolves and blossoms into a column of fire, and the gunners feel the warmth on their faces and a shove against their chests before they hear the sound of the earth folding in on itself with a roar and mud and stones and wood falling around them.

'Take cover! Take –'

Vibrations surge through their boots, and all across the airfield the green grass kicks up at the sky. That scream. Rolling over against the wheels of a truck, holding his helmet on his head with one hand, Bert senses a shadow and looks up to see the crooked black wings of a Stuka stretch out overhead, pulling up from its dive with the wind howling through the trumpet sirens on its claw feet. There are dozens of dive bombers in the air, far and near, high at the beginning of their insane descents and thundering low, daring the tops of the huts and trees to rise up and claim them as they swoop over the airfield.

Then they're gone. So is that demonic noise, lost in the wind and the crackle of flame. Through the wall of black smoke Bert can see a French fighter plane on its side, one wing burning; another has flopped down on its wrecked undercarriage as though in prayer or deference. A third has tilted forward, its propeller churning into the earth and the pilot's head smashed in a purple mess against the glass. Smoke and grit and burning rubber sand Bert's throat. The driver's door of the truck is buckled with holes from the Stuka cannon, and he realizes with alarm that he has just taken shelter under a lorry load of ammunition. Beside him a gunner is being sick, down on his knees, tin hat off and forehead cool in the dew. Arm in arm the two terrified soldiers stumble across the grass and climb down into an underground shelter, legs nearly buckling on the steps. 'I'm shaking,' thinks Bert. 'So cold.' His hands flap uncontrollably up in front of his face, flicking away some invisible pestilence, but he can't see where he is anyway, because the oil lamp has gone out and the bunker is pitch black. Somebody sobs. A voice is calling out and it sounds so young that Bert wonders for a second what a child is doing there. 'Oh, Mum. Mum!'

'Take post!'

The gun position officer shouts down into the dark.

'Get on your posts! Come on! Positions. We're here for a reason. Scramble!'

The shells have not been fused. They were supposed to do it last night, adjust the fuse on the neck of each one with a key, to get it ready for firing. They're still in the numbered compartments. Where is that key?

'Shrapnel!'

What did he say? Shrapnel. Oh glory. They've never done this before. Never fired shrapnel from these guns, on the short fuse that bursts a cloud of hot metal close to the bombers. Then it rains back down on your heads, according to men who've seen it. Bert bends at the knee, takes a shell in both hands, heaves it into the breech and shoves it up there with a balled fist.

'Close breech!'

Number one looks across to the command post but the position finders who send signals to each gun are useless against dive bombers. They were expecting flotillas of high-level aircraft, moving slowly and predictably through the sky, not these falling, screaming demons.

'Fire at will!'

Fire at what? They move so fast. Here they come again.

'Where's QE?'

There's nobody to turn the wheel that moves the barrel of the gun up and down. His seat is empty. Must have run off.

'For God's sake. Bloody kid. Bert, get on.'

Gunner Moreton takes his place, grasps the elevation wheel, puts one eye up against the gun sight and can't believe what he sees: a pilot's head, black and bulbous, goggle-eyed, looking over the side as the force of the dive pushes him back into his seat. The Stuka comes impossibly low over the guns, ignoring their explosions, trailing fiery lines from the Bofors that are meant to protect the anti-aircraft crews. This isn't supposed to happen. There's no way of fighting these things off.

'Fire!'

The force kicks into Bert's gut. His eyes water and his blackened hands tremble on the metal wheel. Here comes another. How many more?

18

The Germans attacked Reims airfield in the early morning and late evening every day. The gunners loaded, aimed and fired until their eardrums were shattered, their backs broken and the lack of sleep made them zombies. The strength and speed of the enemy seemed impossible to resist, but Bert kept those thoughts to himself. Others were doing the same. The blitzkrieg was like a terrifying creature or a natural disaster, an act of the devil that could barely be understood let alone defeated. Numb and fearful, Bert became convinced France would fall and Britain follow. Years later, as we talked and matched his memories and anecdotes to the official records and the grand perspectives of military historians, the despair he felt in 1940 came back to him.

'We thought it was all over. They were too big and too strong.'

The action had started early in the morning of 10 May, when sixty-four German soldiers crossed the border into Holland. This symbolic gesture announced a huge and sudden action: within three hours stormtroopers were dropping by parachute to destroy fortifications in Belgium and two lightning armies of troops and armour supported from the air had begun to move into the Low Countries. Breached dykes and blown bridges could not stop them. The Luftwaffe made a terrifying bombing raid on Rotterdam on 14 May and Holland gave up the next day. Belgium declared itself neutral, then surrendered. The French troops along the border fought hard and won valuable time for their allies to retreat, but there was nothing behind them when the enemy broke through. The Germans just went around the Maginot Line and panzers drove straight into the apparently impassable Ardennes and out the other side as easily as if they were on parade in Berlin. They had to go past Reims to get to Paris.

'The news come through there were a lot of soldiers at Dunkirk waiting to get on boats. It was a good job, too. We couldn't have gone on with all that chaos, having them come back and bomb the life out of the aerodrome all the time. We never did see the boy who was on the elevating wheel again. We retreated too.'

The roads were packed with French civilians trying to get away from the coming invaders. The army trucks could only move slowly through the crowds, watched by the angry, desolate eyes of people who felt they were being abandoned. A member of the Durham Light Infantry who was also trudging along those French lanes wrote an eyewitness account. 'The poor pathetic people that were walking along the roads, you had to see them to believe them. Old horses and carts, farm carts, big ones, little ones, all loaded up with their family possessions. All the people looking frightened and desperate, walking along the roads, not knowing what was happening, not knowing what to do. They had dog carts laden up with stuff, they had bicycles laden up with stuff, the men were carrying big loads on their backs, the children were plodding along the side of the road. Old people, they were collapsing exhausted, and people were trying to recover them. You could see them huddle about the person and they'd eventually lift her or him onto a cart, and they'd move off on the road.'

'We offered them the only comfort we could,' said Grandad. 'I had been saving up my tins of Gold Flake fags for people at home, because I didn't smoke, so I got them out of me pack and just chucked them out of the back of the truck to people. They were grateful, I suppose.'

The artillery unit had not got very far before the lead car pulled over to the side of the road and the trucks did the same. The crews jumped from the back and came to attention. There was a problem, said the commanding officer. The heavy guns had been abandoned but in their haste to leave nobody had disabled them. They could be fired against British aircraft in any counter-attack.

'There's no alternative,' he said. 'Some of us are going to have to go back and sort this one out. Any volunteers?'

Nobody stepped forward. To return would mean becoming detached from the convoy and probably losing any chance of getting home.

'No? Fine, I will nominate.'

The same gritty Scottish voice that had barked its disapproval of a mouth organ at midnight now called out names, each man's shoulders slumping as he heard his own, and the last was inevitable:

'Moreton, you're going.'

The airfield was quiet when they got there. The surviving fighter planes had flown south, migrating away from the bombardment, and their ground crews were on the road somewhere. The wreckers chatted nervously about their families as they worked, pulling the breech pins out and vandalizing the machinery with hammers and wrenches. Jerry wouldn't be bombing the place any more, there was no point, but a panzer division might roll through the perimeter fence at any moment. The gunners only had rifles, which would be almost useless against machine guns, so the only sensible thing to do if the enemy came was to put both hands in the air. In the meantime the place was so still and the air so warm that these shattered, nervous men who had barely slept for a fortnight lay on the benches they had built themselves, next to the guns, and one by one they closed their eyes for a bit.

'I thought we were going to be there for the evening,' said Grandad. 'They must have all gone off that night and left me. When I woke up in the morning the chaps that was with me had disappeared. I don't know what happened to them since.'

He was on his own. The enemy was very near, to his north, east and west, but Bert had no idea. 'I spent a couple of nights on my own in an empty French farmhouse. I didn't realize then that the people who owned it could have been shot for harbouring an English soldier.' Then he started walking, not knowing where he was going. All his kit had been lost: mess tins, washing and shaving gear, water bottle and sterilizer, gas cape, rifle brush, all gone somewhere in the chaos. He still had his gun, and a helmet and gas mask slung over his shoulder. 'I saw some French people praying in a Catholic church, and I went and stood by the door at the back. One of them came out. "Tommy," that's what he called me, "the Germans are close."' They were indeed: the advancing tanks were no more than a mile or two away, as close as my house to his. How did he escape? 'An English truck came along out of nowhere, full of soldiers. They pulled me up with them and we sped off. One of them said to me, "Well, gunner, you're in the infantry now."'

They were heading for the battle, looking for a fight. 'I thought I'd sit right at the back because they usually dropped the first people off furthest from the action. But that didn't work. They drove straight to the front, didn't they? Gave me an anti-tank gun.'

⋆

'Wait here,' the man said. 'Keep your eye on that railway line. There'll be a tank coming along on the back of a train and your job is to shoot it.' Bert knows he'll miss. He has never fired one of these things before. He doesn't think he's nervous though, not after all that has happened to him lately. The twenty-one-year-old is not the boy he was before he left London, but he doesn't expect anyone from home will ever know that. Not his mum, nor his dad, nor his brothers. Nor Vi. One day they'll see each other again, but not alive. Why should he survive when so many others around him have fallen suddenly, caught by bullets, or disappeared in the bright rose of an exploding bomb, or been burned? Hunger, tiredness, excitement and the sudden memory of the scent of burning flesh all twist his stomach as he waits, crouching by the window in the first floor room of a small house, somewhere in France. He wants a crap, badly. The muscles in his legs and arms, and those across his chest, are tight with the unrelenting anxiety, the fear that burns away constantly without him really knowing it; breathing hurts but he doesn't register why, just feels grateful for the chance to sit in one place for a while. The metal of the Boys Mark I anti-tank rifle is cold on his cheek, the prickle of his rude beard brings him back from the edge of sleep with a shudder. He looks down the long barrel, past the magazine and jiggles the weapon on the stand he has wedged against the frame of an upturned dresser. Bert knows enough about guns to jam the stock right up against his shoulder, because this thing will recoil like a heavyweight's punch. Don't want to be flat on your backside when the tank crew sees the flash, he thinks. Then the turret will turn slowly, the barrel will point straight at the farmhouse, and the tank commander will give the order. Then Bert will die. Simple as that.

*

'I was expecting to be killed. You see it happen, you get used to it. At the time there was no way of getting out of it, nothing to do to stop it. The end could come at any time. It's only now, being old, that I realize what all those blokes I knew missed.'

'Move your arse, gunner, come on.'

The Boys is heavy, the barrel hangs by his feet as he staggers down the narrow stairway of the farmhouse and out into the courtyard. The engines have started, the men are pulling one another up under the tarpaulin covers. He pushes the gun along the bed of the truck and takes somebody's hand, looks into a pair of eyes as crazed and dark as his own. It stinks in there, they haven't washed their bodies for days and the khakis are rigid like cardboard on their shrunken frames.

'Where we off to now?'

'Dunno. Out of here. The Frogs have given up.'

'What, surrendered?'

'Packed it in. No point in a last stand now. We're going for a boat.'

They were too late for Dunkirk. The survivors of that epic evacuation were already home, describing what they had left behind. 'It's an inferno over there: a hell made by man,' one soldier told a reporter among the crowds at a railway station in London. Another spoke of the awesome swarms of German troops and tanks and planes, and the destruction they had caused. 'Villages and towns had just been brought to the ground,' said a soldier who had been forced to eat raw swedes from the field and drink boiled ditchwater, because there was nothing else. 'And there was water and smoke and fires in the streets. And I can still remember that terrible smell of death after a bombing or shelling had occurred. And people were in these houses, they hadn't been taken out and there was still that horrible stench which we had to go through. As we went past some woods all the trees had been uprooted, the tops had been shelled away, and it was just like walking through a hell.' This was the landscape through which Bert and his new unit were still making their slow way. They came across soldiers who had lost contact with their commanding officers and been given suicidal orders by others who had appeared from nowhere then disappeared again. There were rumours of mutiny. As the remnants stumbled west hoping to avoid the enemy they could not know that some of those lucky enough to get their bodies home had lost their minds on the way. A dispatch rider was sitting up in bed, looking well, in a psychiatric nursing home in Sussex at that moment. 'Shall I tell you what happened to me in France, sir?' he asked the officer who had come to visit him. The story began when the Germans bombed a crossroads crowded with refugees. 'It was a dreadful scene and I found myself beside a little boy of about five and he'd had his legs blown off. And he was blinded in one eye and he was in terrible pain and I took him in my arms and I could see he was dying and I took out my revolver and I shot him, sir. I did do right, didn't I?' The officer said yes, he would have done the same. Then the rider said, 'Shall I tell you what happened to me in France, sir?' He recited the whole tale again, and again, until a nurse asked the officer to leave.

'He never stops,' she said. 'Over and over and over again he tells that story.'

Winston Churchill knew Dunkirk had been a shambolic retreat and he warned on 4 June that wars were not won by evacuations. Then he stood up in the Commons to deliver the very speech that would define the myth of Dunkirk: a stubborn hymn to resistance that promised to fight on the beaches, on the landing grounds, in the fields and in the streets. 'We shall fight in the hills,' he said. 'We shall never surrender.' And as MPs all around him bellowed approval at these inspirational words, Churchill hissed to a colleague: 'And we'll fight them with the butt ends of broken beer bottles, because that's bloody well all we've got!' The British Expeditionary Force had left behind 38,000 vehicles and a thousand heavy guns like the ones Bert and his mates wrecked in Reims, but the miracle was that three hundred thousand troops had somehow made it back across the Channel. Grandad was not one of them.

19

This must be the end. Bert had ridden his luck, but it's all over now. The infantry unit is strung out along the edge of a ploughed field somewhere in France, waiting for the enemy. The trucks, all out of fuel, were abandoned a mile back. Every rifleman lies on his belly in the ditch, hoping to blend in with the earth and the hedgerows in the dark. Bert looks along the line of barely visible soldiers from a corner of the field, where he sits with his knees crossed and his finger on the trigger of a Bren gun. Back in training camp they taught him how to take one of these powerful machine guns apart and put it back together blindfold. The instructor cut down a tree with a hail of bullets, spitting sappy chunks into the air. A tarpaulin covers the gunner and the men on either side of the tripod, one a sergeant and the other carrying ammunition for the Bren. Another crew like theirs is hidden away at the far end of the field, out of sight from here. If the Germans come they will probably let the tanks go by and hope to surrender to the troops that follow. But if a fight is needed the enemy will get one.

'Listen, gunner, is that right you're a believer?' the sergeant whispers.

'Yeah.'

'Well, it might be a good time to say a prayer.'

It would. Yes, it would. Right now. He can't think of anything but a couple of lines from a hymn he was singing to himself earlier as they marched:

'In seasons of distress and grief, my soul has often found relief. Lord –'

A sudden whoosh, and a bright green ball of light flares in the sky, hanging like the star over Bethlehem, illuminating the silent field. Bert pulls the gun into his shoulder and guides the barrel up to point at the Very light to shoot it out.

'Hold your fire, Moreton. You'll give us away.'

The Germans must be close. This is it. Bert wipes a sweating palm on his tunic, breathing quickly, and finishes his prayer.

'Lord, save us. Take our souls into thy care. Amen.'

'Amen.'

Bootnails crunch on the tarmac, behind them. Swing the gun, he thinks, they're coming from the road. Why haven't the rearguard fired? Where was the warning? Then he hears a voice straight off the Old Kent Road.

'Come on, you bastards, get your filthy hides out of that ditch.'

'They was Tommies,' he told me. 'They called us some right names, but we were glad to see them, because they had lorries that worked.' And food too, salty grey bully beef that the starving survivors lapped from borrowed mess tins like dogs. 'They took us down south, away from the fighting, to some seaside place. I don't know where.' Troops were still being evacuated from Cherbourg and St Nazaire, beyond the reach of the advancing ground forces, although the whole coast was under attack from the air. 'I've never told many people this, because they wouldn't believe it, but when we got to the harbour the French soldiers there didn't want to let us get on a boat. They said the war was over so we should just surrender and become prisoners. Our commanding officer went to theirs and said to him straight, "If you don't allow my men to leave we will open fire." That changed their minds.'

The only vessel available was an old barge used for transporting coal, but at least it was a way back. Bert found a ledge at the front where he could set up the Bren gun to fire on any planes that came over. 'The bloke next to me had a Bren too, and he said, "Here, have you ever fired one of these things? I don't know what to do." I said, "Don't worry, mate, just stand by and I'll fire mine. We'll be okay."'

Their barge was easing out from the protection of the harbour walls, pitching as the waves of the open sea hit the sides, when a fighter aircraft came low across the water at high speed. The soldiers opened up on it with at least sixteen machine guns that Bert could count, and saw smoke trail from the engine as it followed a graceful arc into the water, then exploded. 'I was delighted. I said, "Look at that!"'

The man next to him raised a hand, but did not take his eyes off the oil spreading out from wreckage on the surface of the sea where the plane had gone down. 'No,' he said. 'No. It was a Spitfire.'

There was silence on the barge then, not a word from the soldiers lined up along the side, just the smoky grind of the engine and the suck and rush of the waves. The senior officer was the first to react, and he began to work his way among them on the rolling deck, looking each man in the face and talking slowly with as much authority as was available within his aching, thirsty, hungry, scared and exhausted frame. 'He told us not to worry, that our pilots had orders to stay up high and never come down as low as that, so although it was a Spitfire it could well have been a captured one, flown by a German.' They did not really believe him.

There were further shocks out in the Channel, as the barge made slow progress against the wind and tides. Feverish, soaked by salt water that crusted white in the burning sun and made every pore howl, every sore weep, they gave some men up to hallucinations and madness, and wondered how long it would be before the thing happened to them, or whether it was already happening. Blinding lights danced in their eyes. 'We must have been out there for four days on that deck, in the open, and we saw the wreckage of so many boats that had gone down. The oil on the water was burning, and there was a lot of wood. Then we saw the hull of one really big ship, upside down. It was a terrible sight. Somebody said, "That must be the *Lancashire*."'

The rumour had reached them in the chaos of the port before they went out to sea. Thousands of soldiers had been packed on to a former Cunard cruise liner just off St Nazaire and they all drowned when the ship was hit by dive bombers. The story was almost true: the ship was the *Lancastria*, repainted in battleship grey and sent to pick up evacuees from the Loire estuary. By mid-afternoon on 17 June there had been six thousand soldiers and a few women and children on board, twice as many passengers as was thought safe, crammed into every possible space above and below deck. The captain sent word that no more could be taken, but still they kept coming, and there may have been eleven thousand on the *Lancastria* when she was attacked from the air at ten to four that day. Bombs exploded in the sea on either side of her and one broke open the fuel tanks, spilling tons of oil into the water. The ship shook and pitched as more bombs fell, and one of them was said to have gone straight down the single funnel and blown up the hold where troops were standing shoulder to shoulder. It took twenty minutes for the *Lancastria* to sink. The survivors who managed to get clear of the whirling water and cling to floating wreckage looked back and saw their friends huddled along the ridge of the upturned hull. They were singing 'There'll Always Be An England' when a German aircraft returned overhead and cut them all down with machine-gun fire.

Bodies would be found all along the French coast in the following months. The lucky ones who were dragged out of the sea alive were taken back to Plymouth but made to stay out of sight while newsreel cameras filmed other returning soldiers marching in full kit, looking fit and happy. The British press did not report what had happened. Churchill refused to let the truth be known in case it damaged morale, saying: 'The newspapers have got quite enough disaster for today, at least.' The sinking of the *Lancastria* was hushed up.

'When I got back I told people about that ship, and what had happened, but nobody would believe it,' Grandad told me. 'They called me a liar, so I stopped talking about it, until now. What's the point, if nobody thinks you are telling the truth?'

The whole country was preparing for invasion. German soldiers had been issued with English phrase books, but more than a million British citizens were armed and ready to resist. The King had been practising with a revolver in the grounds of Buckingham Palace, apparently determined to die fighting. Local Defence Volunteer groups had no more than pitchforks and shotguns but they pointed them at the skies anyway, in case stormtroopers really did start dropping down dressed as nuns. Most of the country's best troops were already back safely, Mr Churchill said, leaving some people to assume that the ones who were still returning must be slackers or incompetents. There was little patience for stories from the front line when it seemed the battle was about to rage in English streets; particularly when the tales those haunted soldiers wanted to tell were of destruction and defeat and the astonishing might of the German army. There was a government campaign to stop people like that spreading alarm and defeatism. Mr Glumpot was Hitler's best friend.

There was nobody to meet Bert at the station, despite his having sent word, so he pushed his own way through the crowds to the taxi rank and hired a cab. He did not know that Vi and her sister were still waiting on the platform, unable to make his face out in the crowd. There were so many soldiers gathered under the clouds of steam, still filthy from the smoke of battle and the boats, and the weeks of living rough on the run. Most had shaved and done their best to clean up, but all any of them had to wear was the ragged uniform he stood in. The experiences of the last month or so had rearranged Bert's open, enthusiastic face into a grim mask. He must have walked straight past his wife without being recognized.

There was nobody at Vi's place either, so he got the cabbie to take him down to his own family's house in Nunhead. There was no extra charge. The door was unlocked. He pushed it half open and called out a greeting.

'Who is it?' His father's voice came from the kitchen.

'It's Bert.'

The old man moved to the front door as quickly as his frail legs would allow.

'You're a sight,' he said, struggling for breath. 'We've had all our letters back, saying, "Missing, Untraced."'

The words my grandad used to finish the story of that homecoming were restrained, a curious reminder that he was only one of fourteen children born to a man who was alcoholic and liked to stay out of their way.

'Although he had a big family,' he said, 'I think he was pleased.'

20

The bombs keep falling during the late summer of 1940 and the short, simple letters Vi gets from Bert are not much of a comfort. She has no idea where he is stationed, but thinks it must be close because the envelopes are always stamped with the same London code. Correspondence from military units all over the country comes through the one sorting office, but Vi does not know that. Or maybe she does. Either way, she thinks it might be worth going along to that office to see if her Bert is working there, or if anybody will let on where he is stationed. Wearing her Salvation Army uniform, naturally.

'I'm sorry, madam, we really can't give you that information,' says the clerk at the front desk. He is in his fifties, astonished and saddened to find himself back in khaki after spending two decades as a postman. He envies this woman's husband for having been out in France. At least the boy can say he's done his bit.

'I see,' says Vi. 'I understand. There is a war on, after all.'

'Yes, that's right,' says the clerk, a little concerned. Vi seems close to tears.

'It's just that I need to see him. To speak to him.'

She puts her hand up to her mouth as though forbidding herself to say more.

'Is something wrong, madam?' asks the clerk. 'Would you like to sit for a moment?'

'No,' she says. 'No, thank you. I'll be fine.'

She turns, slowly, towards the door but he speaks again: 'Is it important?'

Vi turns back, purse close to her chest, and gives the man her best unbroken gaze.

'Yes, it is very important.'

'I'm sorry to ask, madam, but is it personal? Something about, shall we say, married life?'

She offers a half-smile that says thank you for understanding, for offering a poor wife assistance, for being so kind. The tears still glisten. She nods.

'Hold on here, just a moment. I'll see what I can do for you.'

He is not gone long. She stands there in the dusty office, with the sun lighting up the counter, trying to read other people's correspondence upside down.

'Here we are,' he says, surprising her. 'Look, I'll tell you where they are. All Hallows on the north Kent coast. It's quite a hike, but you can get a train most of the way.'

She leans against the counter to see the address he is writing down. He stops and puts a hand on hers.

'You know I'm not supposed to do this, don't you?'

She nods, and then she smiles. Properly.

Bert is dozing with his back to the sandbags and his face to the sun. The limber gunner has a space of his own in the round pit, a wooden bench where he can sit to dismantle and polish the breech of his gun, but that job has been done for today. He has also checked the shells, opening each of the long metal boxes in which they are packed, carefully, two by two, and wiping away condensation. The Tannoy crackles and the sea wind almost carries the words away: 'Moreton to the office.'

What, he wonders, have I done now?

'It seems your wife is on the way here,' says the battery commander when Herbert Moreton 1491177 is standing to attention in the hut that serves as his office.

'Is she, sir?'

'Yes, she is. Do you know anything about this?'

'No, sir.'

'Are you in any trouble, Moreton?'

'I don't know what you mean, sir.'

'I mean, Moreton, have you got any married trouble?'

'I see, sir,' he says, silently and furiously trying to work out what is going on. If Vi is coming he has to see her, obviously. Better play along.

'Yes, sir. I have, sir.'

'Right. Well, when she gets here you had better meet her at the camp gate. I can only give you an hour, understood? After that I think you should see her back to the station.'

'Sir.'

He does. He sees her back to the station. Then he sees her on to a train, then back to her house, and then he sees her go to sleep. And in the morning he panics, and races back to the coast as quickly as the train will take him. It is alarmingly slow. The guns have been in action overnight, and he is in danger of being classified a deserter.

'You were missed last night,' says the OC. 'Where were you?'

'I thought you said see her home, sir. Sorry, sir.'

He gets away with it, too.

I'd like to think my father was conceived that night. The dates fit. Vi had used her cunning and charm to see her husband, whose combination of apparent innocence and bare-faced cheek saved him from being put on a charge.

'You've got to remember we were all in a state at that time,' he told me. 'People didn't know when they were going to be with each other again or when the Germans were going to come. We wanted to see each other as much as we could.'

21

The first Saturday of September 1940 was a lovely hot day. Bert was back in London on compassionate leave because his father had taken a turn for the worse, but he and Vi decided to have some time alone together with a stroll along the canal. It was 7 September. 'Somebody close to us did a little cheer because they saw a lot of planes and they thought it was the RAF. I said to my wife, "They're not ours." You could see puffs of ack-ack fire underneath them where the guns along the Thames were firing. The road was full of people, but when they started dropping bombs everybody disappeared.' They were still looking for shelter when the explosions reached them. 'We couldn't find anywhere to go. We knocked at a house but they wouldn't let us in. Scared, I expect. It was terrifying, really. You could hear the bombs coming through the trees. They caught some of the streets in Peckham as well as the docks. They caught me brother's house, but he wasn't in it. I spent that night with my wife in Nunhead, where Mum lived. She wouldn't go down the shelter, so we were in the house with her. I couldn't sleep so when the rain started I got up and stood in the doorway. All you heard was the growling noise of the planes. They were loaded with bombs, weren't they? Horrible. The next day I saw my brother. He said: "You'd better go back, Bert."'

The gunners at All Hallows were ready, shells primed, for whatever came at them out of the mist. Bert climbed off the lorry and went straight to his post, legs still shaky from the long and bumpy journey. The codeword had been sent through, warning of imminent attack. Across the water at Calais there were squadrons of dive bombers and a fleet of troop barges ready to invade. The moon and tides were right. Church bells rang in the Kent countryside, warning the people: the enemy is coming.

But he wasn't, at least not that way. The Germans did not invade Kent or any other stretch of the coast. There was a change of plan: the Luftwaffe would build on its surprising success and launch an assault even fiercer than the one on Rotterdam that had shocked Holland into surrender. London would be bombed into submission. The English would give in. They had to.

At anti-aircraft headquarters in Stanmore it would have been hard to disagree. The top brass had been wrongfooted by the change in tactics and the guns were in all the wrong places, defending ports and estuaries against attacks that were never going to happen. London had only half what it needed to resist the bombers, not least because so many guns had been left behind during the evacuation from France. Reinforcements were needed, urgently. The battery at All Hallows was told to move out and drive to the capital as quickly as possible, and as it did so there were other units travelling from much further north. Guns that had been guarding the Humber, for example, took twenty-five hours to get from Cleethorpes to London, where the crews found the new site they had been sent to was unusable. They had to clear it of rubble and level the ground before the guns could be set up, work that had only just been finished when the alarm was raised. They fired through the night and finally got to sleep at 9.30 a.m., only to be woken up half an hour later for the first of many alerts during daylight hours. There were so few gunners available that the same men had to go back on duty for every alarm. They stayed up firing the guns for eight consecutive nights.

Grandad had even less chance to get settled. 'My first stop was at a park in Catford. We didn't get to put the guns down before the Germans set the blinking field alight by dropping incendiary bombs. They only had to catch one round of ammunition and up we'd all go, so we got away from the pit. You know those big park benches? I lay right underneath one of them until it was all over, then we went round putting the incendiary fires out.'

Experienced gunners were needed at different posts all over London, so the unit was split up and Bert was sent to Hyde Park. Some of the other crew members had come straight from training school without ever having fired a gun in real conditions. They found the roar petrifying. The vibrations from the guns were so great they shook huts and cookhouses apart, and blew false teeth out of your mouth. Being so close to that roar for eight hours at a time scrambled your brain, and there was no respite as they slept by their guns. The rain turned the fields to mud and filled every trench.

There was another very serious problem with the new recruits: some of them were useless, the worst the army had to put up with. Major-General Sir Frederick Pile, the man in charge of them all, was disgusted at being sent the dregs: 'Out of twenty-five recruits to one battery, one had a withered arm, one was mentally deficient, one had no thumbs, one had a glass eye which fell out whenever he doubled to the guns and two were in the advanced and more obvious stages of venereal disease.'

'Here, Bert, have a butcher's.'

'What's that?'

‘Look, over there. Let your eyes adjust. See them?’

‘Strewth.’

The two soldiers take it in turns to look through the telescope at the command post they are supposed to be guarding, just south of Speaker’s Corner. There may as well not be a blackout, because the flickering of flames and swaying of searchlights mean you can see bodies moving in the shadows, in the line of trees by the bridle path, towards Lovers’ Walk.

‘Once you see one they all start appearing, don’t they? How many do you think?’

‘Haven’t a clue, mate. Blow me.’

There are dozens of ‘Piccadilly warriors’ out there in the dark, working women who don’t need to rent rooms while the blackout is on. They’ll do a soldier a favour for a couple of quid, but it costs more if you’re out of uniform and more still if you’ve got a posh accent, as many of their secret clients have. The police have got other things to worry about now, even if they catch a girl flashing her torch on and off to attract business. Maybe that is why so many ‘amateurs’ are giving it a go, taking advantage of the absence of their husbands and boyfriends, and the pimps who run these streets in peacetime, to earn a bit and help the war effort. It doesn’t take long, and you don’t get pregnant standing up, do you? No wonder the parks at dusk have been described as ‘a vast battleground of sex’.

‘Let’s have another look, Bert. Time’s up.’

The gun Grandad fired in Hyde Park, when he didn’t have his mind on other things, was left over from the First War. It would still have been a decent weapon if they had been given enough ammunition. ‘They shouted “Fire!”, then there was a long pause. You had to be careful with your shells, not to use them up too quickly, because we were short. All the time the Germans were dropping bombs. You're supposed to have a hell of a lot of shells, but we didn't.'

He was not kidding. At that stage of the war the guns fired thirty thousand shells for every plane shot down. The crews were worried about blowing up their own aircraft by mistake, but the truth was they had very little hope of hitting anything at all. Their first problem was to find the target. A new system had been set up, based on sound, but this only told the gunners how high the Germans were flying when they were ten miles away from London. There was no way of knowing what the enemy did after that. The fuse had to be set to explode within one hundred feet of the bomber or the shell would do no damage at all, but fuses were unpredictable and sometimes went off early or late. It took a shell half a minute to get as high as a plane, so the gunners had to guess where the aircraft would be in thirty seconds' time, but pilots seldom fly in a straight line at a constant height when they're being attacked by fighters from above and guns below. Atmospheric conditions could easily deflect the shells off target. Oh, and the Blitz crews were firing at night, while under bombardment. Even their official history, published while the war was still going on, conceded the whole thing was absurdly haphazard. 'It is like shooting a pheasant with a rifle in the dark.'

With a blind man shouting directions in your ear, the author might truthfully have added. And beating you around the head.

'Where the hell are the guns?' The question was being asked all over London, from the Dog and Duck to the Cabinet Office, after three days and nights of heavy bombing. There had been no audible resistance. The docks were burning, clouds of black smoke hung over the city and smaller fires burned everywhere. The streets were impassable in some places, just holes in the ground or mountains of rubble. Desperate people formed queues to get back in to underground stations as soon as they were ushered out of them in the morning, and refugees fled for the forests. The Germans seemed able to fly over and do whatever they liked at no danger from the anti-aircraft batteries that were supposed to scare them away, or at least push them up higher where Spitfires and Hurricanes could get at them. The defences were a joke, but it wasn't funny.

General Pile, the man responsible for this mess, did what decisive men have done down the centuries: he called a meeting. Every gun position officer in London was summoned to Kensington on Wednesday morning to hear what must be done. They were sceptical, and ready to remind the general of the many very good reasons why their units could not hit anything. The officers from Gunner Moreton's emplacement in Hyde Park had only to walk down past the Serpentine to reach the Drill Hall in Brompton Road, so they would soon be back at the pits to give the ordinary soldiers their extraordinary new orders.

Stop worrying about your aim, General Pile told his audience. Just fire, and fire again as quickly as you can, and don't stop. He would get them more shells. The RAF would be told not to fly over London during a raid. The new equipment would not be abandoned, but if it was still no use then commanders must use their own ears to guess the height of the enemy. The general did not say how he thought anyone could listen out for Heinkel drones with a battery blazing away and bombs exploding all around them, but he did admit the new tactics were a 'policy of despair'. Something had to be done, he said. Anything. The only option left was to fire as many shells as possible into the sky, to intimidate the Luftwaffe and encourage Londoners.

It worked. That night the London guns sent up more than thirteen thousand shells. The astonished bomber pilots flew higher and higher to avoid being hit. Some turned away completely. This is more like it, thought Bert, clearing the empty shell cases as they clattered from the gun. He would remember that night as fun.

Newspaper editors in Fleet Street heard the thunder like everyone else, and their headlines the following morning were ecstatic: 'Terrific London Barrage Meets Greatest Raid' said the front of the *Daily Express*. The Germans had attempted their most intense attack yet but been repulsed by 'a new super-barrage' unlike any seen before. 'Chains of shells burst high in the sky, a curtain of steel. The sky must have been full of flying shrapnel. It spattered on the rooftops at times like machine-gun fire.' Which was bad luck if you happened to be beneath it at the time. Shrapnel was hurting as many people as the bombs, but the newspapers chose not to say so. Only a few raiders got through, said the *Express*. 'Most had to drop their bombs haphazard on the outskirts.' Which was, again, bad luck if you happened to live on the outskirts.

East London suffered badly, north and south of the river, but the newspapers that rejoiced in the spirited barrage were already creating a myth of the Blitz, the idea that cockneys could somehow cope with all this and come out smiling, with a cuppa and a singsong. Those who lived among them knew differently. 'The whole story of the last weekend has been one of unplanned hysteria,' a woman wrote in her Mass Observation diary. 'The press versions of life going on normally in the East End are grotesque. There was no bread, no electricity, no milk, no gas, no telephones.'

Nobody was whistling, she wrote. Nobody was laughing.

'I know this isn't a pleasant story to read,' wrote an American reporter called Quentin Reynolds. 'It isn't a pleasant one to write. It's much better to read and write about the fighter pilots, the "gay, laughing-eyed knights of the air". Sure, that's what war is. Glamorous and exciting . . . but that isn't the war I see in London every night.' He watched volunteer ambulance women bring the corpses of three adult sisters out of a burning house, followed by the body of a child, her long golden hair 'strangely untouched by fire'. 'This is the war I see. If you want a front seat to the war, come and stand over this three-year-old child with me. Don't be afraid of the bombs that are falling close, or the spent shrapnel that is raining down on us. You want to see what war is really like, don't you? Take another look at the baby. She still looks as though she were asleep. This is war, full style, 1940.'

22

Bert is elated. They've given something back. Early in the morning of 12 September, after firing all night, he steals away from the gun pit for a few hours to walk back south of the river and see what has happened to his own people. The elation vanishes as exhaustion hits him along with despair. So many houses have gone, including the one his sister Hilda rents. She might have been in the shelter at the back of her garden, but is not there now. The terrace where his mother and father live is a row of half houses, their roofs and faces missing. Little licks of flame spring up here and there in the dusty confusion, and water oozes along the gutters like blood. A crowd surrounds a tea van, talking, weeping, shouting, but none of these people are members of his family. They must still be under the ruins. Why is nobody pulling back these timbers and broken walls to find them? The shop on the corner has lost its plate-glass window, and the shelves have been stripped of all their tins and packets, but the grocer is writing on a box top with a bit of charcoal, 'business as usual'. He thinks he saw Ma Moreton heading for a rest centre.

Sixteen people are dead in Camberwell. The Germans turn for home overhead, releasing any bombs that are left over, and this is also where they fall when the aimer misses the docks or a pilot gives up before reaching his proper target. There's a story going round about an air raid warden from Peckham who crawled into a bombed and burning house to pull away debris and free a woman who was trapped under the stairs. The gas main had been fractured and the roof was about to collapse but he went in anyway, and saved her. He deserves a medal, people say, and he will get one. A married couple in the same road could not be rescued. They are not alive to read a warning against euphoria buried at the bottom of the *Express* story. The encouraging new anti-aircraft barrage will make the enemy's bombing less accurate but 'this does not count for much when bombing is intended to be inaccurate'.

Bert is not the only one walking through these bombed-out streets in a daze, struggling to take it all in. Other people are seeing pitiful sights they will never forget. A girl wandering naked, all her clothes blown off by the blast of a bomb that had killed her mother, and father, and baby brother. A man who will not leave the rubble of his home, although his own wife and son have been dragged out dead. He clings to the iron bed frame as women from the ambulance service try to pull him away. The man will not speak but grunts like an animal and his eyes flicker madly, as though he cannot register the reality, cannot believe the roof will not rise and the bones of his loved ones live again. His neighbours were lucky: their house was still standing when they returned from the railway arches where they spent the night. The door was ajar. A bookcase and a dresser have gone, looted with a family photograph in a good brass frame. The thieves were there before daylight, moving in the shadows past the chain of people who were passing buckets of water across the street, trying to stop a blaze.

'We tried to take it in our stride,' my grandfather told me. 'That was the idea, but the soldiers were really upset that their parents were at home getting bombed. Ordinary people went through hell, lying in bed listening to the bombs. They were helpless. At least we felt like we were doing something.'

As we sat in his garden, remembering that summer long ago, he raised his voice in anger for the first time since the stories had begun to flow. 'They used to complain some people never went further than Dover, but the war was here at home. People were dying in their thousands. You don't hear about that. You never knew if your wife was going to be killed. Everyone was in the firing line. The civilians suffered more than the soldiers. The difference was they had nothing to fight back with.'

23

It is on his mothering that a young child can depend for the building up of a real sense of security. If the circumstances of his life change too sharply his sense of safety may be greatly shaken. His adaptability must not be over strained or he will become anxious and insecure.

Gwendoline E. Chesters, *The Mothering of Young Children*

The silence is what people remember. The sudden quietness, a violent absence, just after the bomb has hit and the flash of light and the roaring sound and the shattering glass and the screaming metal and the dust and the bricks and the plaster clattering, raining, pattering down around your ears, and the falling to earth of things that have no business in the sky. After all that, the silence. A dripping tap, or a burst pipe, or a cat scratching, but these small sounds wrapped up in the big one, the big nothing. No need to hold your breath now, to count to ten as one whistle becomes distinct from the others and grows louder, no need to wait those long awful seconds to see if it is you, knowing that if there is no bang, just the light flooding everywhere and the thumping of your blood in your ears then you are dead. If you can hear the explosion it will probably not kill you. Just maim or blind or trap you. And afterwards, after the impact, comes the silence. All quiet like a sleepy Sunday afternoon in the garden. Before the pain kicks in, and the crying begins, and the bells ring, and the voices call out.

Vi had to pass her baby out of the shelter through a hole someone had dug in the earth that had fallen all around the entrance. He didn't even whimper, just looked up at his rescuer with unblinking baby eyes, little Arthur, a few months old. Vi was fine, eventually, when they got her out. The house was gone, another place lost, but nine months of bombing had persuaded her to go down into the Anderson, despite the damp that did your chest no good and the spiders that ran across your face if you tried to sleep. The baby didn't like it down there but the shelter saved them all. Perhaps that was why they still had one in their garden so long after the war was over.

This is my father's first memory of his father. He is three years old, so the year must be 1944. The anti-aircraft emplacement on the edge of Richmond Park is by a wood and a pond, and to the child reared in terraced streets this is like being in the real open countryside. How wonderful to live out here, he thinks. And a great laugh to fire that huge gun.

Daddy is a strange, strong man in a beret who picks Arthur up under both arms and holds him tight against his prickly tunic. It hurts.

'Do you want a go?'

Arthur nods. Of course he does. Lowered on to a cold metal bucket seat, he sits with his feet dangling over the edge, pushing hard against the lever his dad says will make the gun go up and down. It doesn't budge.

'Come on mate, push!'

'I can't!'

Mum and Dad are both smiling as they glance upwards, at an aircraft droning overhead, in the clear sky above the barrage balloons.

'See this button? Put your finger on it. That's how you

fire the gun. Go on, son.'

Arthur looks down at the button, then up at the plane. He presses, hard.

'Bang!' says his dad, making him jump. At that moment the sun reflects on the cockpit glass and the silver silhouette flashes. 'You hit it! You shot him down!'

Arthur jumps off the seat and runs away from the gun, howling. He doesn't hear them laughing behind him. It will be at least a year before the little boy stops worrying that someone is going to come and arrest him for bringing down a British plane. He will never forget the day.

This is the story my grandfather told me about those months in Richmond Park, his keenest memory of that time. It is very different. He is playing the drums in the Nissen hut on a Saturday night, brushes pattering out a waltz as one of the other blokes sits at an upright piano he has nicked or borrowed from one of the big houses up the road, and another blows a trumpet. There are women working at the Richmond site, reading the instruments in the command post and setting the dials the gunners follow, and if there is no raid the battery is allowed to hold a dance. The ATS girls are smart, and pretty, and most of them can do a bit better than your average gunner, so they often get their posh boyfriends along. The men invite outsiders too, in retaliation for the unspoken snub, which is how Vi comes to be present, dancing with one of the other ammunition numbers while her husband sets the rhythm.

'What brings you here then?' asks her dance partner, trying to get a conversation going.

'Oh, I'm married to the drummer,' she says.

'Really?' He looked over at the kit, raising his eyebrows. 'Fancy that. Bert never told us he was married.'

'Is that right?'

She gave him earache that night.

They shared a memory, a story they had picked over on the day we three sat around with fish and chips. It involved rockets falling out of the sky, so must have happened after Richmond Park. Gunner Moreton was moved back to the coast then to fire at the new V1 flying bombs, small jet aeroplanes with no pilots, that came over too fast for a Spitfire to catch and too low for the anti-aircraft targeting systems to work. The gunners had to use their wits. They took aim with their own eyes, following the wavering flight of each sinister drone as it approached across the water, then fired magnetic shells. This wasn't like the Blitz, it was proper shooting at a target that kept up a constant speed and height because the flying bomb couldn't see what was coming. Much safer than the beaches of Normandy, which was where Bert and some of the other men would have been if the German scientists had not devised this new threat. Experienced gunners were needed to stay in England instead, for the time being, and guard the coasts against these pests they called doodlebugs. They were grateful for that. If they missed and the rocket flew over their heads they had to let it go, hoping one of the RAF's fast Tempest fighters could shoot it down or tip the wings to make it fall on an empty field. Sometimes the others laid bets, but the game was a serious one for Grandad, who was stationed out on the desolate marshlands of Essex by Burnham-on-Crouch. He would watch a stray V1 disappear inland and wonder if its engine was going to splutter out over his own part of London, and come down on his family. They had two boys by then. Arthur was walking with his mum and Les in the pram at Goose Green when he heard a sound like a motorbike with a bad engine and saw an aeroplane with its tail on fire. 'Look, Mum,' he called. 'OK, just keep walking,' she said, reaching for his hand. 'Listen.' The engine did not stop. The sound faded away. Somebody else's problem. The next one might not be though. There were so many coming over every day that people tried to carry on with life. You only hit the floor if the engine cut out.

Then the V2s started to arrive and everything changed. 'I am writing this story in the front-line,' wrote someone called W. A. E. Jones, from somewhere in southern England, announcing on the front page of the *Daily Herald* of 11 November 1944 that a terrible new weapon was upon them. 'There is no siren warning now. No time to take shelter.' These rockets were launched from two hundred miles away, they flew faster than sound and seventy miles above the earth, and there was no warning of where and when they might strike, the reporter said. This was only confirmation of what Londoners knew or feared: that the mysterious explosions they had heard with increasing frequency in recent weeks were not gas mains going up, as they were told by officials, but something much more frightening. The bang, followed by a sound like a distant train, could be heard for miles. Some people said they had seen explosions in mid-air. 'Must be flying gas mains.'

Churchill had known the worst but said nothing about it for two months. No official reference to the rockets was made until the Germans started boasting about them, and then the Prime Minister was forced to stand up in the Commons and bluster: 'No reliable or sufficient public warning can, in present circumstances, be given. There is, however, no need to exaggerate the danger. The scale and effect of the attack have not hitherto been significant.' Hardly stirring, or indeed Churchillian, stuff. The note of impotent panic in his language was underscored a fortnight later on 25 November when the worst V2 attack of the war happened on my grandmother's doorstep. Not even Churchill would have dared tell Vi she was exaggerating the danger that day, as she cried and cried at the loss of her friends who had been in the queue outside Woolworth's when the rocket came down. Nobody saw anything before the explosion, which destroyed a whole block and killed 160 people. Two women who cleaned trains at New Cross Station had gone to Woolies with their babies for afternoon tea. They were not counted among the dead, because their bodies were never found. Nine others were also missing, even after a long, floodlit rescue operation.

A thousand V2 rockets would fall on Britain. They were listed at the time as 'Big Ben' incidents, and I believe it was number 363 that nearly killed my father and grandfather. The timing of this attack, at five to seven on the night of 17 December, fits both their stories. This vindication of his memory by the official records surprised my father, who sometimes had trouble remembering where he put his car keys yet could recall fragments of his childhood in remarkable detail. He remembered there were black ribbons hanging down the back of his dad's tunic from the collar, for example, but was not sure what they were. Research revealed them to be the mark of the regiment Bert had just joined, the Royal Welch Fusiliers. The flying bombs had become less of a problem after the capture of their launching sites on the Pas de Calais, so Gunner Moreton had been retrained as an infantryman to help chase the Germans back to Berlin. He must have been home on leave in December before crossing the Channel. Bert had just left their basement flat to walk over Denmark Hill with his eldest son on the way to the fish and chip shop run by his sister when he saw a flash in the night sky. To the experienced soldier that meant a V2. 'Get down!' he shouted to anyone who could hear, pulling his son to the pavement just as waves of pressure from the explosion flooded through the street. 'I remember the warmth,' my father said. 'The light of the bomb was like the sun falling down behind the houses, by the railway line.' He thought it must have hit a factory that made Liquafruta, a tonic for the anaemic. 'I remember that smell so well. There were two smells from my childhood that always made me sick: Liquafruta and Camp coffee.'

Memory sometimes lies. 'Memory is about therapy as well as remembrance,' says David Reynolds in *Rich Relations*, a book about the American soldiers who came to fight in Europe. 'Its function is as much to forget the past as to record it. What GIs recall about their sojourns in wartime Britain is inextricably tied up with what they want to remember *and* forget about the war itself.' His book tells the story of a 'young, idealistic religious boy' from the South who wrestled with the ethics of taking another man's life. He fired three shots during the whole war, one of which was deliberately off target and the other two were only meant to wound. Early in 1945 he was hospitalized with pneumonia after a patrol one night, and sent to convalesce in Hereford, where he had nightmares about decaying bodies and blood gushing all over his gloves. He had an SS buckle with him but did not know how he had come by it. The war was over by the time he recovered, so he went home to America and eventually became a horticulturalist. The nightmares came back sometimes, but by then he was convinced he had not been responsible for anyone's death except perhaps by calling down artillery fire. A return to the battlefield in 1961 was traumatic, when he became so numb with fear that his wife had to help him back to the car. Finally, in 1986, he met his old platoon leader at a reunion and asked the question directly: 'Did I kill a man?' The platoon leader said he had staggered back to their positions after a solo patrol suffering from the cold and shock, his nerves gone. He was covered in blood. The memories that had been denied came back then. He was in the woods, running a fever. Somebody tapped him on the shoulder and he saw the outline of a German helmet. Instinctively acting as trained, he stepped aside, hit the soldier in the back with his knee, took hold of his chin and cut his throat. There was no sound, but blood gushed out all over his glove. He took the man's wallet and buckle. Later, trying to recover himself in the English countryside, he suppressed the memory almost completely. It took forty years to come back.

When I asked my grandfather what he had done in Holland and Germany he said: 'Not much. We were just in barracks all the time. In the Fusiliers they do everything with proper ceremonial guards, a band and everything. Big battalion bands. Even if you all went out to the pictures you had to march. The Germans like red tape and they used to stand around watching. You had to be very smart.' They were training to fight the Japanese. 'I didn't want to go, I didn't like the sound of the Japs. They used to cut your eyes out and goodness knows what. Some of the training we did was horrible, it was hard work: digging trenches, dig and dig. When it rained all night the hole filled up with water with you in it.' So that was it: marching with bands and splashing around in holes. I didn't believe him. Were there no bullets at all? 'Oh yes. We were in the guardroom once, sitting around like me and you are now, and one of the men had loose springs on his rifle. There was a bullet up the spout too. It went off and flew right past me into the wall. The guard came over and he was as white as a ghost. It was a shock to me too.'

I let it go. Maybe I was guilty of trying to impose a story on him. He had told me enough, far more than I had expected, and was obviously reluctant to go into that period of his life. Maybe nothing did happen. Then he took a book out of a plastic bag and showed it to me. The covers were made of cardboard, frayed at the edges and a little warped. It had yellowed with age. This was a book the fusiliers were all given to commemorate their part in Operation Overlord, 'ten months of hard, almost non-stop operations' from the deadly beaches of Normandy to the German city of Hamburg. 'Only those of us who were there remember the scenes of devastation of a beaten enemy,' said the book. 'The wreckage of vehicles, tanks and horse-drawn guns, the stenching carnage of man and beast. We recall the hectic chase of a disorganized enemy, the crossing of the river Seine at the end of August, the almost romantic drive across northern France and Belgium with its cheering crowds, welcoming banners and fruitful gifts with which the liberated people of Western Europe greeted us.'

I knew Bert was shooting doodlebugs in Essex when all that happened, but he was surely at the front line in time for 'the bogs of Holland, the ice and snow of the Ardennes, the mud and floods of the Reichswald Forest and those appalling roads built by the ex-master race'. Was he there by Christmas Day? The fusiliers were given orders to move immediately at dawn, to protect Brussels against a counter-attack, and for their festive dinner they ate cold bully beef out of the can in slit trenches, shivering against the ice and snow. It was a vicious winter, ending as the thaws came and the fields filled with thick mud you could drown in. Even the caterpillar tracks of tanks struggled. Long lines of armoured vehicles became bogged down, useless. Someone had sketched battle scenes for the souvenir book in a hand made shaky by the dreadful sights of torsos in craters, horses flailing in the mud, smashed tanks and trees black against the sky like old bones. There was a photograph of an ambulance wrecked by shelling, all jagged twisted metal and tyreless wheels sticking out at weird angles, the red cross no protection. The battle for the Reichswald Forest that February was one of the filthiest of the war in every way, fought out between hordes of sodden soldiers who trudged through seas of mud in the half-light, shot blindly in the thickets, or were blown apart by artillery barrages that came without warning. They fought by hand in Stygian forests, 'the ruthless, vast and gloomy woods' as the regimental book called them, quoting Shakespeare.

The description reminded me of something, but what? Then it struck me: the television drama he had been watching the night before we went to see him, the one he said brought back the bad dreams. It wasn't the usual Hollywood warfare but a frightening, visceral re-creation of close combat under artillery fire. In the Reichswald Forest. Was he there? I could not prove it, but if he wasn't – if all he did was march up and down on guard duty somewhere safe – why did the nightmares return?

German prisoners walked across a page of his book in their bulky greatcoats with hands in the air, smiling. 'Happy, alas! Too happy,' said the caption, quoting Virgil. The fusiliers behind the prisoners looked miserable. They were the ones who were still wearing their helmets, and who would have to fight on. Was Grandad among them? He had mentioned guarding prisoners of war. The Royal Welch Fusiliers took 35,000 on their way to Hamburg and another forty thousand when they got there. They travelled nearly two thousand miles, ate six million rations and drank 352,000 gallons of rum on the way, the book said. Nearly ten thousand men were wounded, killed or went missing. There were figures for the number injured by gun shots, mortars, mines or bombs and even those hurt by accidents in camp or petrol burns, but it is impossible to record warfare in statistics without becoming absurd, and the author knew it. 'Perhaps you are interested to know what parts of the body are most vulnerable,' he wrote. The answer, with 1,038 injuries, was: 'Lower extremity (including buttocks).'

'There was a lot of shagging going on when we got to Germany,' Grandad said, seizing a cue to talk about something other than death and fighting. 'There was a house near our camp where the women would take you upstairs. Not me though.' Of course not. There was a complete ban on 'social intercourse' of any kind with German women, punishable by a fine, but the military police ignored it most of the time. When they did crack down the fine was considered worth paying. The ban on fraternization was lifted by the end of the summer, and more than a few men had their 'bit of frat'. At their final destination the fusiliers strung up carnival lights on a building to make the regimental sign, an underscored letter W. The world had turned upside down on their journey from the beaches to Hamburg. Fifteen years later the Beatles would play there.

24

After the darkness, the light. The nights have been blind in London for six years, even at the centre of the city where searchlights and flames could not penetrate the deeper shadows of the blackout. Now, though, so many people have come to celebrate; so many bodies, swaying and cheering, drinking and kissing strangers, or just standing in the drizzly gloom, looking around and wondering what this moment really means, Victory in Europe Day, and how to mark it. They have all known the suffocating dark, the stumbling feet, the posts and pillars coming from nowhere to slam cold in the face, the tiny glowing slits the only visible signs of an approaching truck, the voice of a warden crying 'Put out that light' and the disembodied whispers of lovers huddled under the forgiving blanket of night. And it is over . . . now.

Streetlamp globes and bulbs flicker and flash, bus headlights scatter gold, searchlights throw V-signs in the sky; arrows and eyes and signs glow from shops, theatres and bars; and the end of a huge Craven A burns again for the first time since the last day of peace. Gasps, and tears, and wordless moans of wonder greet this sudden cacophony of light and colour, a blazing riot, a victory salute that says Guinness is Good For You! For Vim And Vigour! Keep Looks, Figure & Sparkle! Diamonds! Now see the bold colours of the star-spangled banner hanging beside the union flag, and the hammer and sickle. 'What else can you do but drink, my friend? Have a little of this, help me get up for a better view. Can you see them climbing on Eros, or the boards where he used to be?' So many voices, people squeezing in. 'Pity the Poor Unemployed' says a badge on a soldier's tunic, but he's smiling now anyway. There are haunted faces, people who wish they were dead like their friends, and boys who do not want to go home, but they do their best not to show it. The grand buildings of London are suddenly floodlit: Admiralty Arch, Buck House, they're milling in the Mall, the cross on top of St Paul's is gleaming, how in the world did it ever survive? And away from the centre, over the river, south past the taverns and warehouses, down to the back streets and bombsites that run along by the docks, out to the war-weary tenements, bonfires crackling in the black. It is still half-dark down here, they don't have the wealth of the West End, neither money nor electricity to burn, but there is wood, from doors and broken window frames, and shattered furniture, left lying where it was, now gathered up in a pyramid in the centre of the street as the focus of a party. The grocer's bunting dug up from the basement, and a few dozen sparklers and rockets that fizz. It is all a bright wonder to a boy of four, who should have been in bed hours ago but is standing in the street, barely noticed, watching the leery faces and the straying hands, and the dancing feet, smiling at the giggles and waiting for his mum to finish jigging so he can ask the only thing he wants to know: 'Will Daddy be home soon?'

The answer is no. Bert is in a gatehouse in Germany, waiting for his watch to finish so he can join the VE party in the camp mess hall. Relief at the victory has quickly yielded to doubts about what happens next. If he is not sent to fight the Japanese, please God, how will he cope with going home? He hardly knows Vi, after all. Seeking some comfort, although it is against the regulations, he turns on the radio. The soft, educated tones of a padre come over the British Forces Network, pretending to read a letter to a soldier whose wife he has met.

'Germany's just a vast transit camp. You won't be here forever, even if it seems like it sometimes.'

No, thinks Bert. That's the problem.

'Some day you are going to try to find your way back not only to the old homestead but to the old happy relationship, and if you haven't kept the lines of communication open, well it's just too bad. You probably won't get there.'

That's easy for you to say, padre, thinks the soldier. You've got time to sit around writing letters, and fine words to go in them. She's probably at home with you anyway.

'No, I'm not trying to frighten you; your wife has seen it already. The amber light is on, and if you aren't careful it will turn to red. She is beginning to think you don't need her and that is the amber light, Bob.'

'It's Bert, actually,' he says to the radio. The Reverend Frederick Levison, whose broadcast will soon be available to troops as a booklet, cannot hear him.

'Not to write is a breach of confidence. You are refusing to share your thoughts. You are saying in effect, "You have your life and I'll have mine; but we won't share them: the partnership will be temporarily dissolved." If that's how you feel, Bob, it isn't only defeatism it's sheer suicide. If it's impossible for a husband and wife to confide any more, then it's goodbye to their marriage . . .'

Give it a rest, mate, thinks Bert. You're supposed to be cheering me up. Don't you know what day it is?

'Have you ever considered that neglecting your letters is more than a minor omission; that it's a sin, and a good-sized one? If this makes you uncomfortable I can't help it, it has to be said. We blame ourselves least, if at all, for the sins of omission. Yet we shall be judged for the things we didn't do as well as for those we did wrong. If he's committed no crime a fellow sometimes thinks he has done well. But sin and crime are somewhat different. And this is a sin against loyalty and love. To fail there, in our personal loyalties, is to fail indeed . . .'

Funny to hear someone talk about sin on the radio. Bert mentioned the word once and was jumped on by a firebrand from the valleys. 'What about the sin of unemployment? What about the scandal of the slums?' If he'd been able to get a word in after that Bert would have told him about the Sally Army and the things it did, but there was no point, really. The sergeant major is coming to the gatehouse. Must be time to change guard.

'The chap who can't be bothered to write becomes the middle-aged husband who behaves like a spoiled child; whose slippers have to be brought to him while he monopolizes the best armchair; who has always to have first read of the paper; who tells his wife to keep the door shut and his children to be quiet. You don't want to become like that, do you? So for heaven's sake, Bob, start now; there may even be time before you go to bed tonight . . .'

'Stand easy, Moreton,' says the sergeant major. 'Kill that bloody radio. I hate to say this, but enjoy yourself.'

VE Day was 8 May 1945. A week later the Minister for Labour and National Service, Ernest Bevin, announced that soldiers, sailors and airmen would begin to be released on 18 June. There had been more than four million men in uniform during the war, and he hoped to have 750,000 of them back in their old clothes by the end of the year. There would be no mass unemployment, promised Bevin, who was driven by the memory of an encounter with soldiers at Portsmouth harbour the previous year, as they were leaving for the invasion of Normandy. 'Ernie,' one shouted, 'when we have done this job for you, are we going back on the dole?'

It was a fair question, given the chaos and misery after the First World War. More than three million servicemen were demobilized during the first five months of peace in 1918. It was chaos. The plan, which was poorly thought out and hurriedly brought in, suggested that men with key jobs such as miners and farmers should be first out – but many of them had been the last in for the same reason, and some had been in uniform only a few months. Richer people with the right contacts found it easy to get themselves listed as a priority, and some just came home on leave and never went back. Men who had served for four years and been sent to the front several times were rightly furious when they found out about the queue jumpers. Soldiers mutinied on the docks at Folkestone and three thousand of them marched on Whitehall with loaded guns demanding to be let go. For a brief while it looked like there might be an armed revolution, as in Russia. The poet Robert Graves, who was hoping for the bourgeoisie to be overthrown, put the failure of the uprising down to British men being 'content to have a roof over their heads, civilian food, beer that was at least better than the French beer, and enough blankets at night'. But they did not forget what had happened, not least because two million of them were still unemployed by 1922. There were hunger marches in London and rent strikes the police stopped with violence. The sons of those First War soldiers, born like Bert into poverty and hunger, did not forget their history. They ducked and dived to get a few bob on a barrow or a van, with no job security at all but a much better chance of a living than their dads, who were getting too old or frail to work even if any could be found. Getting called up was an escape from the constant fear of poverty and hunger, a way of guaranteeing you would be fed, and clothed, and kept fit. They knew none of them would ever become officers (you were fourteen times more likely to do so if you went to a public school) but they trusted Churchill and they beat the Germans a second time. Then, as the Second World War came to an end, they asked if the same mistakes were going to be made all over again.

Bevin promised otherwise. There would be a new system balancing age against service, advice centres to help with resettlement, retraining for those that wanted it, grants for education, and eight weeks' pay on release. The men and women it was supposed to help were highly sceptical, but they had their own secret worries too. 'Civvy Street is at once the conscript's peace-dream and his nightmare' said a report into their attitudes. 'He longs for the comfort and warmth and personal affection of it after the cold, impersonal, regimented life of the forces. He dreads the insecurity of job-scrambling, money worries and personal responsibility.' Fighting was simple: you did as you were told, and either killed someone or died. Going back to normality was a lot more complicated.

'The army's a good life, when you think about it.'

Half a dozen men are sitting around a table in the mess, talking over the sound of a band. 'If you fancy a game of football or something, you go off duty in the afternoon and play. Can't do that at home, there's nobody about.'

Bert pulls up one of the canvas chairs, turns it round and

sits astride the back. His friends are in various states of relaxation, a couple with boots up on the table, one lighting a cigarette for another. It's stuffy in the hall, thick with smoke.

'We've got it all on a plate, see?' says the soldier with the biggest mouth, who worked a barrow before the war. 'Mates, a dance and that, the women if you want them.'

Bert listens. Some of the German girls have been very friendly.

'Most of all we've got no responsibilities.'

That's true. His two boys will be a handful.

'When we get back it will be every man for himself. Not pulling together like now. Just do your job, clock off, go home for your tea, down the pub.'

'I wouldn't mind that, mind.' The speaker had been a tin miner until D-Day.

'Sounds good to me.' Sparky was an electrician.

'Yes, but for how long? We all dream of a beer and the missus, but then what?'

'I'm going to make some money,' says Sparky.

'Good luck, big man,' says the miner. 'If you can get a job. Remember last time.'

'No, I mean serious money. Screw the law.'

'Well, maybe you'd better shut up until you have, eh boy? Then drop us a line.'

That raises a half-hearted laugh, but the subject is serious. They talk about this stuff every week, at the current affairs meeting, politics and all that, what's going to happen after the war. Which is now. It's not hypothetical any more.

'The secret is to get back as quick as possible, get a good job before all those other buggers do,' says the barrow boy.

'Yeah, but who's gonna go first?'

'The married ones, obviously. We've got wives to see.'

'Oh right, that again. But I've got a girl waiting for me. I want to get married.'

'Sod off, kiddo. It wants to be older fellas, we're not hanging about.'

'Take my place if you want,' says the miner. 'I'm thinking of signing on, staying in the army. She doesn't want me back anyway, as far as I can see. Might as well take my chances. Help myself to a bit of frat.'

Bert stands up as the rest give a beery cheer. He's got to get some air.

The world was going to be better after the war. Sir William Beveridge said so. His report into what should happen when the fighting stopped had been a publishing sensation, a runaway bestseller in 1942. The Army Bureau of Current Affairs thought it too bolshie for ordinary, unsophisticated squaddies to discuss in their weekly gatherings, but those meetings were encouraging many soldiers to think about politics for the first time, to express their hopes for the future and believe that there might be a way of bringing them to life. Maybe they didn't have to leave it all up to the ruling classes after all. They got hold of copies of Beveridge anyway, of course. Banning the report was a surefire way of making certain a lot of people read it who would not otherwise have bothered. 'A revolutionary moment in the world's history is time for revolutions, not for patching,' Sir William had written, promising to conquer the five giants of Want, Disease, Ignorance, Squalor and Idleness. In 1945 many of his readers believed the time had come.

His words sounded suspiciously Communist to some generals, but real Commies were talking not about revolution for the moment but nationalization, putting the natural resources of the nation into the hands of the people. 'The debt we owe to the fighting men and women who have written the most glorious pages in our history will only be paid if the victory over Fascism is accompanied by the victory over all the reactionary forces which stand in the way of a new Britain,' said a Communist Party pamphlet about post-war Britain. Labour also advocated nationalization, and the brightest young Conservatives realized they could not stand in its way. Churchill did not get it. Neither could he accept the polls that said the vast majority of people admired him as a wartime leader but did not want him to run their peace. A sour mood had spread through Britain very quickly after VE Day, a feeling of anticlimax. 'I feel no elation,' wrote a member of the Royal Observer Corps. 'No uplifting of spirit, only a sort of dumb, inarticulate thankfulness.' Food was still in very short supply, men were still fighting in the East and people even started complaining that things were not as good as they had been during the war. There wasn't the same community spirit, they said; kindness and manners had disappeared, queues were rowdy, strangers didn't talk to each other. Those complaints seem both astonishing and familiar now, but the truth was, in part, that people were exhausted, it was harder to be patient and forgiving when they had no common cause. They were impatient for improvements, and the general election in July gave them a way of saying so.

Churchill was the clear favourite to win but he misjudged the public mood in a way that would have been inconceivable a few months earlier. The people gathered around their radio sets to hear the great man who had cajoled and inspired them through the darkest days, and what he gave them was not generous and statesmanlike but patronizing. He spoke of 'you, listening to me in your cottages'. He said a Labour government would lose their savings. And, worst of all, he said the socialists would have to introduce a form of secret police. He used the word Gestapo. The most disastrous election broadcast in British history cost him at least a million votes. Churchill was cheered on a tour of the North, but booed and jeered in London. The political histories don't really explain why, not adequately and certainly not as eloquently as the words of a woman who lived down the road from Vi, whose name was Lil Patrick. 'You see, what is difficult for you to understand is the depth of deprivation that we lived in,' she told an oral history project in Southwark. 'The things you read about in Dickens were happening. If we wanted assistance in those days our parents had to go before a board; they were called the Board of Guardians. And if you had anything in your home that was saleable, you had to sell that before you could get any assistance whatsoever. And you got food tickets, and you got tickets to get children's shoes. You didn't get money. This is the way they treated people. We're talking about the dignity of human beings, and this is why we feel so strongly, this is why we all voted Labour.' The Labour Party won by a landslide. The economy was in pieces, the country owed huge amounts abroad and the cities were in ruins, but Labour politicians promised a solution. Women like Lil and Vi, and men like Bert, believed them passionately. It had to be true.

'What's the matter, Mum?'

'Nothing, lovely. Nothing. You go and play.'

She turns away from him, carrying a box under her arm. A parcel that arrived this morning from a woman she does not know who lives in a country she has never been to. An enemy land that has been blown to smithereens and occupied by the army in which her husband serves. Arthur has been trying to get a look in it all day but she won't let him, just keeps putting the box in the cupboard below the sink, and taking it out again. The street is quiet. Out in the front yard he pulls up a corner slab to look at the ants, and can hear the woman from two doors down talking to her neighbour.

'Can you believe it?'

'It's an insult, is what it is. A flamin' insult. She should write on the label and just send it back.'

'Do you think he's got a masher out there?'

'What, Bert? Don't make me laugh.'

'No, that's what they say though. I heard her sister. There was a woman's name on the label, she said. A kraut. Fancy that, mixing with one of them.'

'Been out a long time, ain't he?'

'Yeah, what else could it be? I mean, who'd have dreamed it? A food parcel, to here, from bloody Germany.'

'A great big bloody insult.'

25

Did Bert have a lover in Germany? His brothers and sisters talked about it while he was away, and so did the neighbours. 'We were told he had a girlfriend out there,' my father said. 'I don't know. He lived well in Germany, he admitted that. He was doing better than us. The major effrontery was that these people out there were sending us food parcels. I remember all this because it hurt.' Dad had never challenged his father about it and was not about to do so. That was down to me, apparently, but what right had I to ask such a question? Grandad had been more open with me than with anyone else, it seemed, but I was uneasy about pushing him too far. Not that he seemed to understand or care why I was there so often, drinking his tea and listening to his stories as they were released from captivity. It was exhausting, trying to maintain the narrative in my head and fill in the details, while he meandered and digressed, and climbed in and out of the pulpit. He would be lucid for an hour or so, then gradually start to ramble, and our chat would end in another little sermon about how grateful he was to finish his days as well as this. They were not homilies, he didn't moralize, he believed in live and let live. Forgiveness, he talked about that a lot. So who was I to insist on knowing what it was he had to seek forgiveness for? And yet I had to know. This had gone too far to stop now. I would have to wait for the right moment.

Bert must have had a lot of time to think as he waited to

be released from the army. There were plenty of people wanting to give advice about what to do next, and some of their writings offered strong clues about my grandfather's state of mind at the end of 1945. J. B. Priestley, who had been wounded and gassed in the trenches during the First World War, knew what he was talking about when he said the conscript found himself sharply divided. 'There is a conflict in him, and I suspect it is this conflict that makes him appear less radiantly happy, far more weary and wary, than people expect him to be. One half of him wants to settle up, the other half wants to settle down. Sharing the same billet in his mind are an earnest revolutionary and a tired and cynical Tory. Both of them cry incessantly "Never again!", but one of them means that never again will he allow the world to drift into the vast lunacy of war, whereas the other means that never again will he quit the safe old shelter of home for any communal adventure. One wants to re-organize society and the other wants privacy and a domestic life. The red half cries: "It's your duty now to fight for security and social justice for all"; and the blue half retorts: "You've done enough. Find a job, keep quiet, and try growing tomatoes." One demands real democracy and the end of economic brigandage, while the other asks for a bungalow, a car, and a good wireless set. The reformer shouts at the cynic and the cynic sneers at the reformer. And both are performing inside the mind of a tired man, who is homesick and wants to wear his own clothes, to eat what he fancies, and to do no more parades.'

Priestley had become enormously popular in the months after Dunkirk with a series of postscripts to the news on the radio every night. Graham Greene described him as a leader of the people second only to Churchill in those times who 'gave us what our other leaders have always failed to give us – an ideology'. That was the problem. The Tories complained he was too left wing and Priestley was taken off the air. He received two letters: one from the Ministry of Information saying the BBC had made the decision, and the other from the BBC saying it was the Ministry's fault. In his essay 'Letter to a Returning Soldier', published in 1945, Priestley said the squaddie's inner battle had been won by the cynic, last time around. 'The revolutionary, the one who said there must be no more of this murderous nonsense, lost completely. He never really had a chance. The politicians and most of the Press told him he was a hero and that everything would be all right if he took it easy. His women, who still believed they were living in a nicely settled world that happened to have had a nasty accident, told him to dig the garden or take the baby out and not talk so much. The pubs and sports grounds and race tracks were ready to welcome him. Living was dear, but there seemed to be plenty of decent jobs about at good wages. Now and again he would exchange a few drinks with chaps he had served with and they would grow reminiscent and a trifle sentimental, remembering a comradeship that seemed difficult to fit into this civilian world of social classes and profit-and-loss relationships, with its surface softness and its queer underlying hardness . . .' Meanwhile the world played power politics again. 'Dragon's teeth, of a new and marvellous fertility, were sown freely. And the harvest – well, you know.'

Priestley offered a grim vision of the future. A third world war would leave people living underground, half-starved, making giant rockets; or mass unemployment would provoke bloody uprisings. Unless ordinary people were educated they would fall victims to 'any catchpenny tactics of mass suggestion', civilization would decay and the world swarm with barbarians and robots. Cruelty would overtake construction and violence rage. There was hope for the future after the election result but as 1945 ended the victory parties became distant memories. Jerusalem was not going to be built unless somebody put in the back-breaking work. Priestley urged the returning soldier to fight for change, while admitting from his own experience: 'I know, my dear lad, that all this is just what you don't want to do. You've had it. All right, go off with the girl and enjoy the loneliest possible holiday, among the mountains, on top of the widest moor, with –

The silence that is in the starry sky,
The sleep that is among the lonely hills.

But when you come back, be a real citizen and not a hermit in a bungalow. Remember that even if you are not interested in politics, the fact remains that politics are interested in you, and indeed are busy already shaping your future. Remember that we are in history, and are not merely watching it stream past us, as if we were sitting in the balcony of the Odeon. If we do not control our lives then somebody else, probably a rascal, will do it for us.'

The challenge faced by the returning soldier was immense. Go home, the heart was saying, but it won't be easy. Give up the army and all its hardships, yes, but also the comforting routine, the orders that save you the trouble of thinking, the food and the cash that come without question. Go back to live closely with people you barely know and have hardly seen in six years, and to forget all that has happened to you. Don't bang on about your sufferings, because people there have suffered too, as you well know. They have complained to you in their letters over the years while you, anxious not to worry them, did your best to make the news from the front seem not too depressing. So you didn't tell them about seeing the back of your best friend's head blown off. The censor would not have allowed it anyway. And it is too late to tell anyone now, because this is the time to look to the future. Nobody wants to know about your bad dreams. So go home, sleep on a soft mattress rather than in a slit trench, drink tea from china cups not mess tins, spend your days in the company of children who do not know you rather than your brothers-in-arms who understand what you have been through. Get a job, if you can, and take orders from men who never went near a gun. Or worse, women who no longer know their place. Go back to the woman you married in a hurry, who has changed as completely as you have, and has been just as toughened and scarred by the war. And remember it is your duty to transform society. Throw off those old shackles of class, expectation and poverty, and demand a better life for everyone. Fight for the common good, soldier. If you don't the world will go to hell. The stakes are that high.

Talk about pressure. It's no wonder some of them preferred to grow tomatoes.

I have a book that makes me think of Grandad standing in the line in 1946, waiting for his demob suit. *Call Me Mister! A Guide to Civilian Life for the Newly Demobilised* was published that year and is long out of print. Leaving the army will be like getting into a tub of tepid water, it warns: it won't be an icy shock like joining up was, but neither will it have 'the heart-warming glow of a hot bath'. The farewells will be surprisingly subdued, and very English. 'The whole idea that you are Really Getting Out seems too improbable and dream-like to be true.' The departing soldier will notice that the meals in the NAAFI are better in his last few days in the army – 'you are fed like a fighting cock' – and all the sergeants are smiling, says the book. This is a belated attempt to get the soldier to remember his service warmly, so he will come back again if needed. The only person who will say goodbye as though he is losing an old and valued friend is the commanding officer. 'The point is, of course, that he realizes in a very few months you will be installed as the manager of his bank or his laundry or something of that kind and he'd better be careful.'

That was certainly not true in Bert's case. The CO was anything but kind when he ordered him to stay in the army one extra day for going absent without leave. It was daft, really: the night before demob he stole into the West End to meet Vi at her work, to tell her he was coming out next day. The commanding officer caught him and didn't like it. 'You're still in the army, Moreton,' he said. 'Do another twenty-four hours.'

So here he is in my mind, standing in the demob line a day late, holding Army Book X801 and looking along a row of tables.

'Herbert Moreton?'

'Sir.' The officer at the first table just wants to check his name and address, stamp a page in the book and tear it out.

'You get fifty-six days' paid leave,' says a man from the Ministry of Labour. Stamp and tear. When the leave stops so will his ration allowance, war service increment and married man's credit. Not to mention his free food and lodging, heat and light, of course. He'll be on his own then.

'Health Insurance card,' says the third table. Stamp and tear.

'Release record?' Stamp and tear.

He works down the line, receiving a railway ticket, a

ration card and temporary civilian ID. Stamp and tear, every time. And a fortnight's pay.

'Six pounds, private. Sign here.'

'Yes, sir. Thank you, sir.'

'Keep this page,' says a sergeant major at the last table. 'You'll need it for your suit.'

The clothing store is full. The good thing about having been kept an extra day is that he's one of the first out in the morning, so gets first pick of the sizes. Those who arrive here in late afternoon don't have much choice but to accept trousers that ride two inches short or jackets that fit them like potato sacks. *Call Me Mister!* has something to say about this room: 'The most surprising thing about the whole business is that Officers and Other Ranks get precisely the same suit from the same store at the same time. This is most significant and rather frightening. The sight of all those High Officers, with their medal ribbons, red tabs and all, trying on little cardboard hats in the hattery, prior to going back to their old jobs as bus conductors and costing clerks, is touching enough to melt the stoutest heart.' Except of course it won't be the only suit some of them own. The colonel in the corner will be changing back into his old tweeds as soon as he returns to his family's place in the country. If the clothes fit. 'It will at once be apparent they have all shrunk – so much so that it will be quite impossible to button any of the jackets in such a way as to permit breathing' says the book. But rationing will soon sort that out, as all but the best connected and wealthiest of ex-soldiers will have to do without army portions. 'In three months they will fit perfectly.'

They are eating horsemeat at home, or great big slabs of whale meat that are supposed to taste just like beef. You soak them for a day in vinegar before eating. They actually taste of vinegar. The guide has strong advice on what to expect at the domestic table: 'Lunch consists of Bone Soup, served with Diced Bread; Fried Bread Rissoles coated with Bread Crumbs; and Bread and Butter Pudding. Smile graciously and make complimentary remarks in adoring tones as each course appears. Always praise to the skies everything your wife gives you. It may seem difficult on the second day to praise the congealed remains of yesterday's bread and butter pudding served cold – but praise them just the same.' Wait until she is back in the kitchen with the emergency cookbook 'reading up how to serve bread to resemble Coquilles de Turbot' then throw your pudding out of the window. 'If, on the third day, she serves the same thing up again, deal with her in the same way as the pudding.'

Bert is handed a white shirt with two collars, a checked tie, two pairs of plain blue woollen socks, a pair of black shoes, a pair of cufflinks, a brown pork-pie hat with a band, raincoat, and, of course, the demob suit. Grey pinstripe, better than anything he ever had before the war, but other men will still complain. The trouble is they stand out a mile, the newly returned, tanned and fit in their regulation suits, looking for work. Or sitting at the public bar in huddles of three or four, consoling themselves with talk of the old days. They shave every day with their old army razors and keep their cap badges in their breast pockets. Their faces give them away as much as their identical suits. 'You are a marked man' says the book. 'The Regular Civilian wears shabby, toil-stained clothing; and if you mean to get anywhere at all in civilian life you must, by hook or crook, obtain clothing of this kind as quickly as possible.'

The lad in the alleyway outside the demob centre is wearing a fawn gabardine number. Very nice. Neither shabby nor stained by toil. He has had a profitable war, by the look of him.

'All right, mate. Tenner for your box?'

Bert looks at the square cardboard box containing his new clothes. He's still wearing battledress. Is it a good deal? He can't be sure. How much can you get for ten quid these days? That's one of the things he's going to have to find out.

'Sorry.'

'Suit yourself.'

And that's it. He's out. No fanfare. No bunting. Just drizzle on the flagstones and a chilly wind.

'You have an uneasy sensation that something is missing' says *Call Me Mister!* of those first steps as a civilian. 'There has been no welcoming speech from the Mayor and you have had no instructions as to where to report in the morning. In fact you rather feel that nobody will mind very much if you never report anywhere again.' He could get on a train and go north, where nobody knows him. Or go down to the coast and catch a ferry to the Continent. To Germany? Or a bus over the river, back to Vi. And the boys. 'You are free' says the book I am reading while I think of my grandfather standing out in the street. The burden of freedom is great. 'An old soldier of my acquaintance found this last-mentioned state so oppressive that he began to develop a psychopathic longing for an order. If only someone would command him, in a crisp, parade-ground voice, to do this or that, all would be well.'

26

What did he do next? He couldn't remember, or so he told me. We had worked our way back to the source of the silence. There at the door of the demob centre, on the bus home, as the footsteps fell, was where it started. Who could Bert talk to? The army did not provide counsellors. The official advice was not to discuss your service too much. Nobody would understand, everyone had suffered. The men in his unit had shared the same experiences but they were lost to him, making their ways elsewhere in the world. Probably doing better than this too. Each man felt he was alone, that the disorientation and panic were unique to him. He was the only one in danger of losing his mind. For Bert the isolation was worse, because he was not a drinker. He couldn't go to a pub, fall in with other old soldiers and drown his sorrows. The women and the older men at the Dulwich corps of the Salvation Army would be glad to see him home, but behind every handshake would be a sadness and an unspoken question: 'Why you?' He was the only young bandsman at that corps to have come back from the war. He couldn't say why. If he felt guilty there was nobody to tell, and nobody to reassure him. After the *Lancastria* he already knew that his own family would not believe his stories. They would call him a liar. Best keep it all to himself. So he did. And so did all the other members of this silent generation, going back to their homes around the country. Only their rages and nightmares were eloquent but those were not understood. They suffered in silence. The habit lasted, for some of them, until death.

Or a nosy grandson. So far my sympathies were with Bert. I had listened to his stories, tried to decode them, imagined him in France, on the guns in the Blitz, trudging to Germany, turning for home. He kept his head down, never volunteered for danger but did not run when it came, and he got through it all. I knew I would have been found wanting, would not have survived. But the story was unfinished. There was still no answer to the question he had been asked at the beginning of all this: 'Where were you when all the other dads came home?' If he could not tell me, then I had to go back to his son, my father, and hear his version. No more coyness. If there was an accusation it had to be made in full. Dad was ready.

We met at a pub called the Three Rabbits, in the countryside near his home, and sat in the beer garden with two pints of bitter on the table between our two benches. The mumble of the motorway drifted to us across a field. The tape recorder was by his pint glass. I wanted him to know it was there again, an indicator that this was serious. He was in a good mood, introducing himself to the microphone as though it were a therapist. 'My name is Arthur Moreton. I am sixty-two years old. I was born in Musbury in Devon. Near to Beer, which I have been near to ever since. I am eighteen and a half stone. Overweight. Underpaid. Sitting in Essex one hundred yards from the M25, looking at a clear blue sky.'

'And what is your problem?'

'My problem is I've got a son who's a prat.'

'Charming.'

Then, without missing a beat, he changed the mood.

'One of the things I hoped to get out of this exercise of ours was coming to terms with things I should have talked about before.'

'Have you?'

'Not exactly. It has brought some things up, and I've been dreaming about them. But I can't alter history. I can only face what happened and try to deal with it.'

Telling me about his visit to the guns in Richmond Park in 1944 had stirred memories of the contrast between the way his father lived in the army and what was going on at home. 'He was there in his gear, turned out smart, eating well, and we'd be ponced up a bit to go and see him but then we went back to the state we lived in.'

Then came the food parcel from a woman in Germany. Who was she, and how could anyone in that bomb-flattened, devastated place get things they did not have under rationing in England? What was Bert doing with her out there anyway? He finally came back to London in the spring of 1946, a year later than young Arthur thought he should have done. But it was not a happy homecoming.

'He looked around and saw the hovel we lived in and he didn't stay.'

Now we were getting to the point. As far as he could remember there was a blazing row and his father left again on the same day. Rather than remain with his family, Bert walked out and arranged lodgings.

'That is the final effrontery: he's gone and lived on the other side of the hill with me aunt, who's a flighty little nineteen-year-old whose husband is away in the navy.'

'Was there anything in that?'

'I don't think so. They had a nice big house. It would have been just like him to enjoy the roof over her head but not the woman.'

The Salvation Army was one of the few organizations offering help to ex-servicemen at that time, and it gave Bert a job as a lift man at headquarters in Denmark Hill, opening doors and pulling levers for the likes of Frederick Coutts. Then he went to work for R. Whites in Albany Road, by which time Vi and the boys had been thrown out of their basement flat and moved in opposite the church in Wells Way.

'We would see our dad cycle past our house on the way to work and back. You think, "Hang on, what's happening here?" I wasn't thick, my mum was a clever and astute lady who taught me to read the papers by the time I was five. I was working it out: "Dad isn't here. Why isn't he here?" He would go past our house, where we were living in shit, and cycle to hers so he could be in a good environment. How would you feel?'

It was not supposed to be that way. The war was over, each homecoming was meant to be a happy ending and a new beginning. All around them people were sharing tender moments, like a woman whose story I read at the Imperial War Museum. She stayed up late to welcome her husband back from the Far East but the doorbell never rang. Exhausted and disappointed, she fell asleep in her chair – but woke at six in the morning to feel his arms wrapped around her and hear his voice whispering into her ear: 'Darling, I'm home with you at last.'

Forget your romantic notions, my father said. Forget about returning heroes. 'They were better off in uniform and they knew it. You never hear a soldier say he didn't enjoy his army life. They bonded together as comrades and those were the happiest times of their lives. This business about hand-to-hand combat? More people died in training than in the whole of the war. More people died on the Atlantic convoys delivering cigarettes and things we didn't really need from abroad. My mum had seen more people die than Dad. We lived on the hill, we could see what was happening all across London. I had seen more people die than him. A million men had been demobbed by the time he got out – can you imagine a million immigrants suddenly rushing through the Channel tunnel? They had no idea what life had been like in England because they had been overseas. Put yourself in Dad's shoes: you've had six years of being kept fit, fed and educated, and only a relatively small amount of that time has been spent on doing any actual fighting. It has all been regimented: you obey to survive, right? Then suddenly your country says, "Piss off, sunshine." You come back to the brave new world and the first thing you see is there are holes where houses used to be. There's no work. There are touts on the street, there are tallymen, there are people living in filth. Your home is a cesspit. There's not enough food, but you have to pay for what you can get and you've got to provide for others instead of it all being done for you. The spivs, profiteers and money-lenders have won. It was like being a virgin in a whorehouse. You think, "Jesus, what have I come home to?" Somebody who has been just surviving through the war finds he hasn't got any skills – he was loading bloody guns – and no social skills either, but he's got three kids, nowhere to live, a wife who's a nutter and the debts she has run up. Can you imagine, son? There were a million men like that on the streets with long faces going, "Fucking hell, what am I doing here?"'

Good question. What was Bert doing there, as he cycled past his sons every working day, morning and evening? The case for the prosecution, as my father put it, was that he had stayed in Germany longer than he should have done, and then ignored his own wife and family rather than face up to their problems. He could and should have done something about the state they were in but chose not to. 'Where were you?' did not just mean why were you so long abroad, but why were you absent from our lives when you did return to the country? Bert did finally start sleeping under the same roof as his family in 1948, but that did not improve things much, according to his son. 'He decided he couldn't do a runner after all, but he was always going to take the easy way out: go to work, go swimming, go to play music. All his life happened outside the house, as opposed to being indoors and seeing the shit heap we lived in. This is where my bitterness grew up. He knew what was going on in the house, but he didn't want to know.' Vi kept him away from the kitchen and the small room next to it where the boys slept. He didn't need much persuading, despite (or because of) the stench. The kids had no such choice. 'Our home was the biggest pigsty the world had ever seen. Apart from being crowded it was always in a despicable state, no matter where we lived, because of my mother's problems. So my father would always be somewhere else. The contrast is the important thing: Dad was always in a white vest, always well scrubbed and fit, off with the Sally Army or to camp with the Scouts; but there was his family, living in parts of the house Mum wouldn't let him go. He knew the state they were in.'

Bert had always been a sharp dresser, well turned out whatever his job or lack of money, in the best tradition of the rag and bone men he had once worked among with their gleaming white scarves and carts full of junk, and he was still like that after the war, even if he did have to turn a blind eye to Vi pawning his best shirts while he was at work. The army had made him a fitness fanatic who hated to be indoors. Young Arthur was understandably keen to follow his father whenever he went out. 'He would try and take you with him, as long as that fitted in with what he was doing, but he had no interest in you as a person. And no awareness of what you were going through. He was wrapped up in his own world. It kept him sane, to be fair.'

That was the way he had been brought up, I said: as the ninth child in a crowded house with an absent father. It would have been hard for anyone to give personal attention to so many children.

'There were only two of us when he came home. You can give personal attention to two kids.'

'Don't you have any sympathy for him at all?'

'Yes, I do. I can imagine coming back from the army to a place where the rules have been thrown out of the window and I have to take on responsibilities I have avoided in the past. Did you know he was made up to bombardier but deliberately came back down in rank because he didn't want the responsibility?'

Grandad had not told me that.

'You've heard him talk about how he kept his head down and never volunteered for anything? That's my dad. He knew what my mum was and he wouldn't face up to it. He would clear up her mess afterwards, so if the bailiffs came round he would deal with that. He would react then. But for the rest of the time, over and over again, when we kids saw what was happening he was away. That wasn't good enough. There is no excuse. He could have done something about all of these things, but his attitude was the same: keep out of it. I could never, ever forgive him for that.'

Then he signed up as a postman. Joining the General Post

Office was an achievement for Bert, because it involved taking exams, giving references and waiting for months while your credentials were checked. The job meant he left home very early in the morning but was back by lunchtime. Most days he would go swimming at an open-air pool or sit in the park and read his Bible all afternoon, then spend his evenings and weekends with the Salvation Army.

'The amount of time he had to be back in that house was infinitesimal. It was the same attitude as he had in the army and he has now: keep a low profile and get on with your life. He didn't see the damage that was being done.'

'What damage?'

'The damage to the future development and mental stability of his children and his wife. That wasn't his priority. His priority was to survive in a manner that made him feel comfortable.'

'What do you think he should have done?'

'He should have been a man. He should have said, "OK, let's face up to what is happening here and sort it out. We've got kids to think about." But no. We thought our family was better off because we didn't drink and we went to the Salvation Army, but that was a façade. He was the same as the dad who went to the pub every night to escape. We suffered because of his folly and he still hasn't come to terms with that.'

I listened to my father rage and I thought again of Bert standing outside the demob centre, considering his options. He had none, really. He had his orders. If he was one of those men who felt lost without someone telling him what to do, he had only to speak to the captain at his Salvation Army corps, who would remind him that marriage was a contract he had entered into before God. He knew that in his bones already, and he really did love his Vi. Perhaps the mystery of his absence was easily solved, if not easily understood by his children: he was trying to work out how he could bring himself to live with her again. I once met a woman who was the illegitimate daughter of a married housewife from Birmingham and a black GI from Mississippi, conceived during the war. The two lost touch, and their girl spent forty years of her life wondering what had become of her father, fantasizing that he was a rich man or a movie star. He was a hero, she was certain of that. She didn't know he was also dreaming of her, and that he even returned to England to drive slowly through the streets of her old neighbourhood, hoping to recognize something in the face of one of the little girls playing out. She finally managed to trace her father, by a combination of persistence and remarkable luck, but when they met it was a disaster. This was not the man she had dreamed of. He was not a hero. He was a huge letdown. Both of them had to overcome disappointment in each other. They managed it though, and slowly developed a mutual respect and love. They are not the reason for telling the story now, however: the husband is. He was in Burma fighting the Japanese when his wife gave birth to another man's child. When he came back to England and saw the black baby in his house he could not handle it. But he didn't do anything extreme. He moved out for a while, to his sister's house, until he had thought it all through. Then he came home and suggested they adopt the girl. She called him Daddy for the rest of his life.

Bert did not have to bring up a stranger's baby but his return was not easy. Other soldiers used their army pay to buy a market stall or start a business, but he settled the many debts Vi had accumulated during the war. His commitment to her meant he was hamstrung before he started civilian life. No wonder he struggled to cope. My dad did not think that was much of an excuse, and perhaps he was right, but I could not dismiss Bert's war as easily as his son had. I knew much more about it than he did.

'Did your dad ever tell you about what happened to him during the war?'

'No, not really.'

'Did you ask?'

'A number of times, but after a while what is the point?'

27

We go into the park as children and come out haunted by the wisdom of old age.

Ken Worple, *Here Comes the Sun*

'Look,' said Dad, rolling over to whisper. We were lying on our stomachs, beach towels our only protection from the heat in the sun-cooked concrete. Our skins touched.

'Look at that kid.'

It was the last hot day of the summer and the schools had gone back, so that the open-air swimming pool in Brockwell Park was almost empty. A pensioner in a bright pink rubber cap worked her patient way across the pool, which must have seemed like an ocean, a flat, shimmering ocean in perfect blue, to a baby whose father was bobbing her in and out of the icy cold at the shallow end. The sun setting in the trees formed a dappled halo behind the head of a skinny, mop-topped boy as he tugged off the grey flannel trousers he should have been wearing to school.

'It's me,' said Dad so quietly I didn't realize what he had said at first.

Wet feet slapped on the poolside and a blur of puppy fat ran past, leapt into the air and bombed the water with satisfying force.

'That could be my kid brother.'

The baby was out of the pool and wrapped up warm in

an all-terrain pram when her crop-headed father took a call on his mobile.

'Amazing,' said Dad. 'It's still being used for the same purpose.'

The Brockwell Park lido was built in 1937, one of many pools opened in the cause of making London life healthier and more bearable by enabling ordinary working people to enjoy sunlight, fresh air, open space and clean water. Few of these beautiful buildings and shimmering pools survived the municipal madness of the eighties when they were torn down, filled in and replaced with humid, claustrophobic, glasshouse leisure centres. This lido was still being kept open for the people by a cooperative, however. 'Yeah, come any time, really,' one of its members had said on the telephone. 'It's a nice day here.' Flags of lilac and gold flew above the main entrance, which was locked. We found a side door, eventually, and passed through a dark, damp corridor into an enchanted space full of dazzling, dancing light. Leaves on the trees blended with ivy on the low, bark-brown buildings so that we seemed to have stepped into a forest clearing whose living sides protected us from the wind and trapped the sun. The courtyard was curiously intimate; but the sky opened up as the swimmer stepped carefully, reluctantly, into the breathtakingly cold pool, and the reflection of the wide, cloudless canopy overhead in the water all around gave the sensation of floating in a constantly shifting airy haze of sunshine, glitter and blue.

The diving board had been taken down and the fountain that once bubbled in the corner, aerating the water, was gone; but the same paving slabs were underfoot, blackened by the years, and as my father looked around him he saw stray boys, a pensioner, a man and a baby using the place just as his family had done every day, passing the hours at an oasis in which belief was easily suspended and it was the rest of life that seemed unreal. The lido was where he grew up, where his hormones raged and the best days of his early teenage summers were spent.

'This is where you sat to get a tanned body because the sun was always on it,' he said. 'All those bronzed bodies: the scooter gang in that corner, the motorcycle gang in the other, and us in the middle putting coconut cream on our skin.' Those were the days when the sun was a symbol of health, cutting through the smoky gloom of the city to heal war-scarred skin or give pale, bony youths the lustre of gods. Dad would swim until the skin on his back blistered, and his father would lie on the steps with his eyes closed, blocking out the sounds and cares, sizzling; a habit he never lost even in later life when sunlight was declared a danger. 'What we were doing was burning, really.'

Bert swam almost every day, from April to October. Whatever the weather, even on days when goose fat would have been more useful than coconut cream. It could be pouring down with rain and blowing a gale but Bert would be there, doing the breaststroke, with one of his boys shivering in a towel by the pool side. Vi usually met them at lunchtime before slipping away, saying 'I've got things to do'. She worked several jobs for a while without telling her husband: there was the picture house and the tea room, and sometimes she left the boys alone in the flat in the early morning, just after Bert had gone off, and caught a bus into the city to clean offices. If he knew about this he never said. The boys had to fend for themselves until it was time to walk to the park.

'The best thing he ever done for us was to make sure we went swimming every day with him,' said my father as we lay beside the same pool. 'We stayed relatively healthy that way. The pools were important places for people like him. There were lots of men who had enjoyed a healthy lifestyle during the war but it didn't match the way their families were living afterwards so they got out of the house and came here.' Suits and shoes were left behind a counter with one of the dozens of people who worked at the lido then: the locker attendants, the mop-swingers, the women who served tea and sandwiches in the Beach Hut cubicle, and the lifeguards, a tribe of muscular Brylcreemed boys who swaggered among the muscle men and dolly birds enjoying the cult of the body in a way their ration-fed parents could never have done. 'When Mum was here she always made a point of going around talking to everyone.' For those like Vi and Arthur who were too old or young to watch their reflection in the water or worry about joining a gang, the joy of the lido was that everyone went semi-naked, however fine or moth-eaten they had been at the gate: there were no ragged clothes to shame, no bedsits to compare with parlours, no separate hours for men and women; just fun, flirtation and the gloriously free nourishment of sunshine.

The lifeguards still swaggered as they walked by the water, watching from behind sunglasses, but one was from Australia and the other South Africa, and they had no other staff to help them take the money or keep the pool clean. The locker rooms had been abandoned to the dark and dirt, crowded with old trestle tables, shades, boxes and other jumbles of swimming-pool junk. Rays filtering through the bars on frosted windows formed a golden grid in the steam as it billowed from the shower room. The truants flicked towels at each other, wet bodies squelching against the Mediterranean-blue plaster. Chunks of it fell at their feet.

'Can you imagine,' said Dad, 'a guy who is so out of touch he doesn't realize his wife is having a baby?'

'Go on,' I said. 'You're kidding.'

'Nope. He goes off to work in the morning, she drops the baby at lunchtime. I forget how old I was, running down the road to tell him he is now a father again. He had no idea. Genuinely no idea.'

'How could that be?'

'Me mum was getting on a bit by then; you didn't have babies at her age. She was a big lady, too. She was at home, she didn't feel too good, and out came the baby. Imagine the shock it was to us, particularly to me as the oldest? And it was a girl. Everyone had given up on a girl coming along. We called a neighbour, and she said: "You'd better tell your dad." I knew he would be walking down Albany Road from work at one o'clock, so I went to meet him. I don't remember much, just him saying: "What, your mum?" "Yes, Dad, Mum!" He said, "Oh. OK." He didn't run, didn't go any faster. We just walked home, and he said: "Hello, Mother, what's going on?"'

'What did you think of that?'

'I thought, "Hang on a minute, what is this?"'

He was dressed now, pacing the steamy room, waiting for me to tie my laces.

'What would you have done, in his shoes?' I asked him.

'I would probably have divorced Mum.'

'He didn't feel like he had that option.'

'No. I would have had a go at her. I wouldn't have kept shagging her and bringing kids into the world, that's for certain.'

We walked away from the lido, over the sloping fields of the park to the big Georgian house that stood alone at the top of the hill. They used to walk up there as a family, the children running on ahead, then waiting, breathless. I asked if he thought his dad expected his mum to change, to get better. 'Obviously. He could put up with most of it, but not the money problems we had, all through our lives. Even later when I was growing up and going to work. If I earned something it got nicked. If I bought something it got nicked. Anything. I went out and bought myself a pair of hand-made Italian winklepickers, green suede. I had them made. They were the cat's whiskers, cost me about £22, which was a lot of money. I had them for one day, then they disappeared. I knew what she'd done. I'd rant and I'd rave and I'd call her all the names under the sun but I couldn't do a thing about it. I called her the most disgusting names, again and again. Then she'd go to the other extreme, she'd buy something on her book and she'd say, "This is yours. I got this for you." She'd give me the most magnificent double-breasted bum-freezer jacket. I would wear it to go out with all my mates on a Saturday night and on Monday morning it would be back in the pawnshop. I'd never see it again.'

Vi had friends that Bert never met. 'They congregated together at New Cross, Brixton, Brockley. They would try to work a flanker: Mum would buy some sheets off this tallyman, give them to a friend to sell on, then pay the man off with some of the money. All the families would be doing the same but it backfired on them. There are a lot of vicious bastards who will capitalize on that kind of stupidity.'

At the same time she was unfailingly generous and kind-hearted. 'We always had an open house. Any Tom, Dick and Harry. They would come in their hundreds. We didn't have half a penny to put together but they would both give money to these people and feed them. Whatever little spare money they did have was spent on other people, not their kids.'

'And she would never tell a lie?'

'Never. She'd put tears in her eyes. She had big eyes. They would all swallow it: the tallyman would swallow it, the magistrate would swallow it, the judge would swallow it. Not us though. She wouldn't say, "I've taken your shoes to the pawnshop" or "I've sold them". No, she would say, "They're not here." I'd say, "Come on, Mum, you're a nutter, you know where they are. Tell me." And she would say, "You can think what you like." Her attitude was just soft like blancmange. Blurgh! None of this can be blamed on anything except my mother's mental instability. I can understand that now, but how can you explain it to a kid? She was disowned by her own family. They warned him not to marry her, but he knew what he was doing, so there you go.'

When Arthur was still a child, long before he learned how to confront his mother, he would sometimes drift off on his own down to the canal, or on a bus ride to the docks, and wander for a couple of hours, reading the names of faraway places on the sides of barges and boats. The Thames was still busy in those days and it was easy to think of escaping on the tide, but as we stood on the hill in Brockwell Park and tried to trace the route of the river through the distant cityscape, it seemed more like a gutter or a drain, or a fat sluggish thing, rolling behind the houses, from which Londoners habitually averted their eyes. They might have a drink by the river on a hot day, but would never go down to the water's edge, where the solitary treasure hunter trudged through sludge and bodies were found: the gangsters, the suicidal and the victims of voodoo. Swimming was out of the question. The stinking river was filthy, poisonous, and the current would drag a body down to bump along the bottom, then resurface, months later, bobbing like a waterlogged balloon off Canvey Island. How strange, then, to be told by my father that the Thames had been his beach, his Benidorm. On the hottest of days before he knew about the lido, when his family was getting on his nerves, the eight-year-old boy would make his own secret way to Tower Bridge and walk across to the northern bank of the river. There under the high wall, on a narrow ledge of shoreline just by Traitors' Gate, men and women would be dozing in deckchairs with handkerchiefs on their heads, their trousers rolled up or skirts hitched and sand drying on their ankles, as children splashed in the water. It looked like Blackpool at the height of summer, he said, but with ships unloading into warehouses across the way. Fifteen hundred tons of sand had been brought from Essex to make the beach, which was opened in 1934 by the Lord-Lieutenant of the Tower. Half a million people went there in the five years before the war, East Enders from north and south of the river who wanted to swim and paddle and build sandcastles in the five hours a day the beach was exposed, or to hire a boat for thruppence and row under the bridge and back. Sometimes the strong undercurrent swept a pair of legs away and a child was drowned, but those were hardier times and nobody seemed unduly concerned. The number of survivors infected by contact with the rubbish and chemicals and sewage in the water went unrecorded. I grimaced at the thought, and Dad laughed.

'We didn't really worry about the filth I suppose, but you did have to be careful of the tides. Still, it was great fun, our first chance to see what it was like at the seaside.' King George V declared that the children of London should have 'free access forever' but the gates were locked in 1971. By then even the lidos were considered too risky, too hard to keep clean, too unmanageable, and were beginning to be closed down.

When he was not down on the beach young Arthur was up on the cobbled paths around the Tower, killing the time before his mum got out of the Lyons tea shop by offering to act as a guide for visiting American soldiers. 'They knew about Tower Bridge but I showed them little churches where you could get into the crypt. They loved all that.' At eleven he was working in a café, and selling the wooden blocks dug up as tramlines were replaced with tarmac. The blocks were covered in tar that had soaked right into the grain over the years, and they burned beautifully at a time when coal was in short supply and expensive. They cost sixpence a bag from the council but Arthur and his mates would chop the contents up and divide them into smaller bags which they sold door-to-door for a profit of ten shillings.

He could also be found on the steps of the Tower cinema in Rye Hill three or four nights a week, with a knitting needle in his pocket. 'Take me in, mister?' You needed to be with an adult to see *The Lavender Hill Mob*, but getting in was a risky business. 'The biggest danger was from men who had returned from the war. They had been together, in a man-to-man environment, and some were not capable of having a relationship with a woman so they turned to young children. As a fly little boy you learned how to manipulate without getting touched. Get the money and run. Or a guy would try something on and you'd stab him with your needle.'

'Taking a needle is something you only learn by experience,' I said. 'How did you find that out?'

'You find out by people offering you money. A lot of money.' He shook his head. 'Let's leave it at that.'

The biggest thrill of 1951, however, was the Festival of Britain, which opened on the South Bank in May. The posters promised 'fun, fantasy and colour' and the minister behind it, Herbert Morrison, said the event was all about 'the people giving themselves a pat on the back'. It was not entirely clear what they were supposed to be congratulating themselves for. Rationing was still in force, and the meat ration was the lowest it had ever been, so the spivs were making bundles of money on the black market, which meant they were the only ones who could afford to heat their houses during the fuel shortage. The Moretons were not the only ones who had to jam a whole family into a couple of rooms. The alternative was overcrowding, or living in the semi-derelict huts of the old army bases that had been occupied by squatter families. Ernie Bevin had promised five million new homes for the returning heroes but he died in April having fallen a very long way short of that. The people who had moved into prefabricated houses on the bombsite behind Wells Way would have to put up with them for a lot longer than anticipated. Aneurin Bevan, father of the National Health Service, stormed out of government when his own chancellor imposed charges for false teeth and spectacles. The Labour government that had promised so much and raised so many hopes now seemed toothless, and the widening divisions in it left the leadership in a blind panic as it hung on to power with a majority of just five seats. The second election in a year would be timed to take advantage of the optimism that was supposed to flood Britain as a result of the festival, which had been billed as 'A Tonic For The Nation', but Labour was still heading for defeat. Churchill would return as Prime Minister in the autumn but he was old and tired and the country felt the same. One of the main attractions of the Festival of Britain was the Skylon, a spot-lit aluminium cigar with no visible means of support, which some wit said was 'just like Britain'. Children were amazed by it, however. 'The Skylon was just a piece of metal balancing on wire,' said Dad, 'but to me it was, "Wow! Why? How?"' Icons of the modern age such as the *Golden Arrow* train and the car in which John Cobb had set the land speed record were displayed under the Dome of Discovery. 'Everything that had been discovered in the last one hundred years, together in one place. There was a thing about the polar ice caps and you put your hand in through a hole to feel incredible coldness. Now it sounds funny but then it was amazing.' The boy who would come to love reading about Dan Dare, Pilot of the Future, found himself riding an escalator to look at the night sky in a planetarium, and peering through a giant telescope into space. In the Television Pavilion he put on peculiar specs and watched images move in three dimensions, while his ears were dazzled by 'Stereophonic Sound'. This was a way out of his grey, austere world into a bright, shiny, glamorous future of whizzing rockets, bleeping radar screens and the miracle of atomic energy. Then there were the acrobats and marching bands, and an enormous funfair upriver where the allotments had been in Battersea Park. 'The festival was right on my doorstep. What they did was just unbelievable. I was lucky, I had aunts and uncles who were interested.'

'Did your dad not want to go?'

'He never went there with me. Nor did Mum. But I found a way to bunk in, and I did that as much as possible. There was so much in there and it made you want to learn more. I realized there was a wider world and I wanted to be out in it.'

28

Arthur has gone missing. It is almost midnight on 6 September 1952 and he is not at home. Nobody knows where he is. They haven't seen him since early this morning and they are worried. He is a very independent boy of eleven and he doesn't think his parents give a toss where he goes, or what happens to him. He doesn't know they are knocking on the doors of friends and neighbours, asking if anybody has got Arthur with them, and appealing for help at the police station. Neither does he know, although he would guess if he stopped to think about it, that the news from the Farnborough Air Show has been heard on wirelesses all over the country. 'A prototype jet aircraft, the De Havilland 110, disintegrated in the air and items of debris fell into the large crowd of people who were watching the display. Twenty-six people are believed to have died, including the pilot and his observer. Another sixty-five are being treated in hospital.' Bert and Vi do not think their son can possibly have gone all the way down there to Hampshire, but you never know with Arthur. One of his brothers did hear him say something about an air show. Their fears are well-founded: the child did save up his own money and buy a seat on a coach this morning from Victoria to Farnborough, where he was among 150,000 spectators. He got there late, having failed to realize how far it was from London, and was standing on top of a hill overlooking the crowd when there was a loud boom. The silver twin-tailed jet had broken the sound barrier just for the show of it. The noise like a clap of thunder sent a thrill through the crowd then the plane appeared, coming fast towards the hill, so low that Arthur was almost looking straight at it. In a moment the metal at the leading edge of a wing peeled away, wrenching the plane into a sudden lurch upwards, and the two heavy Rolls-Royce engines were torn off, hurtling down towards the earth at great speed. One of them hammered into the stand halfway up the hill where the richer people had gone for a better view. There was no way to avoid the molten missile as it exploded into the wooden structure and the bodies of those who were sitting there. Arthur watched the impact and saw bits of the shattered fuselage falling twisted on the runway, and heard the shrieks of frightened people, but it was all too quick to take in. There was smoke, and voices asking 'What happened?', but the next plane, a Hunter, was already swooping down on the airfield as the emergency services cleared up the mess. The show went on. Arthur couldn't move at first, the bodies were packed so close together, but as the masses recoiled the small boy was able to push past less mobile bodies, duck into tight spaces, squeeze through gaps. He rode the coach back to London replaying all he had seen and heard, over and again, as voices around him worried away in quiet tones. Then he walked, and walked, from Victoria to Camberwell; and now he is in a café on the Albany Road cramming his face with crackling, the greasy scraps of chip and batter they scoop from the bottom of the fryer and sell to kids who can't afford anything else. The door rattles in its frame and his dad strides in with a policeman behind him.

'They said you were here. Where on earth have you been?'

*

I can hear his voice in my head, telling me off. 'If you're going to steal my memories get them right. They didn't come to find me at all. I just had something to eat and walked home, because I didn't think they would be concerned. They were, of course. I don't want to tell you any more about that. It's real to me. The memories are traumatic.'

We had reached the big house on the hill in Brockwell Park, where sausage, egg, chips and beans were available for three quid, an offer neither of us could refuse. The wood panelling had been painted pale blue and white fairly recently and there was a modern steel counter, but otherwise the refreshment rooms were much as they been when Vi walked up the hill with baby Christopher in his pram, and Arthur and Les beside her. 'I can still see my mum here with us now.'

London was laid out along the horizon, from Battersea power station on the left to the London Eye on the South Bank, the NatWest Tower in the City and the light at the top of Canary Wharf blinking at us away to the right.

'This place is what made me who I am,' said Dad. 'It made me realize there was a world beyond the one we lived in, gave me the dreams to get away.' A helicopter crossed our line of vision, the sound of its rotors trailing in the wind and mingling with the lazy clatter of a train hidden in the trees at the bottom of the hill. The view had given the boy a new perspective. 'We are only a short distance from the centre of London but the changes in lifestyle between here and there are unbelievable. The people who lived where we did were the worker bees for the ones who lived further out in houses like the ones you can see over there on the edge of the park. That is still true. It wasn't any different living in an inner city then than it is now. If I went up to

Whitechapel or somewhere now I would find people like us living in exactly the same way as we did then. Their skins might be a different colour but they would have proportionately the same amount of money: not a lot. They would think twice about spending it on anything other than food. That's how it was then, and how it is now.'

The park was, for him, much as the idealists and planners had intended: a place where the city met the country, the sky met the earth, and the rich met the poor, sometimes without prejudice. A place of escape from cramped, noisy and decaying flats; a spacious green garden in which it was easier to think.

'This place is like the centre of a vortex, a bit of calm in the middle of everything. That's poetic, isn't it?'

'Yeah. I'm filling up.'

'I'm talking about my life here, have some respect. You could sit up here in the peace and quiet, look at everything around you and learn from it. You say I'm obsessed with aeroplanes and you might be right, but the thing about aeroplanes was that they could take me away from the environment in which I lived and played.'

'I always thought your obsession was all about the war. Spitfires, and Hurricanes. Trying to understand what happened.'

'No. It was about flight. It was about freedom. I hadn't realized that until now.'

There were other kinds of adventures to be had in Brockwell Park as he grew older. Wandering off from the lido or the tea rooms he met other boys and girls who were hanging about the place, and they came from posh homes. Well, posher than his anyway. They went to grammar schools, and public schools some of them, and lived in the big houses around the edge of the park. They didn't seem to mind him hanging around, and he was a fast learner. In time the park itself became more important to him than the lido, he said.

'This is where I discovered nookie.'

That word made me laugh.

'We were introduced, actually. I was forced.'

This, I supposed, was the Angela he had mentioned in passing.

'Yeah. Angela . . . Rosemary. Susan. Elaine. I dunno. I can't remember. It wasn't nookie really, of course. Grunt and fumble, that's all. Middle-class girls, you know? Grunt and fumble.'

I really did not want to go there, mentally. I could see him walking up the hill in his black jeans, tartan lumberjack shirt and fluorescent socks, with his hair greased back, looking like he wished he had just got off a motorbike, but I didn't want to think about my dad over in the bushes with some girl whose parents were sitting in one of the big gardens down below drinking gin and tonic and wondering where their little angel had got to. There were tea dances on the hill, in the open air on a parade square, and the teenagers would stand around the edges, taking furtive drags on cigarettes they hid behind curled fingers, watching elderly feet glide as though on rails.

'We watched the old people –'

He stopped, and smiled. 'They were as old as I am now. We watched them dancing and we took the piss. So someone said, "Why don't you have your own dances?"'

They did. The new sound of skiffle was easy to re-create: you just needed a guitar to strum, a tea chest bass and somebody who could warble out 'Don't You Rock Me Daddy-O' in a rough approximation of an American accent. It was not sophisticated, but it was also nothing to do with big bands, or crooners, or any of the things the old squares listened to. Arthur couldn't hold a note but he knew plenty of lads who had been raised around the pub piano, and they took to skiffle easily. So the hops on the hill at Brockwell Park became a regular thing. Arthur was growing up fast. He had given up on school. The next step was to get a job.

It is too easy to massage another person's life into episodes and epiphanies, particularly when they are only sharing fragments of it: the bits they remember, or want to tell. There is one story, however, that illustrates how far removed his experience of the wider world was becoming from that of his parents. What would Bert have made of it, if he had known?

The year is 1956. Arthur is not long into his first proper job as a shop boy with Dunn's, the hatters in the Strand. This big break has been arranged by his maternal grandfather, who manages another of the company's stores. Arthur is done up like a kipper in his first ever suit, with a hat and a chin still sore from shaving every morning. You have to be smart to work for Dunn's, which is hard when you have only one set of good clothes and go back to live in squalor every night. On the bus to work of a morning the fifteen-year-old struggles to forget his home life and become a salesman presentable enough to serve the wealthy, powerful and famous, because the shop is next to the Savoy Hotel. He is already confused and exhausted by the stress of living two lives when the boss asks him to run an errand that will expand the boy's horizons to breaking point.

'Take this parcel into the Savoy, Arthur,' he says, 'and deliver it to the suite occupied by the gentleman who goes by the name of Liberace.'

Liberace? He's big news, Daddio. There were crowds in Southampton when he arrived on the *Queen Mary* last week. Arthur saw them on a newsreel at the pictures. The announcer called him 'the well-known American leader of fashion', adding 'by the way, Liberace also plays the piano'. He certainly does, with flair and panache and a great big candelabra. Plays anything from Rachmaninov to Tin Pan Alley, and makes whatever comes out of that gleaming grand sound like a multi-tiered wedding cake dusted with icing sugar. Good-looking bloke, too. 'No male attraction has devastated the opposing sex in these terms since Rudolph Valentino,' said *Variety* magazine, reporting that he received 27,000 Valentine cards. Not everybody is convinced. 'There must be something wrong with us that our teenagers longing for sex and our middle-aged matrons fed up with sex alike should fall for such a sugary mountain of jingling claptrap wrapped up in such a preposterous clown,' says Cassandra in the *Daily Mirror*. 'He is the summit of sex – the pinnacle of masculine, feminine and neuter. Everything that he, she and it can ever want.' Liberace takes exception to Cassandra calling him 'the biggest sentimental vomit of all time' and 'this deadly, winking, sniggering, snuggling, chromium-plated, scent-impregnated, luminous, quivering, giggling, fruit-flavoured, mincing, ice-covered heap of mother love'. There are some things you can't say and some things you can't be in 1956 unless you want to be locked up or forcibly subjected to hormone treatment.

Dad won't talk about the encounter, even now. All I can do is imagine him as a gawky young lad awkward under the gaze of the Savoy commissionaires – who must realize he ought to be kicking around in shorts rather than an itchy suit – and walking through the lobby, under the chandeliers, past the oil paintings, not looking any of these people in the eye. 'This world is not my own,' thinks the shy half of him. 'Well, it bloody should be,' thinks the teenage rebel eager for an escape from home. His red cheeks and stooped shoulders suggest the shy boy is winning. He knocks and the door opens. The perfume is smothering, it tickles his nose. The curtains are drawn. The artiste is not in the room, but other members of the entourage are. What did it say on the newsreel? 'His brother and wife, his arranger and wife, his violinist and wife, his manager and wife. Liberace. And his mother.' They're ordinary enough people, smiling and showing him where to put the package, on a table by a vase of lilies. His reflection looks back from the table surface as he stoops to place the box.

'Ah!'

Arthur turns as he straightens up, nearly catching the vase with his elbow. The most extraordinary man he has ever seen in his life is looking him in the eye. His expensive pinstripe suit is sober enough but the star also has a diamante tiepin, hair fluffed up in a bouffant, and the mouth of a medieval king about to enjoy a feast.

'Good morning, my friend.'

The others have gone. Liberace speaks through a smile, as though something is funny.

'And what is your name?'

Arthur stutters out the answer. He doesn't know where to put his hands. The artiste flicks both of his behind him to tuck in the tail of that beautifully tailored jacket and eases down on to a small, red leather sofa, occupying slightly more than half of it. He gestures to the space beside him.

'Won't you come and join me for a moment?'

What happens next? I don't know. He won't tell me and I can't imagine any more. For some reason I can't go all the way in my version of this story. It was easy to listen to Grandad's stories and think of him as a soldier; and it is slightly more difficult to imagine my father as a child, but not impossible – but that all stops in his teenage years, with the girls in the park and with Liberace in the Savoy. I have a mental block. Perhaps it is the same impulse that makes me want to run from the room when my mum and dad talk about their sex lives. When he first dropped a hint about this encounter we were walking back down the hill in Brockwell Park and he gave only the barest of details, but enough to make me laugh at the thought of him, dizzy in those clouds of perfume, awkward in his new suit, all alone with the maestro.

'What did you do? What did he say?'

That, of course, was another way of asking my dad if he had sex with Liberace. Now *there's* a question I never thought I would have to ask. The pianist who once took to the stage in a shocking pink coat made from llama skins decorated with sequins never admitted he was gay, and in 1956 he sued Cassandra for insinuating it. The trial was a sensation, a fabulous confrontation between the Establishment and the most dazzling and absurd of all the young American peacocks who were stealing the hearts of British children.

'Are you a homosexual?' Liberace was asked in court.

'No, sir,' he replied.

'Have you ever indulged in homosexual practices?'

'No, sir. Never in my life. I am against the practice because it offends convention and it offends society.'

He said that under oath. And in the park fifty years later my dad insinuated that Liberace had made, to use the language of the court room, certain proposals guaranteed to offend convention.

'I couldn't comment. My memory may be faulty.'

He was smiling, but what did that mean? Was he embarrassed and hiding the truth or using his silence to exaggerate an innocent meeting and tease me? Was I horrified by the idea he might have said yes to a quickie with a man who could fill Carnegie Hall? Or absolutely delighted?

'Come on, Dad, tell me. You know you want to.'

He shook his head.

'There's a lot of things about me you don't know, mate.'

29

It was soon after meeting Liberace that Arthur stopped going to work. 'I just couldn't handle it. The difference between who I was at home and the person they wanted me to be up in the West End was too big, it did my head in.' So he stayed at home with his mother, and they sat together by the fire all day, then all week, then all month. 'She said: "Don't worry, everything will be all right, you can stop here with me." And of course when you're feeling depressed you want a cuddle, you want to be with your mum. It doesn't matter what she is like, she is your mum. She wanted me with her and I wanted to be there.' He was sacked, eventually. The manager had no choice. Vi made no demands on her son, who was only fifteen, and she put no pressure on him to get another job. She was glad of the company. His world narrowed again as the months drifted by until it was entirely contained within the four walls of that cramped, unhealthy flat. Then, at last, he got claustrophobic. 'I came to my senses, if you like. I felt like I was being sucked down into that blancmange I've told you about, into my mother's world. I needed to get out. I started applying for work without telling her.'

The job at Dunn's had been a false start. In years to come he would not even mention it on his CV. This was the real reason for his reluctance to talk about meeting Liberace: whatever really happened in the hotel suite between the shy boy and the superstar, if anything, was less important to him than what followed. The encounter had become associated with the memory of depression falling, like a blanket that felt warm and comforting at first but nearly smothered him. The only way to crawl out from under it, as far as he could see back then, was to try that other life again. The West End could be a place of escape. So Arthur became a messenger boy for a print company, and found himself working in Soho, where his dad was a postman. Bert thought the place was a den of iniquity but he kept his mouth shut about what he saw and had certainly never shared it with his son, who was astonished and delighted to be in a world as exotic as the Strand had been posh. He spent the rest of his teenage years milking the coffee bars and dens of Soho for every experience he could. The 2i's in Old Compton Street was the centre of the British rock and skiffle universe and bright, breezy, toothy Tommy from Bermondsey was the sound of the rocket age, briefly, before Bill Haley came shooting in with his Comets. Not that Arthur knew what he was watching. 'You can build a legend up now and say I was there when Tommy Steele was playing at the 2i's, which I was, but at the time I was a kid, I had no idea what the place meant or who he was.' The film every boy and girl had to see in 1956 was *Blackboard Jungle*, a mild tale of teenage rebellion, which included a song called 'Rock Around The Clock' by a chubby former country singer with a kiss curl. Young people rose to dance in cinema aisles all over the country when it came on, to the alarm of their elders. In Croydon youths were ejected by police for daring to jive and chanting 'we want rock and roll'. Crazed by the beat in Manchester they trampled flowerbeds and held up traffic. In London, one or two boisterous revellers even ripped out a seat or two, which was characterized in the papers as rioting and the end of civilization.

The generation gap yawned. The war had made the

mums and dads sceptical about authority, and impatient enough with the old way of doing things to have sacked Churchill for a season, but eventually even the newly politicized gave up hope of politicians ever achieving anything at all. They went back to growing tomatoes; or in Bert's case a job for life with the Post Office. But the sons and daughters of the conflict let scepticism flower into rebellion. It was mild at first, but would get more serious and adventurous later. As for Arthur, he had left home now – in his mind, anyway, if not for real. He did not like the way his parents lived, and no longer believed in the God upon whom they depended, although it suited him to belong to the Scouts and the youth group at the Church of England where his new friends hung out. 'There were some lovely young ladies there, and at the Sally Ann too, so I did go back from time to time. I still sing a song I picked up at a church meeting then. "This world is not my own, I'm just a-passin' through . . ." It annoys the hell out of your mother.'

That song annoyed the hell out of Woody Guthrie too, although Dad did not know it. Guthrie heard migrant workers sing it in their camps in dustbowl America, and he hated the underlying message which he took to be 'hang on, accept the misery, poverty and sickness of your lives because you'll get your reward in heaven'. The same attitude my dad resented in his parents. Guthrie rewrote the song to make it a protest, an attack on passivity. Arthur the teenager was being forced to choose between two worlds: the old and the new, the passive and the aspirational, the Salvation Army and the sexy, sinful world of rock and roll, frothy coffee and girls. There was no contest.

The stories just kept coming as we drove home from Brockwell Park, symbol of his awakening. We passed the market where Dad bought an ex-army motorbike with a fishtail exhaust from a fella he knew was a bit iffy. He borrowed an old paratrooper helmet and rode off down the road to try the bike out, wobbling all over the place, but a policeman stepped out in front of him and put his hand up. He swerved and went off in the opposite direction but there was another copper. They knew who the vehicle had belonged to, and wanted to see what kind of an idiot would buy it from him. Arthur had no insurance, of course. 'So there you go. I was banned from riding the bike before it was even mine.'

We passed Goose Green, where they really did herd geese one day a year when he was a kid and walk them to market in Smithfield. Honest. We passed Ruskin Park where the boxer Freddie Mills trained every day. He saw Arthur's little brother doing exercises with his dad, and took a shine to him. Freddie had been champion of the world. He liked the look of the boy, who was 'built like a little brick shit-house', and said he could toughen him up, make him a fighter, if he was allowed to spend every day with the champ. Freddie got a flea in his ear. He also got a bullet in the face a few years later, and was found dead in a car in a dark alleyway round the back of his nightclub.

We drove down the Walworth Road, where Dad once managed to stop the traffic. He was working in a pie and mash shop and his job that day was to take live eels from one shop to another, to be fished out, chopped up, stewed and jellied. The journey meant crossing the road, which was busy, carrying a heavy bucket of eels in each hand. They twisted and slid in their own natural slime as he walked. There was folded newspaper on top of each pail to stop the glistening black creatures escaping, but one of the newspapers fell off. Arthur dropped the bucket. The slime oozed into the tarmac and the eels thrashed about. He got down on one knee to pick them up, grasping after slippery bodies as the cars went past close to his head, but then he knocked the other bucket over. Now there were eels all over the place, wriggling around on the white lines. Somebody was laughing. The traffic had stopped. His trousers were soaked in slime and the eels were gasping. Car horns sounded. There was gridlock and the cause of it was a sorry pie-boy down on his knees, hands sliding through a writhing mess in the middle of the road. 'I remember the big red bus at a standstill right behind me, and the people on the top floor just staring down. Slippery buggers.'

He was twenty years old when he met my mother. The squint had gone and the startled look had grown into a cheeky grin like Bert's. I've seen a photograph of him on a seafront around this time, leaning against the railings with both hands in the pockets of a sharp, dark suit that he is wearing with a skinny tie. A jack-the-lad. She was only fifteen, just out of school, when he found her. It is an odd, unsettling feeling to look at a picture of your mother sitting on a rug in figure-hugging early sixties fashion, long legs tucked to one side, using one hand to push back her hair as it blows in the wind, and admit to yourself that she is actually very fanciable. Lovely, in fact. 'I thought, "Oh boy, I've cracked it this time",' he told me, and I could see why. Marion was training to be a telephone operator in the summer of 1961 at the exchange in Shoreditch, and at the end of her course there was a dance in the canteen. Naturally enough all the local, single telephone engineers were keen to attend, and Arthur was there. 'I went with a mate who took photographs for the police. We danced with these two girls, one of whom was your mother, and after a while we went out on to the fire escape, canoodling.' Now it was my turn to look away, embarrassed. I wondered what her version of the story would be like, but I knew that if I asked she would laugh and shake her head and say, 'Oh, there's nothing to say.' She was not a natural storyteller like him, and avoided the limelight as much as he sought it. They arranged to go on a double first date with the photographer and her friend but it was nearly disastrous. 'She got the bus in to Liverpool Street, so we agreed to meet there under the station clock. The only trouble was, there were two clocks. We waited and waited, and so did they over the other side, and then we gave up and decided to go home, but as we crossed the station we bumped into each other. The girls were suitably unimpressed. If they had walked the other way you might never have happened.'

Their second date was alone. He took her to the cinema at the Elephant & Castle to see Frank Sinatra and Sammy Davis Jr in *Ocean's Eleven*. 'I don't know why we went all the way over there. I must have wanted to feel like I was on home turf I suppose. The heavens did not open up and the birds did not sing, not at first, but it grew into something really good. A friendship, or love, or whatever.' Such an old romantic. He proposed on the platform at an underground station, then again properly at a Chinese restaurant on the Mile End Road. 'It was called the Golden Bird. You know what I'm like: I tried to put the ring on her finger and dropped it in the chow mein.'

They were married in 1965. On one side of the church were the threadbare Moretons and their pious friends from the Salvation Army, on the other the Everitts, led by Frank, who worked in the print room at the *People* newspaper. His mates could hold their drink. Gladys was a little more refined; she had worked in book binding and her brother was on the board of a brewery, but the Everitts lived in a typical Victorian East End terrace and coveted a place in the suburbs. 'They thought we had made it because we lived out in Ilford by then,' said Dad. 'You can imagine the shock it must have been when they came round for tea.' There were rumours about the bride. 'Everybody said she must have been pregnant to get married at eighteen like that, to me, but they were proved wrong because you didn't come along for another two years.'

Money was short at first. The Post Office offered good prospects but did not pay its juniors well. 'I saw my job as being the head of the household. After all we had been through in the family I couldn't have it any other way. My mum used to handle all the finances, Dad would give his money to her and she would let him have some of it back for himself, but you know what happened: she got in trouble and didn't tell him anything about it. That was not going to happen to us. We did not have much but we were very careful: I would go down the High Street late on a Saturday afternoon, just before the stalls packed up, to buy the food cheap, because they had to throw it out otherwise.' My own first memory is of being three years old and letting the midwife in to see my mother, who was giving birth to my sister in the bedroom. I have tried many times to write about my mum, but all I can think of to say is that I love her, without complications. There have never been any problems between us. For all the fuss about fathers, it is our mothers who often turn out to be the strong and inspiring ones, the ones we run to when we are hurt, and the ones we ignore and devalue in our preoccupation with being men.

'The pivotal person in my father's life was my mother,' said Dad as he drove home at the end of that tiring and emotional day at the lido and the park. 'The pivotal person in my life has been your mother. They were two strong women, and one inherited the problems of the other by marrying her son. Marion could not have known what she was letting herself in for, but she put up with my hang-ups, my depression, my need to keep on working away until things were exactly right. Who else would have tolerated me being out all hours, leaving her to look after you kids? I was so driven, and I didn't have the ability to do all the things I wanted to do, but I was not going to let that stop me. She had to duck and dive just like my mother, she had to go out and do cleaning in the morning and do another job in the afternoon because the money I was earning was so low, but she stuck it and she stuck with me.' His voice trembled. I could not think of a reply, but he did not wait for one. 'She became my best friend. I can talk to her, tell her all my problems. She is my very being. Nothing I have achieved could have been done without Marion. Nothing. She was the cornerstone. You need to know that.'

We were at a crossroads. The lights changed and so did his mood. 'See where that Pizza Hut is? I came roaring down here once, tried to take the corner and ended up going straight through the front door of a bakery.' I knew this story. I was eight or nine when I first heard it, in bed with my mum and dad and little sister on a Sunday morning, sitting on his knees playing king of the castle. 'Get down, you dirty rascal.' The blankets between them were warm. He was telling stories and I could see him in my imagination: a silver and black motorcycle, probably a Triumph, with my father the hero on the back in jeans, a white T-shirt and leather jacket like Jimmy Dean, flying down the hill. There was oil on the road. No, a child stepping out in front of him. He acted bravely so that the child might live. The tyres slipped, the handlebars bucked, he was in the air, then bouncing, sliding, on his leathers, man and machine, in through the doorway. Old ladies screamed and dropped cream puffs. Their dogs howled and ran. Babies yelled. The shop girl, who looked like my mother, shrieked as the bike and the bloke hit the counter, shattering the glass, sending splinters everywhere. The helmet saved his life, but there were complications. The doctors had to operate to prevent the young man who would become my dad turning into a slobbering vegetable. They shaved his head and used a hand drill. He stayed awake throughout the operation, watching the drill wind into his skull, because there was no kind of anaesthetic that would work. It didn't hurt, because they knew what nerve to press to numb the brain. All this was what he told me that Sunday morning, as the sparrows chattered on the telegraph wire outside. I was wide-eyed, and utterly taken in. I believed in that story – the big bike, the flying glass, the medieval doctoring – until the moment in the car with him twenty-five years on when I heard a word that shattered the whole heroic fantasy.

'Sorry, what did you say? What did you say you were riding?'

'A moped. You're quiet. Stop me if I'm boring you.'

He had no idea. Heroes do not ride mopeds. The king had fallen from the castle.

Did I hear it wrong or just tell the story differently in my head? That's what we all do. We think we're getting to know someone but we are actually adjusting their story to fit ours: to satisfy our needs, our cravings, desires or prejudices; to explain the things that have happened to us; justify our actions; or forgive our mistakes. That's what he did with his father and what I have done with mine. It was a moped, not a motorcycle. He really did have that operation on his skull, but it was because of a medical condition, not the accident. My mother did work in a bakery, but not the one he collided with. I must have combined all these fragments to make one dramatic whole. I remembered the story about him jumping on the bailiff's head to protect his mum, but that was wrong too. He did jump from the first floor on to someone who was having a go at her, but it was only the boy who lived downstairs. I heard what I wanted to hear.

We do the same with history. That's History with a capital H, as distinct from the personal histories of people like Bert who do not keep diaries, seldom write letters, and have not traditionally been of interest to the composers of the grand narratives of time. One exception is the historian Angus Calder, who points out that the story of the Blitz on London was instantly mythologized, in the dictionary sense of myth, as 'an ancient traditional story of Gods or heroes, especially one offering an explanation of some fact or phenomenon'. The heroes of this myth were the ordinary people, the cheerful cockneys, who survived the sustained bombardment of their city thanks to humour, phlegm, improvisation, teamwork and gallons of tea. That was not how it felt to those who saw the looting, the hysterics, the exodus to the countryside, and so on, but never mind. It's the myth that counts, and the fact it explains is that Germany did not invade, Britain was not conquered. The instant myth was useful to the government, which wanted to show the rest of its people they could take whatever the Germans threw at them and survive. It was useful to socialists who wanted to show the people it was possible to build a new Jerusalem unbound by class or oppressive tradition; they could achieve anything in even the most extreme of situations if they worked together for good. This version of the myth would later see the welfare state, education for all and the national health as products of the wartime revelation that the working classes could and should demand a role in the running of the country. Even in the sixties the myth was powerful enough to support the right of a telephone engineer like my father to enter the town hall as an Alderman, an honorary position traditionally given to the longest serving local councillors so that they no longer had to suffer the indignity of seeking re-election. Arthur and a couple of his friends were not councillors at all but they had fought unwinnable seats for the Labour Party, which wanted more young bodies in the town hall, so they were given access to power as Aldermen. The system was abolished soon afterwards, and in time he was properly elected.

With him in the chamber, on all sides, were men and women who had served during the war and then taken up the challenge articulated by J. B. Priestley, to go on fighting for good. They had become the veteran councillors, union leaders and MPs, who were ready to give way to young blood, the sons and daughters of 1945. In the Labour movement my dad found a belief system to parallel that of his own father: a conviction that every ordinary soldier was a king and priest, or at least a fully functioning citizen whose voice must be heard. This was a foundation stone of the Labour myth of the Blitz, which survived the collapse of the post-war government as it was dashed on the rocks of reality. The myth survived the corruption of the sixties when the redevelopers were happy to indulge the idealists as long as they paid for those monumental estates. The seventies were a strange time of compromise and confusion, not least for my father who was working as an engineer while serving as the deputy mayor of his borough. The Daimler would arrive on Sunday to carry him off in the chain of office to a garden party at Buckingham Palace, and on Monday he would be back at the depot signing for his screwdriver.

Margaret Thatcher looms large in the story at this point, not so much a politician as a dark force, a cyclone sweeping through the land. She united her natural enemies at first – it was easy to hate 'Thatcher the Snatcher' when she took the decision to end the supply of free milk to every school child – but as Prime Minister she used temptation to divide and conquer. The best example of this was her decision to give council tenants the right to buy their flats and houses at low prices. There were some people, like my father, who argued that this would create ghettos; but other Labour activists forgot their opposition long enough to make sure they were first in the queue. As the years passed and Dad's friends sold their former council houses on for huge profits and moved to bigger homes he began to feel guilty that his principles had harmed his family. Thatcherism was beguiling: it undermined the myth of solidarity by offering riches. Anyone could join the new brash, materialist, compassionless middle class if they were prepared to pull up their socks, get on their bike and clamber over their neighbour's body. The last temptation of Arthur was the chance to move up the career ladder and become a public relations man. He had no training and no credentials other than his natural ability to charm and persuade, but that was not really the problem. The Post Office had just been split up. In the new job he would have to represent part of it, British Telecom, with energy and a smile, although he had bitterly opposed the company's creation. 'It tore me apart,' he told me. 'I took that job because I wanted to prove I could do it and mainly to give the family a better life. But it hurt.'

There was one more flurry of resistance, one last great conflict between the old left and the new right, which also marked the end of the socialist myth of the Blitz. My father and I happened to be in a car together on 3 March 1985, when the radio newsreader announced the end of the miners' strike.

'That's it, then,' said Dad. 'They've won.'

There are many ways to interpret that moment, and one of them is that the myth born in the summer of 1940 had finally been exposed as inadequate. The people could not work together to build a new reality. Old England would always reassert itself. 'They' had won, there was no point in resistance. The only thing left was to grow tomatoes: keep your head down, get on with life. At the time it seemed to me that Dad reacted by doing what his father had done: giving up. There were good reasons for doing so: he was exhausted, and not very well. The strain – and surely guilt – he felt at having to sell BT to the world must have contributed to his breakdown and endangered his heart. The last flourish of the left in his part of the world was a takeover of the local Labour Party by the Militant Tendency, whose members hiked up the rates to pay for services and were rewarded with genuine death threats. The atmosphere in the town hall became crazily intense as the old-fashioned post-war generation of councillors was ousted. As a child I had sat in the public gallery and watched my father engage in passionate but courteous debate with members of the opposing party, knowing they would enjoy a pint together when the meeting was over. Now I was a junior reporter with the local newspaper, watching from the press bench as a new wave of councillors exchanged vicious words and V-signs with their enemy. Mrs Thatcher was out of reach, so the rage and hatred they felt at what she was doing to the country was directed at easier targets: the Tory doctors, lawyers and small-businessmen, who seemed bemused by the changes in the world but glad to be on the winning side. The militants didn't last long. The old struggle was over.

Dad quit the council soon after making his dream move to the suburbs. I happened to be in the room when he got a telephone call asking if he would be prepared to stand as a councillor in his new borough. The call was from people who knew him as a moderate, a man who worked hard for his community. They wanted him, and assumed he would want to join them. They were Conservatives. He declined the offer politely, and put the receiver down, but as he turned away from the phone this man who rarely swore muttered, 'Fuck off.'

There would have been no need for him to leave Labour to join the Tories, because one was about to mutate into the other. In the euphoria of 1997 Tony Blair and his friends made explicit comparisons between their new dawn and that of 1945. Peter Mandelson, grandson of Herbert Morrison, deliberately echoed the Festival of Britain in the Millennium Dome. Everyone seemed to want to believe that things could only get better. We needed a new myth and they were happy to oblige.

The architects of New Labour would argue that they had not given up on their old aims but found new ways of achieving them in the changed world. That was exactly what my father said he was doing in his final years with BT and then as the chief executive of a club for businesses based in Docklands. 'Why should the devil have all the best tunes?' Instead of giving up, he persuaded, cajoled and embarrassed companies into accepting some responsibility for the people who were living around their shiny new offices; and when they agreed he put on free entertainment, tried to give locals a say in what was being planned and visited schools to help children understand the history of their area. Eventually he was presented with an award for this work: and so a man who had once been threatened with the sack for refusing to shake Mrs Thatcher's hand found himself on a platform with the man who had brought her down, Michael Heseltine. All of which passed me by, frankly, until the day he was proposed as an honorary Fellow of the University of East London. That meant putting together a life history, which was why I found myself sitting with an open notebook and a pen asking him questions on the day he first warned me of the family curse. By speech day I knew enough about his childhood to feel a big lump in my throat as he stood in his mortarboard and gown and was applauded by a thousand academics.

And what has all this got to do with stories about Liberace and the myth of the Blitz? Only that there is no truth in politics; the story depends on who is telling it. The future of healthcare may well lie in private insurance, but without free treatment available on the NHS I would probably have died from a fatal asthma attack. The regeneration of the docks must appear a success to anyone who remembers weeds growing in derelict warehouses and long dole queues, but it seems like a con trick to those of us who visit the gleaming offices and notice the apartheid between wealthy white workers and their poorly paid black cleaners, or who know families that have been driven off the Isle of Dogs by inflated property prices. The myth depends on the perspective of its creator. What you see depends on where you stand.

The same goes for people. As a child it suited me to believe that my grandfather, Bert, was a hero. I had no evidence but it made the games real. The idea did not suit my father, who believed there was nothing in the old man's army record to justify the absence that had hurt him so much. He had no more evidence than I did, but Bert's silence allowed both our myths to flourish. One of us said he did not speak because the war had been so horrific. The other said he had done nothing to speak about. Neither of us really knew the truth. That's how family legends arise.

Here's another one. Everybody on Mum's side of the family knows that my other grandfather, Frank, the one this book has not so far been about, played for Orient Football Club between the wars. He was a tough, hard-working player they called Tanky because he charged through the midfield like a Sherman scattering the enemy. The war cut short a promising career, as it did for so many men. Tanky drove trucks in the desert with the Eighth Army, although he spent a lot of his time cheering up his fellow troops by playing for one regiment against another in front of large crowds. They could not have seen much when the game got frantic and the sand rose in clouds. Frank was rumoured to have missed a bullet by inches once, when it came through into the cab of his lorry and hit the metal sheeting behind his head, but I never heard him talk about it. He was supposed to have been there at the liberation of Sicily, when the mafia came down from the hills to help the invaders chase the Germans out, and to have fought in one of the four hard infantry battles for Monte Cassino, but he never told me about that either. I'm told he came home looking like a hero, in desert boots and khaki shorts to show off the deep tan he had acquired; but the reasons for his refusal to drive again after the war remained a mystery. The thing he did like to talk about was football, and the thing he liked to say most often, when he came home for his tea after yet another disappointing performance, was 'never again'.

There were supposed to be three generations on the terraces when I went to my first ever match but Frank was too ill to come, so he lent me a scarf in the red and white of the Orient. The game was an important one, a replay in the quarter final of the FA Cup against Middlesbrough, who were a division above the Os in the spring of 1978. We were not expected to beat First Division opponents but the first match had been a goalless draw. All this was lost on me, of course. I was eleven years old and had never seen so many people; there were millions. Well, about twenty thousand actually, but it seemed like millions. The intense atmosphere, the dazzling floodlights and the emerald beauty of that enormous pitch were all revelations. And the language: words I had thought were playground secrets, loud in the mouths of grown-up men.

'Swear-words are the poor man's adjectives,' my dad told me as we waited for the game to start. When Boro scored from an offside position he called the referee a bastard. So did I, under my breath. I was in the tribe.

The result was a shock. We won. I remember the winner as an overhead kick from outside the penalty area in extra time and I dare not look up the official records in case that is not true. Only one more game and we would be in the final. '*Che sarà, sarà*, whatever will be will be, we're going to Wem-ber-lee, *che sarà, sarà*.'

Frank died before the next match. Time has dimmed my memory of a lovely man, although I do recall his shiny, hairless head and the sound of him snoring on the sofa. I remember Mum crying in her dressing-gown when she got the call, and my sister and I snuggling into her. I remember his absence, the strangeness of his house when he had gone. There was no question of supporting West Ham, Arsenal or Spurs after that, and no doubt that we should go to the semi-final as an act of memorial, a kind of pilgrimage in honour of the man. It was less than he deserved. The Os heard the roar of forty thousand people, saw an Arsenal team of deities run out of the tunnel and gave up before the whistle. The gods were gifted three goals then got bored. It was an introduction to the realities of supporting a lesser team, and further lessons would follow. They sold their best players for peanuts, got relegated, and relegated again. The crowds diminished and the club went broke. It was sold, apparently for a fiver, and began a much-belated mini-revival that led to the verge of promotion. The deciding game would be played at Wembley. No more than three thousand people watched Orient on an ordinary Saturday by then, but the club had to ask for thirty thousand tickets for this play-off final. Dad and I bought two of them. We were not fairweather fans, just people who had got sick of standing in the rain all the time. It was more than twenty years since Frank had died but we both knew this journey to Wembley was in lieu of the one the team should have made for him in 1978. I carried a cigarette card from 1930 with a picture of him on it, posing with a team called Leyton Excelsior. The pilgrimage would be completed at last.

They lost, of course; that was inevitable. But here's the real point of this story: Frank had never really played for the Orient at all. I checked the records after that trip and although they included the names of every man to have made even a substitute appearance for the club his name was not there. He might have made it to the reserves, perhaps, or had a trial, but he did not play in a league or cup game. I was so disappointed when I found that out, not least because two decades of masochistic devotion to a hopeless team had been based on a fantasy. But then it made me laugh. Good on yer Frank, I thought, if it's not true it should have been. The story was better than the reality, but isn't that usually the case? Without thinking, next time somebody asked why I had the misfortune to support the Os, I said with absolute conviction:

'Oh, my grandad used to play for them.'

30

I do here declare that I will never treat any woman, child or other person, whose life, comfort or happiness may be placed within my power, in an oppressive, cruel or cowardly manner; but that I will protect such from evil and danger so far as I can, and promote, to the utmost of my ability, their present welfare and eternal Salvation.

From 'The Articles of War of the Salvation Army'

'I'll be ready for them next time. I'll have a knife or something.'

The first time the burglars came, Bert was watching football on the television in his front room. The sound was up loud because he was getting a bit deaf, but then he was eighty-four years old. They put a ladder against the wall, got in through an open bathroom window up on the first floor, and went through the cupboards and drawers in his bedroom without him hearing.

The second time the burglars came he caught one of them at the back door.

'He was only a little fella. I would have had him. I wasn't afraid.'

The boy must have been, because he scarpered. Nothing was taken. Dad called to see if I would go down with him and check the old man was all right. Grandad came to the door quickly and was obviously shaken up. He said he was fine but his hands were trembling a great deal, and he kept repeating himself.

'I'll be ready for them. I wasn't afraid.'

The bathroom window had already been sealed and the side gate replaced. We jammed the back door shut, and said he should get rid of the tall ladder in the garden.

'Oh no, mate, can't do that. Gonna use it to fix my roof tiles, aren't I?'

His leg was bad and he could hardly walk, let alone go up a ladder, but he was adamant. The burglaries did not stop. A frail old man living alone in a big house down a quiet road was too much temptation. The third time they came he was in the music room watching television again. One of them even had the nerve to say hello.

'Do you know you've been burgled?'

'Have I?' said Grandad, startled to have a stranger in his house.

'It's a right mess in there. I just saw the front door open and came up. You better check they haven't taken anything. Where do you keep your money?'

Grandad recovered himself and told him to clear off. It could have got nasty, he could have been knifed or had his head smashed in, but he held his ground and warned the young intruder he was going to call the police.

'He was only a little fella. I wasn't afraid. Comes from the army, I suppose.'

The boy disappeared. When I visited Grandad a few days later he was still very nervous, and told me all about it in exactly the same phrases he had used after the first and second burglaries. We both believed it would happen again. He was trying to get in the habit of keeping all the doors and windows locked, but it was hard to respond to a threat after forty-two years in the same house without a problem. As for leaving his home, forget it.

'Why should I let them change the way I live? Why should I let them scare me into living differently?'

The remainder of his cash had gone to the bank, but it didn't sound like it would have been much use to the burglars anyway.

'I went on the underground the other day. Somebody had to show me how to put the ticket through. I'm not used to it, am I? Even the blokes at the bank laughed at me.'

Why was that?

'I said, "Is this the Bank of England?" They thought I was joking.'

He had ridden the Central Line up to Threadneedle Street with a bag of money.

'I said, "I want these twenty pound notes changed to new ones. Nobody told me they had gone out of fashion."'

Why not hand them in at your own bank?

'Barclays? They only take a few at a time, not loads. It was a nice day out.'

We were talking about money. Suddenly he stopped smiling and went quiet. Grandad got up and left the room, and I wondered what was wrong. I sat on the sofa I had known all my life, my fingers worrying at a worn patch. The material was tough, hard and shiny, wrinkled grey like an elephant's hide. On the shelf there were bleached-out photographs of the family. Rosemary's wedding. My dad in the robes he wore as deputy mayor. My teenage self standing between Dad and Grandad, Arthur and Bert, in a snowy field. We had socks on our hands for gloves and snow on our coats from a snowball fight like the one my sister was having behind us with an unseen opponent. Grandad was wearing a fur Cossack hat as big as the head it was jammed on. There was another photograph, yellowed with age, of Bert and Vi in the young years of their love, before the children. Before the war. He looked dapper in a waistcoat and tie, that white shirt dazzling as it always used to. She stood by him, arms loose at her sides, in a summer dress with flowers on it. They both peered through round glasses. There were stains in the corner of the ceiling where water had come in through the roof.

'I couldn't face life.'

I hadn't heard him come back. He was standing in the doorway, slightly stooped, as though on tiptoes ready to catch a ball.

'I couldn't face up to it when I found out I was in debt. Quite a lot in debt.'

He was talking about the end of the war. This was it: his answer to a question I had not asked, but that had hung over all his stories since the three of us ate our fish and chip lunch. He had not been able to answer his son that day but I was not him. I was interested enough to have listened for hours and come back for more, but I had not been hurt by the reality. He could tell me about it.

'There were other people coming out of the army who had lots of money to play with. I had nothing. It was all ready to be paid out, owing to people. I couldn't take it. I was wrong, but I just couldn't face it.'

So he kept his distance, stayed away, until his obligations, or his orders, were too strong to resist.

'I did go back eventually. I thought it would change, but it never changed.'

'What do you mean?'

'My wife would spend money but we couldn't afford it. That was her way. That's why I am like I am today.'

We had been shopping together that morning and spent ages looking for the cheap lemonade he knew they sold in the supermarket. I found a bottle that was sixty pence a litre and thought that was a bargain, but the one he wanted cost seventeen pence. His bill for the whole week came to six pounds.

'I want to make sure I don't get bankrupt any more.'

I told him he wouldn't go bust drinking cheap lemonade. Sick maybe, but not broke. He didn't even smile. He knew he had caused enormous pain to his boys.

'I know the children were going through it. I know that now. I did what I thought was right. I stuck on, helping the situation. What else could I have done?'

He was standing in the doorway, half turned away from me, rocking slightly.

'I don't know. I did the best I could.'

Did he have a girlfriend in Germany? I chanced my arm and asked him outright. I believed his answer. Yes, there was a young woman he went out dancing with, whose family were quite well off. He visited their home, and they sent a food parcel back to London because some things were easier to get in Germany while the Americans were around. He thought Vi might like the treats. He didn't think of the impact it would have on her, although he certainly heard the rumours when he returned. But nothing serious or even romantic happened with the Fraulein, he said. I believed him, partly because although he was a wild flirt he seemed never to have shown a real interest in any other woman than Vi; and partly because I thought he was being honest when he chuckled and said: 'I was more interested in her mum, to tell you the truth.'

*

He left the room again and went downstairs. Perhaps this was all too much for him and I should back off, crack a joke, put a record on. What business was it of mine? He came back with a spoon and a large white bowl full almost to the brim with tinned peaches.

'You'll be hungry. I've put milk in it too; that's all right isn't it? Get it down you.'

The milk had curdled slightly in the syrup. There was gallons of it. I couldn't refuse. At least the sickly sweet taste distracted me from worrying about his state of mind. He wanted to talk, he didn't need any prompting. Grandad reminded me he was brought up in a big family, but this time he said something new: that it was his mother who had made all the decisions and taken all the responsibility

'She did it all. My father used to say, "You've got to look after yourself." I suppose I was much the same. I know I took my kids out, but I never told them what to do. I just got on with life, same as my parents did. There's a lot of mistakes I made in me life, I don't doubt it.' My father had never heard him say that. 'It's like yourself, you're always training to be a parent, aren't you? You don't know what to do. You never went to school for that, did you? I wasn't experienced in married life. Some of us suffer through our own folly. I should have faced up to life a bit more.'

They were thrown out of Wells Way in 1960. The debts had become unavoidable and the mess could no longer be ignored. The bailiffs came and nobody fought them off. The Moretons, all seven of them, went to stay with a sympathetic woman from the corps. Then the Lord provided for Bert and Vi. Well, a friend's husband did anyway: he had connections and was able to arrange for the family to make a completely new start in another part of London, a dozen miles away to the north of the river. This was not a flat but a three-bedroom, two-reception house in a wide avenue with trees and nice neighbours. The front garden was bigger than the floorspace of the flat in Wells Way.

'I'm happy today because I am enjoying what my heart used to dream of.'

Arthur was not the only one whose longings had been stirred by a walk in the park. 'I used to go to Brockwell Park with the kids and see people living in nice houses and my heart was falling out,' said Grandad. 'But I wouldn't have been here today if it was not for your father. I said to him, "I've got a chance to get a nice place, could you help me?" The rent was about three pounds, my wages were only six pounds or something.'

Dad was nineteen and earning good money in the pie and mash shop while he waited for his application to the Post Office to be accepted.

'He helped me. He stuck by me.'

They lived in a grove, not a road. Most of the houses were smart, some even had plaster lions at the gate, but there was a handful of rotten teeth in the row, all cracked and dirty with the paint falling off and grey nets at the windows. They belonged to families from somewhere else, somewhere worse, where the bombs had fallen. People who couldn't quite shake off the past no matter how far they walked, nor how much they refused to talk about it. If Bert thought his troubles were over, he was wrong.

'Even here I got into a bit of trouble. Somebody knocked on the door and wanted to throw me out on the street because I hadn't been paying any rent. I was giving it to my wife every Sunday before I went off to the Salvation Army hall and she was signing the rent book, but she wasn't giving him the money.'

They were in serious trouble again but Bert was not prepared to lose their new home. The union rep at his sorting office organized a meeting with the paymaster, who listened to the case and offered to help. 'He said, "Here, Mr Moreton, I don't want any of my staff to be unhappy. We'll lend you the money and you pay it back each week. Do overtime. Pay it that way." That's the lowest I ever got.'

Perhaps. But there was another episode that Grandad did not want to talk about, despite his growing candour. Nobody in the family spoke about it easily either, although my father had told me a little, reluctantly. The loan from the paymaster was not the end of their money worries at all. Vi did not change her ways but secretly ran up new debts, which she was unable to hide, eventually. This time Bert refused to pay them off, saying she would have to face the consequences – which meant going to prison. Vi was sent to Holloway as a result of her husband's decision. My father found it hard to forgive his dad for that, but if being tough, for once, was Bert's way of showing love, a means of forcing Vi to confront her problems, it worked. She was seen by experienced prison doctors who diagnosed severe depression, the first time anybody with medical training had recognized what was going on in her head. My father called it the family curse, an affliction he had seen cripple his mother and experienced for himself, the first time, at the age of sixteen. It was like a blanket smothering the face, he said, describing a collapse into despair that was a relief at first but then left him unable to think or breathe or move. Much of his life had been spent in flight from that paralysis, keeping one step ahead, most of the time, by staying busy with projects that built up self-esteem and distracted him from the fear of sudden attack by the hopelessness that fell without warning like a bird of prey. 'You have a constant drive to keep going, a worry or a fear that you should be doing something better, something more worthwhile, and that if you stop and relax it will get you.' I knew what he meant. When he said he had seen the curse in me I recognized how easy it was to slip into what he called 'the blancmange'. I remembered walking alone by the river, watching the sun play on the water, feeling contented one moment then overwhelmed, suddenly, with a sadness I could not explain and which had no root in anything that was happening to me. My legs were lead, all the blood in my body seemed to have seeped away into the ground and my head felt about to burst. I could not explain why I was crying, nor could I tell anyone why I spent the next three days in bed, ignoring the ringing of the doorbell and the telephone. Some people say it is like a black dog chasing them. I have only known a shadow of the thing that stalked my grandmother, but the shadow was vicious enough. I also have the benefit of knowing that I am being stalked. She did not know what was happening to her and was completely on her own. You did not admit to depression in the war years, it was almost like treason and completely contrary to the supposed spirit of the Blitz. Even in the sixties when the doctors did offer help there was still a great stigma in her illness, and the real danger of being separated from her family. So Vi kept her despair to herself and sought distraction by doing little deals that nobody knew about, and by being hospitable and generous to anyone in need, even as her own secret needs grew. There was always someone worse off. The tallymen who came to the door while Bert was out were just like the credit card companies and loan sharks of today, always ready to extend more credit at rising levels of interest. The

Lord wouldn't mind if she spent money she did not have as long as she spent it on someone else: on cake and sandwiches for a hungry tramp invited to the table; a few bob in an envelope for a mother down on her luck; tasty treats for the kids; and odd, extravagant gestures like the fashionable-bum-freezer jacket she bought Arthur for no reason and had to smuggle back to the pawnshop a few days later. She was forever borrowing a little bit from someone to pay off someone else and avoid violence or the bailiffs, all the while ignoring the bulk of the debt looming and growing behind her. I do recognize echoes of her problems, inherited in tiny ways, like the habit of never looking at my bank balance when I make a withdrawal, and the irrational panic I feel about anything to do with money. And that creeping, tearful sadness that comes from nowhere, for no reason, and has no mercy.

'She was a good woman,' said my grandfather as we talked in the room where she died. Bert could not allow himself to speak badly of his wife. 'A marvellous woman. She just had a weakness.' Vi was a kind and witty person, who loved her husband and kept her vows. They were quite a pair, the rag and bone boy who could barely read or write and the shop manager's daughter who had secret troubles of her own. Nobody thought they should get married but them. Nobody thought it would last but it did, for the rest of her life. She coped with the blackout, the bombs, the rockets, fires, food shortages, con men and looters, and death after death after death among the people she knew, young and old. She brought up the oldest boys on her own during wartime, accepted her husband back on his terms, comforted him after his nightmares, raised two more boys and a girl, endured prison and the severe depression that had dogged her life yet finished it with an enormous circle of friends and the devotion of a family who knew her faults but thought her worthy of love. Her ability to survive was heroic. Bert said she had enabled him to do the same. 'She was good to me. I don't know what I would have done without her, whether I'd be here at all. She was a very educated woman and she helped me, gave me tests and helped me pass all the exams for the Post Office. When she was dying she said, "What are you going to do?" See, she was worried about me even then.'

Vi had been a large lady in her time but she shrank away at the end. I remember my nanny as a small woman with musty hair and watery smile, who sat in an armchair with a rug over her legs and called me Collywobbles. I loved her. We used to watch *Crossroads* together in the darkness some nights when Grandad was out at the Army or upstairs playing his music, with the electric fire glowing red, the black and white television throwing shadows across our faces. She had always looked older than her years, but seemed to age even faster as she got weaker, until she looked like a sick, sallow woman in her eighties, not her sixties. Her quick tongue never slowed, though.

'When she was on her last legs she would answer the phone and say, "I'm still here",' Grandad told me. 'Then, when she was really going, she even made a joke. "Jesus died young, didn't he?"'

She slept downstairs in the front room in her last week. I have often thought of their last night together: of Vi exhausted in her makeshift bed, guessing what was to come, and Bert holding his wife, weak as she was and almost not there, perhaps stroking her hair. A word or two, then the eloquent silence of two bodies breathing, one strong and regular, the other fading, and the tired eyes closing to sleep. After the rushed wedding, and the fearful uncertainty of war and its aftermath, she had spent every day of her last thirty years with her soldier, leaning on him and being leaned on. She could see he was exhausted that evening, so sent him upstairs to lie down. When he came back she was cold.

'Shall I tell you what her last words to me were? She said, "I'm sorry." I said, "It's me that should be sorry, not you. You've got nothing to be sorry for."'

31

Hers was the first dead body I ever saw. I remember the rouge on her cheeks matched the silk lining of the coffin, but her skin was the colour of a church candle. Some people kissed the tips of their fingers and touched her forehead with them, but I did not need to do that to know she was cold. I just stood there, in the corner of the room with the french windows, an awkward thirteen-year-old in a black velvet jacket I had never worn before and a tie my mother had borrowed. Foster, Donaghy, Hatton. The names of the Luton football team, recited over and over in my head, helped me not to think about what I was seeing. I gulped air, so as not to cry. Luton were playing on the telly in the other room, with the sound turned off. I didn't support them, nobody in the family did as far as I knew, but they were playing at my grandmother's funeral. Les Sealey, David Moss. Her cheek had been soft and slack when she was alive; it tickled your lips and nose to kiss her. 'She prayed for you every day,' said my uncle David, putting his arm around my shoulder and pulling me closer to him. I was not a child. I was taller than him. I didn't stop him. Brian Stein and Ricky Hill. We must have been in the garden when they screwed down the lid of the coffin. Drizzle flattened our hair. One or two people were smoking, but not many: this was a Salvation Army funeral, there were bandsmen in uniform and ladies in bonnets, and nothing alcoholic to fortify the soul. When the family had been squashed together into a couple of limousines with tan leather seats, a member of the Walthamstow corps lifted a polished brown pole into a holder that was slung on shoulder straps to sit at his groin, and tilted the army banner to hang so it almost touched the ground. There was no wind to disturb the yellow star on its red background and those words, 'blood and fire'. The flagbearer began to walk, so very slowly, at the front of the funeral procession, a dozen steps away from the hearse like one of those servants who used to go ahead of the car with a red flag. I wanted to be with the people who were watching from the pavement. I wanted to say 'Look at that, what a turn out, they certainly know how to give you a send off', and then go off somewhere myself, back home for some tea, and forget about the whole thing.

I remember it as a humid day, and a long one. The march was slow, the hall was far. When we got there, the grand-sons and daughters sat in a row, in creaking wooden chairs placed too close together, the older ones holding the hands of the youngsters, showing us where to open the red leather song books. The pages were thinner than tissue, they rustled and stuck to moistened forefingers. The songsters sang on the stage but they didn't shake their tambourines, and people went to the microphone to talk about Vi. They said good things about her: she always had a welcome for people, she had her struggles but she loved the Lord. She had been promoted to glory, they said. Promoted to glory. They made it sound like she was the lucky one.

I stayed in their house not long after she died, in the spare room with the psychedelic poster, and I woke in the very early morning to the sound of Grandad moving around in the kitchen downstairs. I unzipped the sleeping-bag I was using instead of bedclothes and went to stand on the landing, by the entrance to the room where they used to sleep. I don't know why. Perhaps it was a dream, or grief, but I would swear I felt her presence in the half-light, like she was making sure I was all right, 'not half left'. It made me smile.

'OK, Nanny,' I said out loud. 'I won't be sad.'

'He loved her,' said their eldest son. 'He still did until the moment she died. And she loved him. Never had an affair, never went off with another man, not at all. Even after all their troubles, when she died he couldn't handle it. We would go there for months afterwards and he'd be crying his eyes out. They loved each other until she died. In some ways, you know, it is a fantastic love story.'

We shall not cease from exploration
And the end of all our exploring
Will be to arrive where we started
And know the place for the first time.

T. S. Eliot, *Little Gidding*

32

To preserve a man alive in the midst of so many chances and hostilities is as great a miracle as to create him.

Jeremy Taylor, from the Royal Welch Fusiliers' souvenir book for Operation Overlord

The little black leather-bound book was on his shelf, between the autobiography of Billy Graham and *The Christian Doctrine of the Godhead.* The book of prayers sent to my grandfather by General Booth at the outbreak of the Second World War had been in the thigh pocket of his battledress at Reims, in the farmhouse, in the ditch, on the barge, all through the Blitz, on the coast, in Holland and Germany, to the end. The little black book came home with him and was a help in the slow process of learning to cope with life as a man, a lover, a husband and not a soldier. He showed me the pages, water-stained and crisp but still readable, with a thought for every day.

'It took a long time to adjust. We had changed, you see, become a bit like savages by the end of the war. You stop caring, become more like an animal.'

Those words surprised me. They were not the sort of thing you would say after spending all your time in Germany on ceremonial duty. Was it hard, I asked slowly, trying to sound casual, to kill someone? At last he gave an answer, of a kind.

'Not in the artillery, we weren't fighting that kind of war.

Then you're killing someone with white gloves on, aren't you, from a distance? Not face to face. In the infantry you've got to defend yourself. Your personality changes. Your life changes, really. You become barbarians.'

Was he trying to admit something?

'Most of the people who were face to face with Germans were volunteers. I didn't fancy volunteering. I kept out of trouble. I was trained for it, mind you, but I wasn't enthusiastic. It wasn't in my blood. If I could get out of killing people like that I would.'

That was a big 'If'.

'When we did house clearing they would tell me, "You go in." I said, "No, I'll stay out here on guard." I used to stand in the door outside. They would search the places for loot and soldiers. I didn't like it really. The Germans were scared alive. I used to hear the kids shouting, "Englander! Englander!" We had to look for arms, you know. Sometimes I think the officers were more interested in finding cigarettes. They did it for a laugh, really.'

Innocent fun? Not quite. He jumped up and put his arms out as if holding a machine gun, pointing it at the ceiling.

'We were told to spray the houses with tommy-gun fire before we went in. Shoot it up, through the doors and windows, whether there was anybody in there or not. Just fire. I didn't like it.'

He sat down, back into the armchair.

'We never did it.'

The memory was obviously vivid though. So, for me, was the thought of children running from their homes and shouting for mercy as exhausted, battle-crazed soldiers fired in through the windows. Or Bert squatting behind walls, covering his colleagues, fighting the Germans street by street and house by house, hand to hand. Or crawling through mud and snow in the Reichswald Forest, watching the trees for movement. There would be no way to opt out of those situations, with the unit relying on you and every shadow a potential sniper. We were both lost in thoughts of battle, real, imagined or forgotten.

'I saw some terrible things.'

He spoke quietly. There was a book about the army on the table, open at a photograph of a flame-thrower. He picked it up and stared at the picture for a moment.

'They would point one of those at a house where a load of Germans were and they would all be burned alive.'

Who were 'they'? Was he one of them? I couldn't bring myself to ask.

'I saw murders. Terrible things.'

Then he put the book down, closed it and smoothed the cover with his palm.

'Murders.'

The little black leather volume from General Booth went back on the shelf.

'I like what Paul says. "My sins are in the past." Do you want a bit more tea?'

There were no more stories after that. I still went to see him, and we talked for ages every time, but he covered the same ground again and again, often in the same words or phrases. Then one day Grandad found something he had looked for often when I visited, but had never been able to find. A photograph of a group of men in battledress, five rows deep, the front ones sitting on the grass with their legs crossed and those at the rear standing on benches. He was right at the very back, behind two taller soldiers, not smiling like some of them but giving the camera a cautious look.

'That's 333 Battery. The commanding officer was like a father to me.'

The officer looked like a caricature, with his brush of moustache, head boy grin and swizzle stick. So did the sergeant major, who was wearing a tam-o'-shanter and a twirly moustache from the pages of Biggles.

'I got a postcard a few years back, it just said "from Rabbit". Didn't know who it was, but now I think it must have been this fella here; we used to call him Rabbit. Can't think for the life of me why we did that.' The smiling, slightly worried face gave no clues to the nickname. Rabbit was in his very early twenties at the time, like Bert, and wore his cap at the same unlikely angle.

'There should be a dog somewhere. Here it is.'

He bent over to look more closely at the blurred shape of a German shepherd.

'What was its name? That was a lovely big group of men. I can remember every one of them, looking now, even though I can't have been with them for more than about three months or so. They were moving us around, mixing the experienced gunners up with the new ones.'

There was a single tear on his cheek, just below the eye, as he straightened up. He neither mentioned it, nor attempted to wipe it away. Then he said something I could not quite believe I was hearing, given all that we had talked about. It was said confidently, almost lovingly, with no irony.

'That was a lovely big family.'

33

This is how my father is on the best of days: walking up the hill behind his house with his grandson, telling him stories, making him giggle, loving without restraint. I watch them together with a pounding heart because I can now guess at the way we were thirty years ago: the things he felt, the feelings I have forgotten ever having. After all that has happened I am grateful for this extra time together, these days of ease and friendship. When Jacob is on his shoulders so am I, chuckling as he bounces me, oblivious to his wheezing, rasping breath. The reluctant adult in me hears the sound as a reminder that I will soon be alone with no shoulders to sit on, no hand to hold. When he laughs I know it to be a relief. But when I see them together I am a boy again, able this time to relish the uncomplicated closeness. As a child I was too young to notice the way he watched me, to know what troubles he shed, briefly, when he got down on his knees and pretended to be a lion. I must have shrieked and run away like Jacob does. This is how it was. Their smiles were ours.

This morning Jacob came into the room while I was writing, because he wanted a spin on the office chair. Then he noticed the book on my desk. It was open at the picture of the flame-thrower that had caused my grandfather to go cold as his memories returned. Jacob was more interested in the facing page, a photograph of an anti-aircraft gun.

'Was Little Grandad a soldier?'

'Yes, he was.'

'Did he fire a gun like this one?'

'Yes, he did.'

'Did he kill anyone?'

'I don't know. Possibly.'

'Were they bad people?'

They had families, I wanted to say. They had sons of your age, and daughters, and they had no more of a part in the decision to go to war than Little Grandad did when he was conscripted. They were scared and did not want to die. But all this was too complicated and it was too early in the morning and I was tired, so I said: 'Yes.'

'Oh,' he said. 'OK.'

He went off to play somewhere else and I wished it were that easy. I wished there were answers as simple as that to hold on to all your life. Good and evil. The Salvation Army way, blood and fire, would be a comfort if I could bring myself to believe in it. At five, Jacob thinks his Little Grandad is a hero because he was a soldier. He thinks Grandad is a hero because he brings home flying helmets from the museum and lets him try them on. He thinks I am a hero because I am Daddy and he knows no better. Yet. I wish we could keep it like this, without the disappointment, forever; but the one sure thing you should know about fatherhood, if you are a man, is that you will mess it up. You probably won't know how or why or when – it could be a misplaced word, a burst of temper, a bad habit, an act of neglect, a character flaw you don't know you have – but it will be found out and held against you and some day, who knows when, your child will stand there and yell: 'Why did you do that? How dare you?'

That's if you're lucky. If there is a yell it means you have a chance to hold up your hands and say, 'I'm sorry, I made a mistake, I didn't know. Please forgive me.' Or, 'You don't know the whole story, let me explain.' Or even, if you must, 'I have my reasons. You'll understand one day.' If there is no yell, if they just brood or resent or stew or plot, you've had it. The silence will grow, keeping you apart. So if he must discover that I am not a hero, please God let Jacob come to me and tell me why not, and perhaps we will have a chance. I am glad to have heard the stories of my own father's life, even if he does not like all the ways I have imagined them. I have always loved him, even when I was angry and hated him, and I am frightened of what life will be like when he is not with me any more. I am grateful that we have come to understand each other more fully lately, and hopeful that everything that needs to be forgiven is forgiven on both sides. The conversation we both needed began because he was ill and seemed to be running out of time so he wanted to talk. I wanted to listen, particularly when he threatened a family curse that would get me one day. But the curse was not really depression, hard as that illness is to bear and sometimes even impossible to survive. I have not suffered like he and his mother did, but neither must I suffer in silence as they did because of shame. Now it is out in the open I do at least have the advantage of being able to recognize the early signs, knowing what might happen to me and where to get help. That makes it less scary. The secrets my father and his father kept for so long also seem less potent for having been spoken out at last. Dad had to make a life for himself without ever being given a clue how to do so. He was brave enough to make sure I did not have to do the same. The real curse was silence. I hope it is broken.

So what do I tell my son about heroes? He wants and needs one and pretends to be one all the time. A fireman, a policeman, a superhero, even an AA man because they rescue people. I tell him he's a hero, my hero, because heroes are brave and strong and clever and so is he, but he is not convinced. I had no such problems at his age, it was all quite clear: the heroes were the soldiers, sailors, pilots and spies who had fought for Us against Them. As I write this there is another war on, and the myth makers who worked so effectively on the Blitz have been reincarnated to tell us the rights and wrongs of the fight. They know who the heroes are. They would know what to say when Jacob asks about the bombs and the bombers, and who are the bad men and who are the good. But what has their version of heroism got to do with the boy of Jacob's age who was held up to the camera this morning so that the world could see a face that was burned when a missile came out of the dawn haze and destroyed the building next to his, without any care for what the generals call collateral damage but he knows as a searing pain, a hideous pain, a weeping pain? My dad was the same age when rockets fell around him. What does it mean to have a father or a grandfather who is a soldier on the wrong side, waiting in a trench with an old rifle while the men with billion-dollar tanks and body armour and microphones linked to the press room prepare to attack? My grandfather had the good fortune to be on the side that won his war, although for a long, frightening time it looked as though he was not. He knew the fear of facing an enemy who had more weapons and more power. He knew what it felt like to wait to be killed.

I watch our heroes on the news, and I watch the way they carry themselves, the way they sit with their legs open, the rifles held like a trophies, the love for each other in their eyes. I hear the way they talk. 'I would love to have such a bond with anyone back home,' says a GI, 'but that ain't gonna happen, never. That would be extraordinary. These are my brothers. When you have been through times, been cold and hungry or wet and frozen or hot and dry out there, you come together.' I watch them and think about Bert on the guns as the Stukas come screaming down out of the sky, and the words he said as he held the photograph. 'That was a lovely big family.'

He never knew what was going on, from one fight to the next, and I was scornful of that as I tried to work it all out with the luxuries of time and history, but now I hear the GI speaking. 'This is war. We're not supposed to know what the hell is going on.' Every televised death, every severed limb, every withered hand, every firefight now makes me think of Grandad then, and I wonder, what would I do? Would I measure myself against him and find myself inadequate? Surely. Would I risk what he risked, or suffer what he suffered – the undreaming waking, the nightmares, the inability to talk – if I had to fight? If I had to pick up a gun and learn to clean the barrel and fit the grooves in the dark and love it so it saved me; and see the light go out in another man's eyes and call him my enemy even as he reached out for nothing; and watch from a hill as the streets where my family lived were burning; and walk through the flattened suburbs of a foreign country with broken furniture and children's toys scattered in the rubble; and turn away as my beloved comrades threw flame into the rat corners burning out survivors, shooting first and counting later?

If I had to do all that I would try to forget and not to remember. I would keep my counsel and thank God for every day I lived, and curse God for every day I lived more than those I loved. And when a grandson came calling and asked me to remember, I would know that he did not know what he was asking. So I would tell him as much as I could bear; and if he kept asking until the dry embers of memory were rekindled into flame, that haunting flame, I would forget myself and the new life I had made and the rules that bound me, and I would rage, and I would weep, and I would say to him, 'Please can you, please will you, please can you not, why don't you ever for God's sake, for my mind's sake, for my life's sake and the memory of them all, will you please just stop?' But Grandad did not. For that he is my hero.

So what do I tell my son? That most of us grow up thinking our father is the greatest man in history, whether he's around or not. Then we learn to see the old man's faults, challenge him and bring him down. And finally, if we're lucky, we grow and begin to see ourselves more clearly, even as we turn into him.

That's when we understand the ambiguous nature of heroism, the truth that all our fathers were heroes. And none of them were.

Acknowledgements

This book would not have existed without the courage and honesty of my father, Arthur Moreton, and the willingness of my grandfather, Herbert Moreton, to share his stories. Thanks, fellas. Rachel, the best of women, made all things possible. Jacob taught me about heroes. The arrival of Ruby, Joshua and Grace while this was being written changed and inspired much of it. Mum was a star. Vix was a sister and a mate. Thanks to Leslie, Christopher, David and Rosemary for their trust; and to Gladys. We'll go to the dance one day.

Thanks to Mary Mount at Viking for taste, sensitivity, patronage and a good ear. Jane Bradish Ellames dared me to do this and Camilla Hornby saw it through with style. Andy Turner, Malcolm Doney and Jo Dillon helped shape the story. Suzi Feay and Steve Richards offered insights into the manuscript. Doug Gay and Rachel Morley shared wisdom about fathers and families. Richard Collins paid kind attention to detail. The support of Tristan Davies, the Senior Common Room and my colleagues at the *Independent on Sunday* was invaluable. Thanks also to the staff at the Departments of Documents and Printed Books at the Imperial War Museum in London and at Southwark Local Studies Library.

In memory of Frank Everitt and Violet Moreton.

Sources

This book's theme song is 'I'll Be Seeing You' as sung by June Tabor on the album *A Quiet Eye* (Topic, 1999). For unpublished diaries, letters and first-hand notes on the experience of people who lived during and immediately after the Second World War, visit the archives of the Imperial War Museum. For more on the Blitz, visit the Museum of London website, and for more on the myth read Angus Calder, *The Myth of the Blitz* (Pimlico, London, 1991).

For insight into lidos and public open spaces read Ken Worple, *Here Comes the Sun* (Reaktion Books, London, 2000), which says, among other things, 'It is a characteristic of buildings and landscapes that they often outlast the belief systems and political cultures that brought them into being, remaining a kind of sedimented geological layer in the changing and developing historical landscape.' So it's OK to go round rubbing old bricks.

For comparisons of wartime London, England or indeed Britain with the present day, the series of 'Then & Now' books is invaluable. I made special reference to the three volumes of *The Blitz Then & Now* (Battle of Britain Prints International, London, 1987). For a good swim, go to Brockwell Park lido and help to keep it open. For a slap-up lunch, go to Brockwell House. Bubble and two toast with mine, thanks.

The following sources proved invaluable:

Bedoyere, Guy de la, *The Home Front* (Shire, Princes Risborough, 2002)

Bourke, Joanna, *The Second World War: A People's History* (OUP, Oxford, 2001)

Calder, Angus, *The People's War* (Pimlico, London, 1969)

Charlesworth, Tim, *The Story of Burgess Park: From an Intriguing Past to a Bright Future* (Groundwork Southwark, London, 2002)

Chesters, Gwendoline E., *The Mothering of Young Children* (Faber and Faber, London, 1943)

Church, Leslie F., *Welcome Home: A Little Book of Greeting and Thanksgiving* (Epworth Press, London, 1945)

Clayton, Tim and Craig, Phil, *Finest Hour* (Coronet, London, 1999)

Communist Party, *Demobilisation: How Should it Be Done?* (pamphlet, London, 1945)

Coutts, General Frederick, *No Discharge in This War: A One-Volume History of the Salvation Army* (Hodder & Stoughton, London, 1975)

Davis, Rib and Schweitzer, Pam, *Southwark at War* (Local Studies Library, London, 1996).

De Hegedus, Adam, *Home & Away: Notes on England After the Second World War* (Hutchinson, London, 1951)

Dobinson, Colin, *AA Command: Britain's Anti-Aircraft Defences of the Second World War* (Methuen, London, 2001)

Fitzgerald, Constantine, *The Blitz* (Macdonald, London, 1957)

Forty, George, *British Army Handbook 1939–1945* (Sutton, Stroud, 2002)

Hennessy, Peter, *Never Again: Britain 1945–51* (Jonathan Cape, London, 1992)

Hylton, Stuart, *Their Darkest Hour: The Hidden History of the Home Front 1939–45* (Sutton, Stroud, 2001)

Leask, Mrs Diane, unpublished diaries in the Imperial War Museum, Department of Documents

Levison, Frederick, 'To a Soldier Who Seldom Writes Home', broadcast over the British Forces Network (pamphlet, 1945)

Mass Observation, *The Journey Home: The Advertising Service Guild's Report on the Problems of the Demobilisation.* The fifth 'Change' wartime survey: six shillings (Advertising Guild/John Murray, London, 1944)

Ministry of Information, *Roof Over Britain: The Official Story of Britain's Anti-Aircraft Defences 1939–1942* (Stationery Office, London, 1943)

Owen Jones, Peter, *Small Boat, Big Sea* (Lion, Oxford, 2000)

Patten, Marguerite, *We'll Eat Again* (Hamlyn, London, 1985)

Priestley, J. B., 'Letter to a Returning Soldier' (Home and Van Thal, London, 1945)

Reese, Peter, *Homecoming Heroes: An Account of the Re-assimilation of British Military Personnel into Civilian Life* (Leo Cooper, London, 1992)

Rooke, Dennis and D'Egville, Alan, *Call Me Mister! A Guide to Civilian Life for the Newly Demobilised* (Heinemann, London, 1946)

Staunton, Mrs V. J., unpublished diaries in the archives of the Imperial War Museum

Turner, Barry and Rennell, Tony, *When Daddy Came Home* (Hutchinson, London, 1995)

Wicks, Ben, *Welcome Home: True Stories of the Soldiers Coming Home from WW2* (Bloomsbury, London, 1991)

The author may be contacted via the publishers or
colemoreton@surefish.co.uk

Permissions

The author and publisher gratefully acknowledge permission to reprint copyrighted material from:

'All your anxiety' by Edward H. Joy used by permission of the Salvation Army. Copyright © Salvationist Publishing & Supplies Ltd, 1 Tiverton Street, London SE1 6NT; 'The Articles of War' used by permission of the Salvation Army. Copyright © International Headquarters, 101 Queen Victoria Street, London EC4P 4EP; *Little Gidding* by T. S. Eliot published by Faber & Faber Ltd. Reproduced by permission of Faber & Faber Ltd; *Welcome Home: True Stories of the Soldiers Coming Home from WW2* by Ben Wicks (1991) published by Bloomsbury. Reprinted by permission of Bloomsbury Publishing; *When Daddy Came Home* by Barry Turner and Tony Rennell (1995) published by Hutchinson. Reprinted by permission of the Random House Group Ltd.

Every effort has been made to obtain permission from all copyright holders whose material is included in this book. Viking apologizes for any errors or omissions in the above list and would be grateful to be notified of any corrections that should be incorprated in the next printing of this volume.